SHADOWS WILL FALL

Dun Laoghaire: March 2003. Frances Shaw finds the body of a young woman, naked, drowned and laid out in the doorway of the hospital morgue. *Coney Island: November 1963.* The body of a young woman, naked and drowned, is left in the doorway of a hospital. A conviction for murder follows. *Dun Laoghaire: October 1953.* The drowned, naked body of a young woman is found in the doorway of the morgue. A conviction for murder follows.

Frances Shaw is too keen a student of psychology to accept the police theory of a copy-cat murder – and she knows a lot more of the facts than they do...

SHADOWS WILL FALL

Shadows Will Fall

by

Rose Doyle

Magna Large Print Books
Long Preston, North Yorkshire,
BD23 4ND, England.

British Library Cataloguing in Publication Data.

Doyle, Rose
    Shadows will fall.

A catalogue record of this book is
available from the British Library

ISBN 0-7505-2398-0

First published in Great Britain 2004 by Hodder & Stoughton
A division of Hodder Headline

Copyright © 2004 by Rose Doyle

Cover illustration by arrangement with
Hodder & Stoughton Ltd.

Published in Large Print 2005 by arrangement with
Hodder & Stoughton Ltd.

Magna Large Print is an imprint of Library Magna Books Ltd.

Printed and bound in Great Britain by
T.J. (International) Ltd., Cornwall, PL28 8RW

For Annette

For the word on Dun Laoghaire, as it once was, much thanks to George Rogerson and Eamonn Russell. For the low-down on New York my thanks to Joe Kennedy (for the kick start) and, for their generosity, forbearance and anecdote while I was in the Big Apple, to Dennis Duggan, Jack Deacy, Bonnie Stone, Ray O'Hanlon, Maureen Sullivan and Yvonne and John Healy. *Good Old Coney Island* by Edo McCullough was enlightening, as was *Wild Nights – the Nature of New York City* by Anne Matthews. And, for their saintly patience, great gratitude to my editor Sue Fletcher and the indispensable Swati Gamble.

1

March, 2003. Dun Laoghaire.

The body was in the doorway of the morgue. The earlier bodies had been left in morgue doorways too, but I didn't know that then.

That morning, with ceaseless rain pouring from an overloaded sky and the town for the most part asleep, all I saw was the dead body of a young woman called Alannah Casey who had liked cappuccino made with non-fat milk and no chocolate. The dog shivered against me. A gull settled on the wall and cawed. It was joined by a second, then a third.

Those are the things I remember most clearly, and in that order.

First her body, then the incessant, dark, disapproving rain on everything. There had been weeks of it, though it was almost April and supposed to be springtime. Then there was the state of the dog and the vitriol of the gulls. I've never liked gulls. I had been walking Lucifer, the dog. He hated the rain and had wanted to stay indoors but I was having none of that. The need to exercise him got me up and out early and walking myself. I also had a business to run, a coffee shop called The Now and Again Café.

Alannah Casey had been coming there for months to drink cappuccinos with her boyfriend in the afternoons.

Lucifer and I were doing a circuit which took us past the back of the hospital that morning. We'd abandoned the pier, which had been too wild, and taken this as a route offering relative shelter. The rain and early hour meant we were the only souls about. It wasn't yet seven o'clock. The Irish are not a nation of early risers.

The dog saw, or perhaps sensed her, before I did. He had run ahead of me, up Charlemont Avenue and through the back entrance to the hospital. He'd been sniffing his way past a row of staff cars when his tail went between his legs and he dropped to his belly.

'What's wrong, Lucifer?' I had to yell, what with the rain falling and an early, Wexford-bound goods train hustling along the distant rail tracks. The Accident and Emergency door was directly ahead and a stone angel on the roof of Outpatients watched from my left. The morgue was to my right, the row of cars blocking my view of the door.

'What's wrong?' I called again.

Lucifer was inching forward, whimpering. He was getting old, my lovely Lucifer, arthritis working its way from one back leg to

14

the other. But he was still game and a player. Cowering wasn't his style at all.

He'd set up a low growl and was standing again by the time I came up to him.

'It's all right,' I said, holding his collar as we stood over her body. He barked. 'Be quiet,' I said.

Alannah Casey's face shone beautifully in the grey light, oval shaped and achingly white in its frame of long, very wet black hair. She was naked and lay on her back on the wheelchair-access slope, eyes fixed in dull wonder on the cloudy skies, hands folded with childlike modesty over her pubic hair. There were goose pimples on her arms and thighs.

She'd shone beautifully in life too, sure of how she looked and seeming very in love with the young Russian she used to meet for the cappuccinos. She'd been nineteen years old and liked to wear leather jackets with low-slung jeans.

Nineteen. So close in age to my daughter Emer. But she was someone else's daughter and for this I gave brief, fervent and guilty thanks.

Thankfulness was overpowered by guilt and my legs ceased supporting me. I sat beside Alannah Casey on the slope of cement and touched her poor, dead face. The shock of its cold stillness was terrible. The dog whimpered, keeping carefully away from her.

I took out my mobile and phoned the garda station. My ex-husband worked there so the number wasn't a problem. I told the guard who answered where I was and what I'd found.

'We'll be with you right away,' he said. He had a brusquely reassuring country accent. Midlands, I'd have said. 'Don't go away,' he added.

'I'll wait,' I assured him.

I'd always fancied myself as someone with a grasp of what it was to be human. But I'd never come up against humanity at its most deceiving, ruthless and damaged. All of that was about to change.

I reached for the dog as the morning became truly dark and the blood drained from my head. He started to bark again as I fainted.

2

Shock affects people in different ways. In my case I felt like a bird caught in a storm; battered and looking for home, mutely hysterical and able only to keep on going. After I'd given my statement in the station, after four cups of sweet tea and two Anadin, after I'd given the names of every customer I knew and a description of Alannah Casey's boyfriend, a young guard was delegated to drive me and Lucifer home.

I told them I'd a business to run, which they already knew, and that I would be in the Now and Again Café if they wanted me. They told me my ex-husband, Det. Gda. Hector Shaw, was away but would be back on duty at four o'clock. I told them he knew where to get me, if he wanted to talk to me.

When they asked I told them I was fine. When they insisted on treating me as if I was elderly and feeble minded, I wanted to scream at them that I was only forty-eight, that I was still two years away from being fifty, that I might be too old ever to be young again but was far too young to be made to crawl into middle age. Wanted to but didn't. Instead I left, with my dignity and Lucifer, and walked in rain turned drizzly to the security of work and the café. I picked up the deliveries left by Ted Cullen, my elderly but ever-reliable delivery man, in the barber's on one side, the paper from the newsagent's on the other, and opened an hour and a half later than usual. The black, café T-shirt felt more appropriate than the passionate purple I'd been wearing and a quick ounce or so of make-up dealt with my drained face.

I felt quite calm, considering. I avoided looking at the table by the window where Alannah Casey used sit with Dimitri Sobchak.

Mrs Anita Crawford, my first and often last customer each day, arrived on my heels.

'You're late,' she said, yanking her wheeled shopping bag through the door. 'You won't last long, running a business like this.'

'Sorry,' I said, 'couldn't be helped.'

'I was waiting in the rain,' she said. 'Lucky I had my brolly.'

'Sorry,' I said again. 'I'll have your tea and scone in a minute.'

'You'll lose customers if you keep this up.' She removed her cotton hat, which was wet. 'People have been coming and going. I'm the only one stayed. Out of concern, and worry.'

'That was good of you,' I said and pulled the chair back at her table so as she could sit.

Owning a café was a singular scourge and bizarre obsession. The Now and Again had been my way of dealing with empty-nest syndrome after Emer left home; I'd borrowed more than was sane and bought it overnight. Alannah Casey had once told me she thought the lime green and black with chrome fittings was 'pretty cool'. I did coffees and teas with the best home baking I could source and opened six days a week.

Mrs Crawford sat waiting for me to put the usual fresh flower on her table.

'A carnation all right?' I said and popped it in the stem vase.

She grunted, not yet ready to forgive, opened her coat, checked the money-bag around her waist and rooted in the shopping bag for the day's newspaper.

'Customers of a place expect loyalty,' she said. 'If you're going to disappoint people you should put a notice on the door.' Her damson lips pursed in the pink of her powdered face.

'Difficult to give notice about the unforeseen,' I said and turned on the radio.

'You can be snappy enough when you want to,' said Mrs Crawford. She opened the morning paper and went straight to the state of her stocks and shares.

I knew most of my customers a little and some of them well. Mrs Crawford, who had a flair for the dramatic, claimed to have been an actress and looked like a sprightly, ninety-year-old cadaver.

Alannah Casey hadn't been anywhere near as forthcoming about herself or what she did. Her style had been cool and mocking – with everyone but Dimitri Sobchak. With him she'd been anxiously loving.

I served Mrs Crawford and phoned the woman who helped me run things. Nina Lisekyo was Russian, had been living in Ireland for eight years and was both a treasure and my right hand. She disapproved of and disliked Dimitri Sobchak. He was 'a man with a cold and corrupt heart' she said. He'd certainly made no effort to smile or be friendly.

'You didn't arrive,' Nina said. 'You must give me the keys if you are going to stay in bed.'

'I'm here now,' I said, 'so could you get in quickly? I need you. Please.' Craven was the only way to be with Nina when she was being Russian and angry.

'I am coming,' Nina said as, too late, I heard the radio announce a news broadcast and saw Anita Crawford lift her head from the paper.

'What's that they're saying about Dun Laoghaire?' She cocked an ear. I listened with her, too disabled suddenly to turn it off.

'...the state pathologist will carry out a

20

post mortem on the dead woman, who is reported as being in her early twenties, later today. Unconfirmed reports say the gardai are preparing a murder investigation. The woman's name will be released after her next of kin have been...'

'Switch it off.' Mrs Crawford rattled her spoon in her saucer. 'I'm too old to have to listen and take on any more of the world's brutalities. I want no more of its wickedness.'

I did as she said and slipped on a CD of Stéphane Grappelli playing in the Hot Clubs of Paris. A celebration of life was what we needed.

'Another one gone.' Mrs Crawford started on her scone. 'Soon that entire generation of young people will have killed itself off. We did everything we could for them, gave them everything we didn't have ourselves and look what it's got us. Turbulence and ingratitude and drunkenness and drugs. And death.'

The Guards knew Alannah's name because I'd told them, so her parents and family must know by now that she was dead. Everyone who needed to know would know by now. Dimitri Sobchak too.

'I'm going outside,' I said, 'won't be a minute.'

I yanked the awning into place and leaned my back against the window, wishing I could see the sea and cursing progress and the high apartment block opposite. When I closed my eyes I saw Alannah Casey's dead body.

'You all right?'

Three young men in construction helmets were standing in a semicircle about me. They came most mornings for coffee from a nearby building site. Every one of them had fancied Alannah. She'd had that effect on men.

'I'm fine,' I said, 'just needed a breath of fresh air. Come on in.'

They looked relieved and followed me like sheep. They needed carbohydrates and coffee a lot more than the town needed the apartments they were putting up.

'Good to be inside,' one of them said, 'there's not an awful lot Derek can get us to do in this weather.'

Derek Moran was their foreman and worked them like mules. They said he was fair but I wouldn't have fancied working for him myself. Dour and driven about described him.

They sat where they always sat, at the table next to what had been Alannah's. I was making their coffees when Greg Slattery, red haired and the only local among them, called out to me.

'There was a young one murdered in the town last night,' he said. 'They're saying she was drowned in the Coal Harbour and dumped at the back of the hospital.'

'We heard it on the radio,' Mrs Crawford said, saving me from an answer.

It hadn't taken long to get around then. By lunchtime I'd be part of the story myself and the voyeurs would start arriving. I must have been mad, opening up.

Ed Mulvey, by far the best looking of the three builders, was close to shouting as he thumped the table.

'Chucking him into the harbour with his ankles in cement's too good for the bastard did a thing like that,' he said. It was the longest sentence I'd ever heard him utter. He held his hat over his knee to stop his leg jerking.

'Yeah, well I'm betting they'll never get whoever done it.' Ronnie Fox, who bleached his hair and wore an earring, helped empty the tray when I arrived with their order. He was the most house-trained of the three. 'Fuckin' bastard's long gone by now. Not even in the fuckin' country, I'd say. Drugs, probably. Drugs is what it's about.'

'Loose morals and foul language have their part to play in all of life's tragedies,' said Mrs Crawford. 'You'll find they've a role in this one too.'

Nina's arrival ended speculation, for then; Nina had a history which involved the KGB and an ex-lover, her mother's death and her own escape and was a lot less tolerant of our customers' foibles than I was. She was

23

thirty-one years old and though I thought her beautiful I could see that her sharp-boned face with its catlike eyes was a matter of taste. She gave me an immediate and hard look.

'Are you not well?' she said.

'I am very well,' I snapped.

'No, you are not. You are put out by something.'

'Later.' I poured strong black coffees for each of us. 'I'll tell you later.'

She grunted and raised a cool eyebrow at Ronnie Fox, leaning back in his chair and trying to catch her eye.

'Yes?' she said.

Nothing she said or did would put Ronnie off. He fancied the knickers off her, had told her so in those words and been warned for his trouble that the Now and Again wasn't a toilet.

Nina was refilling his cup when the door opened, and stayed open. I knew, without looking up, that John Rutledge, another of my elderlies, had arrived and was finishing a cigarette. Smoking in the open doorway was his protest at my no-smoking ban. He didn't usually bother when it was raining.

'Born in a barn, were you?' Greg Slattery called.

'I was born in St Michael's Hospital, if you must know.' John Rutledge held his cigarette aloft, delicately between two fingers. He was gay and sometimes took pleasure in rattling the homophobe lurking in Greg.

'Were you now?' Greg affected patience. 'I'll be plainer. If we'd a wanted to take our breaks outside in the rain we'd have stayed on the site.'

'He wants you to shut the effing door,' Ronnie said, 'and so does everyone else.'

I closed the door myself. 'Same as usual?' I said to John Rutledge.

'I didn't really expect you to be open,' he said, 'but since you are and I'm here the answer's yes, I'll have the usual.'

He sat without removing his coat, a long black number he wore all winter because, he said, he'd lived most of his life in hot places. He put his cigarette pack on the table and fiddled with the sugar bowl.

'Why wouldn't she be open?' Anita Crawford asked sharply.

'Do they not know?' John Rutledge looked at me and gave a dazed shake of his head. 'Did you not tell them?' He sounded bleakly incredulous.

Even the coffee machine fell silent. I looked away, and caught Nina watching me. She moved closer.

'Terrible business,' John Rutledge muttered, 'terrible thing our friend dying like that.'

He took a cigarette from the pack and lit up. I sat down opposite him, my legs giving out for the second time that morning. If I'd been a smoker I'd have grabbed the fag from his mouth. If I'd been a screamer I'd have yelled at him. But, stoic that I was, I sat and waited for the world to come crashing about me, again.

What I really wanted was someone to hold me while I wept. Only I couldn't have that either.

John Rutledge sucked the smoke from the cigarette into his skinny body. He let it out slowly too, in a cloud about a Van Dyck beard that was a tribute to the skill of the next-door barber shop. Nina brought him his usual latte and banana muffin and stood back, leaning against the counter. I felt her eyes on me.

Eddie Mulvey broke the silence. 'You've got the floor, man, and we haven't got all morning,' he called, edgily.

'The young woman who used to have coffee here with her Russian is dead,' John Rutledge said. Mrs Crawford gave a small scream and clutched at her throat. He ignored her and went on. 'She was found at the mortuary entrance. Unclothed, is what I was told, exposed to the rain and...'

'We heard it on the radio,' Mrs Crawford interrupted, her voice shrill, 'we heard but we didn't know it was the girl who came here...'

'Oh, be quiet.' John Rutledge sounded

26

tired. 'Our little friend was the mother of a two-year-old child. Shows how little you know about the people you drink coffee with.' He stubbed out the cigarette and trailed off, into the paralysed silence, and looked at me. Nina was looking at me too.

'Did you know?' she said. I nodded.

'So why...' she looked around the café. 'It is not respectful.'

'The dog found her,' I said. 'Lucifer...'

Nina grasped the situation at once. 'We should close,' she said, but gently.

'I've told the police everything,' I said. 'I had to give them the names of regular customers, employees, delivery driver, the plumber...' I stopped. The silence was back. 'They'll want to talk to everyone,' I said.

Ronnie Fox pushed back his chair and stood. 'Jesus fucking Christ! She's dead ... he killed her...' He was shaking and white faced. 'The bastard killed her!'

'Take it easy, man,' Greg Slattery said, 'take it easy.' He sat very still himself. 'May the Lord have mercy on her soul,' he added.

'Amen,' said Nina, stony faced.

'The Russian,' Eddie Mulvey avoided looking at Nina, 'did you tell them about her gobshite of a Russian boyfriend?'

'I told them.' I felt cold, my face and hands especially. I sat on my hands.

'Saving your presence, Nina,' Ronnie Fox said, 'but your man Dimitri was a right

27

arsehole of a gobshite, like Eddie says. Everyone of us could see it but her. He wasn't just a wanker, he was A1 trouble. He won't last long out there. He'll be got, one way or another. If the guards don't get him, someone else will.' He was knowing and grim. 'He'll be got.'

'Don't be too sure it was him...' John Rutledge began but didn't get far.

'Anyone could've told her the Russians coming in here is all fucking ex-KGB and army deserters,' Eddie Mulvey shouted, 'pouring out of the place like sewer rats since the wall fell. What about the chopped-up body found in a suitcase in Sandymount a few years ago? It was Russians did that.'

'The wall fell in Germany,' John Rutledge said.

'She should have stuck with her own...'

I was the one cut Eddie short this time. 'If you know something then you'd better go to the guards,' I said. 'If you don't then I think you'd better shut up.'

Nina had gone behind the counter and was cleaning up. She'd said more than once that Alannah Casey should be careful of Dimitri Sobchak, though never to the dead woman's face. She knew Sobchak's kind, Nina said, and kept a distance from him herself. I'd never asked her what she meant.

'I know something.' Eddie had stopped shouting. 'Everyone here knows something.

We know he was here yesterday and that he was all over her. We know he's not here this morning. Where's the little pillock now she's dead?'

'Probably down at the garda station,' John Rutledge said. 'You'll very likely be asked to pay a visit there yourself so you can speak up then.'

'Fuckers can come for me,' Eddie said, 'I'm not making their job easier for them...'

'Why not?' Ronnie Fox snapped. 'Don't be a fucking jerk-off on this one, Eddie.' He was staring at the carnation in its vase. 'She was a lovely woman...' There were tears in his eyes.

'I must go.' Anita Crawford rattled her wheely-bag and got to her feet. 'Poor misfortunate child. And a mother too. She never told us that...' She bundled the newspaper into the bag. 'Wonder what else she didn't tell us. A dark lady with dark secrets. Time will tell us her story, time alone. I have things to do now...' She looked at me, ancient eyes distraught under blue lids. 'You should take hot milk and honey, my dear. Get that daughter of yours to look after you.'

The door opened before Mrs Crawford got there. Derek Moran, yellow site hat on his head, held it open as she went through.

'You lot thinking of spending the morning here?' He looked at each of his workers in turn, sour as hell and not seeming to sense the mood. He'd only been to the Now and Again once before and was a man much practised at hiding himself under a hat and behind his moustache.

'We were waiting for the rain to ease a bit,' Greg said.

'By God but you're mightily delicate,' his boss said irritably. Rain gusted past him into the shop. 'There's plenty you can be doing under cover on the site. You don't need me to tell you that.' He became even more irritable. 'The rest of the lads finished their break ten minutes ago.'

'The rest of the lads' took their break on site or filled up on cola and sandwiches in the newsagent's two doors down. My lads, awkwardly embarrassed, began rooting for money in their pockets.

'It's all right,' I said hurriedly, 'it's on the house today.'

'Today's is on me,' John Rutledge said, firmly.

Derek Moran, sour as ever in the doorway, stood waiting.

'The young woman who was murdered last night was a customer here,' I said, abruptly and quickly. Maybe he just wanted to get on with the job. Like I'd just wanted to get on with the job. But he should be told anyway.

'What young woman?' He looked at me, I

think. It was hard to see his eyes under the hat. He certainly turned his head.

'A young woman called Alannah Casey,' I said. 'She was nineteen. Her body was left at the door of the morgue.'

'I'm sorry to hear that,' he said. 'I'll pray for her immortal soul. Are ye ready, lads?'

They filed out past him and he closed the door.

'He should pray for his own soul while he's at it,' John Rutledge said. 'Any chance of another coffee, Nina?'

'If you drink it quickly,' Nina said, 'we are closing now out of respect.'

She gave John Rutledge his coffee and we closed the coffee makers and everything else down and cleared up together in silence. Lucifer's head appeared round the door to the back of the counter and I gave him a scone. He took it and disappeared.

This, more than anything else, made me want to cry. There was no rationality to my feelings.

The door opened again.

'We're closed,' I said and looked up. Thaddeus Shaw, my father-in-law, was almost at the counter.

'You should have come to me when you found her,' he said, accusingly. 'Are you all right?'

I could have asked him the same question. He was wearing his pyjama top under a silver anorak and a yellow woolly hat on his bald pate. I was glad the counter hid the bottom part of him. I didn't want to see if he was wearing the pyjama legs too.

'We're closed, Thaddeus,' I said again. He was agitated and I was tired. Thaddeus had something of the circus bear about him; like a bear too he needed humouring.

'Proper order,' he said. 'I want you to come up to the apartment with me when you're ready. This is no time to go back to the house alone.'

Thaddeus lived at the top of the apartment block opposite. He'd been on the ball and told me when the café premises had come up for leasing

'Go home, Thaddeus, please,' I said, 'you'll catch your death. I'll talk to you later.'

'I'll wait 'till you're finished here,' he said. 'Delayed shock's no joke. I promised Hector I'd look after you.'

This I found hard to believe. Thaddeus and his son Hector, my ex-husband, had an actively hostile relationship going back to Hector's teens. It had endured throughout our marriage and continued still, with occasional lapses. This might, of course, be one of them.

'You were talking to Hector?' I said, carefully. I moved closer to him and smelled what I thought, but couldn't believe, was drink.

'I was,' Thaddeus said. 'He's out of town

32

but is on his way back. The station phoned him, told him about you finding the girl's body in the early morning. You and the dog. He phoned me. I came straight away.'

There was a thaw then. Hector wouldn't want me talking to anyone, would want to go over my statement with me himself.

John Rutledge came up behind Thaddeus and put a fifty-euro note on the counter. 'That's to cover everything, the lads and myself,' he said, 'we'll sort the change another time. Good day to you, Thaddeus.'

Thaddeus grunted without turning and John Rutledge left, black coat wet and flapping.

John and Thaddeus had known each other years before, as young men, but didn't seemed inclined to continue the friendship. Thaddeus's excuse was that John Rutledge wasn't the man now he'd been then. I'd no idea what John Rutledge's reasons were.

'There's something I want to talk to you about,' Thaddeus said.

Thaddeus was seventy-five years old, a recovering alcoholic with a past for which he was constantly making reparation. His blindingly stubborn way of doing things often did more harm than good. But he was a kind grandfather to Emer and an always decent, if fussing, presence in my own life. It all came down to guilt about the damage he'd done his son, but that was all right.

Life's like that.

'Later,' I said. 'I really do want to go home to bed.'

'People are going to plague the place for coffees they don't want,' he said, 'all of them wanting to see where the dead girl and her lover sat. You can have your sleep in my spare room. This is a terrible thing, Frances.' He paused. 'We have to talk.'

'Tomorrow,' I told him, 'we'll talk tomorrow.'

Or the day after, whenever I could bear to hear the gospel according to Alcoholics Anonymous – which was more than likely the sort of talk Thaddeus had in mind. AA, for Thaddeus, had an answer to everything; it was his lifeline and substitute addiction. He'd moved back from the counter and I told myself I'd imagined the smell of drink. He'd been on the dry, as far as I knew, for about thirty-five years.

'Fran is tired, Mr Shaw.' Nina, of whom Thaddeus was wary, leaned across the counter and forced him to look at her. 'She needs to rest. I will take her home, the dog too. She needs to gather her thoughts together.'

Gather my thoughts was just what I needed to do. There was nothing to be done about my feelings, which were numb.

'With all respects, Miss Lisekyo, this is none of your affair.' Thaddeus gave a small bow in Nina's direction. 'There are things my daughter-in-law and I need to discuss.'

'Tomorrow.' Nina came from behind the counter and held open the door. 'She will talk tomorrow. She is shocked now. You are an old man and must understand this.'

'I am an old man who has concerns for his family,' Thaddeus spoke with dignified fury, 'you know nothing of this matter, Miss Lisekyo. You just see what is in front of your nose and know nothing of the history attaching.' He clasped his great hands in front of him, a habit when agitated. 'Go home now, there's a good girl. Frances and myself will lock up.'

Even for Thaddeus, who liked to have his own way, this was an insistence too far.

Nina looked as if she would propel him bodily out of the shop.

'What history?' I said, hastily. 'What *are* you talking about, Thaddeus?'

'There's something you don't know that I must tell you. You must *not* get any more involved in this thing...' He rolled his eyes at me, a signal that he didn't want whatever he had to say heard by Nina. 'Please, Frances, please come and listen to what I've to say, please.'

Such pleading and humility wasn't just uncharacteristic of Thaddeus, it was unknown. Hector's father, though freely admitting his mind was pickled from years

35

of drink, still thought he knew it all.

'All right,' I said, 'but I'm not leaving Lucifer here on his own.'

Thaddeus had an aversion to the dog, whom he liked to call a retarded mongrel. He preferred his animals stuffed and in glass cases.

'Go with him,' Nina said, crossly. 'I will close up. I will bring Lucifer to your house later. Go.'

The rain had stopped as I crossed the road with Thaddeus, and the wind had died down. I was relieved to see he was wearing a pair of track-suit legs.

But I wondered, in the damp stillness, if I was the only one to sense an eye-of-the-hurricane calm in the air.

3

November, 1953. Dun Laoghaire

The small girls look at their mother, then at one another. Their mother's moods are unpredictable so neither wants to be the one to ask if she can see their father coming. Their mother is standing at the window with her back to them, looking out into the street. The girls are sitting at the kitchen table in their best frocks. Framed in the window their mother's hair is a golden halo.

'Is he coming? Can you see him coming?' Stella, who is eight and the oldest, is the one who eventually asks.

Shirley Walsh, their mother, closes the curtains, securing all chinks. She is not popular with her neighbours. They spy on her.

'No. Not yet,' she says.

Shirley has been concentrating more on the dark and the bitter rain than she has on a sighting of her husband. She is sick inside at having to spend another winter in Dun Laoghaire. She had so very much wanted to be back home in Liverpool by now but here she is, still trapped, still watching the street grow colder, the neighbours scuttle for the shelter of their mean homes. The winters have all been the same, every one of the ten since she came to live here. She keeps telling Jimmy she wants to go and he keeps promising he'll think about it. Now she feels, as she always does this time of year, as if she will go mad. The feeling makes her reckless.

'When's he going to be here?'

Stella, her eldest, asks again about her father. Stella is a demanding child. She is eight years old and a daddy's girl. Probably because she sees so little of her father, who is a merchant seaman. But also because she is pretty.

'Soon,' Shirley tells her, 'soon.'

'You always say that.' The child is sullen.

'Don't you give me lip,' Shirley says.

The kitchen is too hot and too small and the fire is burning their fuel too quickly. Shirley, in her emerald blouse and emerald, toeless high heels, sits for a minute on a box holding shoe polish and thinks about her family. She misses her father and sisters. She even misses her dead mother, though she didn't have much time for Shirley when she was alive.

She missed the coronation of the new queen earlier in the year too. She is missing the whole of life.

The kitchen, at its widest, is seven feet. The walls are yellow, the tiles around the fireplace beige and the floor covered in red

38

lino. Shirley keeps all of these surfaces shining clean but allows dust and smoke to settle on a certificate framed over the fireplace. This says the house is dedicated to the Sacred Heart and Shirley has no time for such Roman Catholic witchcraft. It's just more of what she has to put up with.

She goes back to kneading bread at the table. Stella, who is like her mother and will make a lovely woman, fiddles with her hair and watches. Shirley's other daughter, Melanie, is a year younger and is clever but plain with brown hair and glasses. The glasses are a flaw on her father's side. No one in Shirley's family has ever needed them.

'What *time* will he be here?' Stella persists. 'Is he going to be here at eight o'clock or nine o'clock?'

Shirley frowns, irritated by her daughter's resemblance to herself at the same age. It reminds her that not only is her childhood gone but so too is the young woman she'd once been and the fun and men she'd once had.

Shirley Walsh is twenty-eight years old. She has been married to Jimmy, four years her senior, for ten years. They met in a pub in Liverpool during the war. There had been no war in Ireland and he had promised her so much.

She kneads the dough with vigour, the pleasure of its fleshy softness relaxing her.

39

She makes good bread. When Stella starts to speak again Shirley cuts her short. 'Don't ask me any more,' she warns, gently enough.

'You're such a baby,' Melanie says to her sister. 'It's stupid to keep asking.' Her voice is flat and far too old for her seven years.

'And you're just a scabby-faced know-all,' Stella snarls.

Melanie stiffens but doesn't touch the eczema. Stella fiddles again with her golden hair.

Shirley thinks about the endless times she has told Jimmy how the women on the street watch her, how they wait for her to put a foot wrong.

What she has never told him about is the way the men circle her, tongues hanging out like dogs. She cannot tell Jimmy how the women blame *her* for the filthy behaviour of *their* men, nor how she feels she has lost herself, lost Shirley Hudson, the pretty hairdresser who was once young and game for anything.

He knows nothing of her life. Nothing.

She separates the dough into a couple of loaves which she dusts with flour and puts into the oven on a baking tray.

If she'd stayed in Liverpool, if she'd had the sense not to marry Jimmy, if she'd kept her knickers on and not been swept away by a blue-eyed Irishman singing like a drunken angel in a pub...

40

But she'd been so hot, just listening and looking at him, that she'd drenched herself. It was always like that with her and Jimmy; wild as animals they were.

She's wet now too, God help her, just thinking about him on his way home to her. Two children and ten years in this shithole later he can still make her feel like this. Except that he's never here when she needs him, God damn him to hell. Never. What happened was his fault.

She promises herself that that night, when they are alone and he is full of loving her, before the rot sets in, again, she will tell him she is going home and taking the girls. With or without him.

'Maybe he's not going to come tonight,' Stella pipes up again. 'Maybe something happened to his ship. Maybe–'

'I'll redden your legs if there's another word,' Shirley says.

She looks at the clock, a wedding present from her father who refuses to visit Ireland. It's half-past six.

The neighbours will appear, feigning friendship, when Jimmy arrives. No one will call her a 'bloody English cow' when he's around. They'll snivel and grovel and look to see what he's brought that they can get their hands on. He's so full of generosity, her Jimmy, street angel and house devil that he is.

41

'When will we—'

Stella stops when Melanie grabs her arm and squeezes it. Stella pulls the arm away and is quiet. A ceilidh band on the wireless plays a reel.

'Switch that bloody noise OFF,' Shirley screams, suddenly.

Melanie jumps up, kills the music and sits down again.

Shirley rubs her brow with the back of a floury hand. Maybe the child is right and Jimmy isn't coming tonight. Wouldn't be the first time he's been 'delayed' getting home.

'When will Uncle Ritchie be here?' Stella, seeming determined to torment her, takes another tack.

'Soon,' Shirley sighs, calm again as she rubs the flour from her hands and tidies her hair.

'Are Ben and Michael coming too?'

'Why do you think she's making so much bread, dummy?' Melanie says.

'Because you're a pig and eat too much,' Stella sniggers.

Melanie, under the table, shoots out a solid shank and topples her sister off her chair.

'She kicked me!' Stella howls, picks herself up and allows fat, instant tears to roll down her hot cheeks.

Shirley carries the kettle to the sink and begins filling it under the tap. 'My patience is wearing thin,' she speaks in measured tones, 'you'll both be in your beds before your father comes if you're not careful.'

A splutter of brownish water comes from the tap, then stops.

Shirley screams an obscenity and slams the kettle into the sink. When the lid slides from the draining board to the floor she aims a kick at it.

'The water's gone again.' Her voice is a thin, controlled scream in the silent kitchen.

Stella has stopped crying.

'I'll get water from the barrel.' Melanie goes to her mother. 'Can I have the kettle, please, Mam?'

When she holds out her hand Shirley lifts the kettle from the sink and threatens her with it. Stella gives a small, fearful gulp and begins to cry again, this time in earnest.

'We'll do without tea,' Shirley says in the same high, almost scream of a voice, 'and your uncle and cousins and whoever else calls can do without too. Let them see how we live, how we don't even have running water in this dump of a house.'

'Who else is coming?' Stella, distracted and hopeful, stops crying. 'Is your friend coming? Will he bring–'

'What friend?' Shirley stands over Stella, holding the kettle.

Melanie watches the hand holding the kettle. Stella scrambles to her feet and moves backwards to the door.

'The friend who brought us the Lemon's sweets.' Stella is white faced and shaking. 'I want to go to the toilet.' She turns, reaches for the knob and is almost through the door when Shirley jerks her back into the kitchen.

'What Lemon's sweets are you talking about?' Shirley demands. Stella gives a terrified squeal and her teeth chatter. She cannot speak. 'You were dreaming,' Shirley says, shaking her, 'nobody came with Lemon's sweets. Nobody. Do you understand me?'

Stella's head bobs on her shoulders. 'You don't want me to tell Daddy he brought us sweets,' she whimpers, 'I won't. I promise...'

'You weren't listening to me...' Shirley raises the kettle, 'nobody came, nobody brought sweets.'

The child makes a mewling sound and wrenches herself free of Shirley's grasp.

'It wasn't a dream!' Stella is frenzied. 'He *was* here. He brought us a box of Lemon's sweets each...' she escapes into the hallway '...I'm telling me da when he comes...'

Stella flies like a wind let loose along the hallway. But it's not long enough for her to fly free and Shirley catches her as she struggles to open the front door.

'Little bitch!' Shirley's spittle covers her daughter's face as she holds Stella with one hand and brings the kettle cruelly across the back of her skinny legs with the other.

'Let me go, you're killing me, let me go...'

Stella covers her face with her hands as Shirley lashes out with the kettle, again and again, smashing it across her daughter's knuckles until she breaks the skin and it bleeds. Melanie pulls at Shirley as Shirley screams, loud enough to waken the dead. Loud enough too to be heard in the street by her husband's brother Ritchie, when he arrives outside the door with his sons Bernard and Michael.

'Open the door!' Ritchie Walsh ignores the knocker and bangs on the door with his fist. 'What's going on in there? Open the door, Shirley, or I'll have to use my shoulder...'

Crying and terrified, shrinking from the blows of the kettle, Stella doesn't hear. Neither, raining blows with the kettle and made deaf by her own fear, does Shirley.

4

March, 2003. Dun Laoghaire.

Thaddeus's penthouse was one of those overpriced mid-1990s' jobs with a great many sliding glass doors, chrome fittings and white everywhere. He'd overstuffed it with dead wildlife, large sea-birds mostly, which was his concession to a decorating plan. It was otherwise spartan and ship-shape, a way of living learned during his long-ago sea-faring days with the merchant navy. He did all his own housework.

He'd bought it when he'd finally been persuaded to sell the family home, a house I'd never felt comfortable in. I didn't feel comfortable in the penthouse either. It was always too cold, for one thing.

I sat into one of the black leather chairs in his living room and watched the clouds roll by. They were thunderous.

'Would you like to talk about finding the body?' Thaddeus said after he'd made tea and put a plate of chocolate biscuits (which he loves and I hate) in front of me. Attending AA meetings had convinced him that talking was good and must be encouraged at all times and in all situations.

'No,' I said, 'I would not. I've talked about it enough for today.'

He looked disappointed. 'It would do you a great deal of good,' he said.

I tried the tea. It was undrinkable. 'You said you'd something to say to me,' I reminded him, sharply. I was becoming irritable. A sure sign of normality returning, the effects of shock wearing off.

'I didn't want to say too much with the Russian woman there,' Thaddeus said, 'wagging tongues, all of that. She'll know soon enough. It's better you should hear things from me, first hand as it were.' He could be ambiguous to the point of obscurity.

I put my mug of tea down on the shining surface of a small table, hard. 'Any chance I could have a brandy?' I said.

While he was in the kitchen I stepped out onto the balcony and took deep breaths of the cold, damp air. The bay looked sullen and bad-tempered, the massed cloud adding to the general gloom.

Thaddeus appeared at my side with the brandy and a coat which he put around my shoulders. Then he stepped smartly back inside and reappeared with a second brandy.

'Thought I'd keep you company,' he said. I stared at him.

'You don't have to,' I said.

'True,' he took a long drink, 'true. But I want to.'

'You don't drink, Thaddeus...'

'I'm old enough to be the judge of that,' he didn't look at me, 'at this stage the odd glass isn't going to make much difference.'

'If you say so,' I said. This had never been his line on drink before; up 'till now he'd combined zealotry with an obsessional and personal abhorrence.

'Did you know she was strangled?' he said after I'd taken a hefty gulp myself.

'No,' I was startled, 'no, I didn't know that...' I hadn't seen any marks on her, none at all. 'Her hair was partly across her neck,' I said, remembering. Her black, black hair. 'Who told you this?' I said.

'Hector. He got the preliminary word on the phone from the police doctor. He's going to be fairly involved in the case when he gets back to town.'

'Is that what you wanted to tell me?' I said. The brandy was warming. I took another large gulp. Thaddeus made a point of only buying the best booze. And of serving only double measures.

'No,' Thaddeus said, 'it's not about Hector. But he tells me too that the dead child was naked. Is he right?'

The wind off the sea was restless, and growing colder.

'She was naked and she was *arranged*,

Thaddeus, as if she was laid out for coffining…' I stopped. It seemed obscene to go on describing her dead and very lonely body. I downed the rest of the brandy.

'You recognised her straight away?' Thaddeus said. He'd finished his drink.

'I knew her, Thaddeus, she came to the café all the time. Her name was Alannah Casey…' I stopped again. Thaddeus had got me talking about it more than I wanted. 'I'd like another,' I handed him the empty glass, 'please.'

He put an arm about my shoulder and led me back inside. He shut the sliding glass door, tightly, and put me sitting in an armchair. I closed my eyes when he went to get me the drink. I hadn't the energy to even be curious about him drinking again.

He was gone so long I was almost asleep when he got back. When he touched my shoulder I woke immediately.

'I know what her name was,' he said.

There were two glasses of brandy on the coffee table – as well as an old-fashioned leather suitcase. Thaddeus sat on a straight-backed chair, opposite, and watched me.

'She had a boyfriend,' he said.

'Dimitri Sobchak. He's Russian. Nina doesn't like him. She says he's corrupt, that she knows his type and can sense evil in him.' I paused and put together my own thoughts about Dimitri Sobchak. 'All I could see was what Alannah Casey saw in him,' I said. 'He was fair, slightly built, very good looking with a small beard. He had a sort of fierce energy, an exoticism about him. Alannah was tall and slim and dark. They were interesting together. Very intense, the pair of them.'

I was speaking about Dimitri Sobchak as if he too was dead. Or gone. Thaddeus, with a sensitivity unusual in him, picked up on my unease.

'The police are looking for him,' he said. 'they'll be talking to him. Would you have thought he was—?'

I didn't let him finish. I didn't want to hear him say the word murderer.

'I don't know.' I was curt. 'Alannah Casey seemed to me a disaffected teenager in love with a man who might make her unhappy. He didn't seem suitable but I wasn't sure why – married unsuitable? Jobless unsuitable? Illegal immigrant unsuitable? It never occurred to me he might be murderously unsuitable though. Not that.' I'd said the word. It felt shit.

Thaddeus got up and took a small watering can to the white geraniums growing inside the window. He'd hated his wife's white geraniums when she was alive but after she died began caring for them as if they were children. They died anyway. He always replaced them.

50

The watering and silence was clever of Thaddeus because I began to talk again, compulsively. I'd all but forgotten he'd brought me to the apartment to tell me something.

'Dimitri Sobchak was moody, not what you'd call a cheerful type. Alannah Casey wore a lot of black, a bit of a Goth really, but with style. She painted her fingernails different colours. She wasn't particularly friendly but she'd a lovely, rare smile. I thought her a little sad. She was the sort of woman men wanted. At least two of my builder regulars were in lust with her.'

Thaddeus was fiddling with a key in the lock of the suitcase. 'Ah, yes,' he said, 'it fits. It all fits, again.'

I thought he was talking about the key until he threw it down in exasperation. 'Wrong one,' he said, 'be back in a minute.'

He left me facing some of the reasons I felt uncomfortable in the penthouse. One of them, a framed photo of myself as a smiling younger woman, stared from a shelf. I remembered when it was taken, how little I had to smile about at the time. Next to it Thaddeus had placed a picture of Emer in her early teens. She was smiling too, proof that pictures lie. Or at least give a fleeting truth. There were no photos at all of Hector. Thaddeus could be very unforgiving.

On a second shelf there was a wedding

51

picture of Thaddeus and his wife Deborah. I'd never known her. The car crash in which she'd died had happened five years before I met Hector. The photograph showed a dark-haired, handsome woman. Very like Hector. Hector whom I'd loved so much for so long and now couldn't love at all.

A cold-eyed seagull landed on the balcony rail and I watched his feathers lifting in the wind as he walked along the rail until Thaddeus came back. He brought three keys with him and began to try them, one by one.

I went back to talking about Dimitri Sobchak. I couldn't stop myself. 'He always wore a leather coat and he was a fidget,' I said. 'Before he sat down he would lay his mobile, cigarettes and lighter neatly on the table. I told him the first day he couldn't smoke, that the café was too small. After that he would just roll a cigarette between his fingers. He never went outside for a smoke, like the others.' The seagull abandoned his balancing act on the rail and flew away.

'You think he did it, don't you?' Thaddeus said.

'Jesus Christ, Thaddeus, how do I know? I just keep thinking that I should have paid her more attention. Talked to her more...'

'What difference would talking to her have made?'

'We'll never know, will we?' I said.

'We know all right,' Thaddeus said, 'that it

wouldn't have made any difference at all. It's my opinion that whoever killed her had it well planned and wasn't going to be stopped.'

He opened the suitcase and sat looking at the collection of old newspapers inside. He didn't touch them.

'What was it you wanted to tell me, Thaddeus?' I said.

'What I've to tell you is something the guards know already...' He gave me a quick look and went on in a disjointed mumble as he took the newspapers, one by one, out of the suitcase '...I thought to myself ... as I was telling you already...' he put the papers in neat piles, '...that it would be better if I told you... I want you to understand my position...' there was nothing but a small, brown-paper-wrapped parcel in the suitcase now '...it's sad you have to be told at all but in the circumstances it's the best thing for everyone that you hear it from me, not the newspapers or gossip...' Thaddeus was distressed, no doubt about it. Distressed enough to start drinking again. He was also beginning to distress me. For both our sakes, and to move things along, I got tough.

'Tell me *now*, Thaddeus,' I said, 'whatever it is you have to tell me. If you don't I'm leaving.'

I stood up. Thaddeus, who was holding the brown parcel in his hands, didn't move.

'I mean it, Thaddeus,' I said, 'I'm leaving.'

'You're right,' Thaddeus said, 'I'm a foolish, prevaricating old man. Soon I'll be a drunken one, too.'

A single, slow tear rolled from the corner of his eye. It's said that the tears of old people are as terrible as those of children are natural. I'd never understood why until then. Thaddeus's tear was unbearable.

'Please, Thaddeus.' I hunkered beside him and covered the hands holding the parcel with mine. 'Please tell me.'

'I will,' he said. The tear rolled into the crevices about his chin and disappeared. 'I'll tell you now.'

He unwrapped the paper and took out a framed, black and white photograph of a young woman. I waited while he dusted and looked at it. His hands shook.

'She was a good-looking woman,' he said and laid it, almost reverently, in the open lid of the suitcase. 'It's not a face to forget.' He looked at it again. 'She was the first one to die, the start of it.'

It wasn't until days later, until the story of the past began to fill out in earnest, that I thought about the way he'd told me the story, and what he hadn't told me.

'Your young friend is the third woman to die as she did,' Thaddeus said. 'Two other women were murdered, a long time ago, and left at the doors of morgues. This woman

54

was the first of them,' he tapped the glass over the photograph, 'her name was Shirley Walsh and she died in nineteen fifty-three, here in Dun Laoghaire. The second was called Lilyla Borodin. She died on Coney Island, New York, ten years later. Around the time that John Fitzgerald Kennedy was assassinated, to put a date on it for you.'

At first I couldn't get what he was telling me together in my head. My initial reaction was that he was having his way with the truth, as he often did, turning facts on their head to make a better story. Then I looked at the wide-eyed, blond-haired woman in the photograph. She was heavily made-up and she was, as Thaddeus had said, very lovely. Then I looked again at Thaddeus. He was looking at the photograph too, and he was absolutely motionless. I sipped my brandy.

'Tell me the rest,' I said and listened without any of the terrible suspicions which would come later.

'It was before you were born. Hector was a baby. Shirley Walsh was the English wife of a merchant seaman named Jimmy Walsh. I knew him and I knew her.' He cleared his throat. 'Her naked body was found in the door of the morgue on a morning in November, nineteen fifty-three. She'd been half strangled, then drowned. She was twenty-eight years old.'

'Who found her?' I said.

'Couple of youngsters mitching from school. The morgue was in a different place then, down by the coal harbour. The youngsters knew her, same as you knew this morning's unfortunate young woman. Took them a while to get over it.'

'I'm sure it did,' I said. It would take me a while too.

I couldn't sit and I couldn't stand still so I paced in a circle round a gannet on a pedestal and a fox with useless teeth bared. I felt ill.

'Did they find the person who did it?' I said.

'There was a conviction,' Thaddeus said.

'Who did they convict?' I asked. Thaddeus, who had been holding the photograph, wrapped it up again and put it back into the suitcase, face down.

'Her husband Jimmy was found guilty,' he said. 'He protested his innocence but there was any amount of evidence produced in court proving he was a jealous and possessive husband and a bad-tempered drinker.'

'What was she like?' I said.

'She was a restless creature...' Thaddeus hesitated. 'Jimmy Walsh met her in Liverpool and married her within weeks. She was eighteen and he was twenty-two. When he was half-drunk he used to say that meeting her was the night his ship came in. When he was arseholes it was another story. Sorry about the crudity.'

He put a hand on the piles of newspaper cuttings. 'Jimmy Walsh could be violent when drunk,' he went on. 'That was what did for him in the end, that tied to circumstantial evidence and the stories about Shirley's infidelities. She didn't have much time for women but she liked men and they liked her. There was a lot of gossip.'

'How did she come to be murdered?' I hadn't wanted the practical details but Thaddeus gave them to me anyway.

'The court decided Jimmy tried to throttle her before throwing her into the harbour in a drunken rage,' he said. 'The evidence showed she was hauled in when dead, her body stripped and carried to the back door of the morgue. The conclusion was that the stripping had to do with shaming her in death for being unfaithful. Jimmy Walsh was sentenced to hang.' He was sitting very upright in the chair. 'He did the job for them himself, hanged himself in his cell with a belt just a week before old Pierrepoint the hangman was due to arrive from England to do the job.'

He stopped. I sipped the brandy and waited. I was beginning to feel light-headed. When Thaddeus began to talk about Pierrepoint I let him ramble for a while.

'They used to get an Englishman by that name over to do the job of hangman because no one here would do it. I saw him once in the street. He didn't have a lot to recommend him. He was about six feet tall and wore a long overcoat and an Anthony Eden hat and he'd a face like a constipated bulldog. There wasn't a place in Dun Laoghaire would give him a bed so he used to stay in a hotel in Dublin. He got a fee of twenty-five pounds for a hanging.'

Jimmy Walsh had cheated him out of that, at least.

'They were confusing times,' Thaddeus went on, 'confusing times for everyone. Most people thought Jimmy Walsh did it. The weight of circumstantial evidence was huge.' He put his hand on the papers. I couldn't even read the headlines from where I was sitting and didn't try. Not then anyway. 'When it was all over, after Jimmy had hanged himself, his brother Ritchie emigrated to Coney Island, New York, and took his own two sons and his nieces, the daughters of Shirley and Jimmy, with him. Ritchie Walsh was a timid, bookish sort who'd made an unfortunate marriage to a harridan who'd left him with the two boys to rear. It was a brave thing for him to do, to take the young people away to have a second chance at life. Can't have been easy for him and by all accounts he wasn't really up to the job. He went at the drink in a big way in America.'

There was an unremitting sadness to it all:

58

a young mother murdered, a young father dead to suicide, their children taken away to America.

'Was it Ritchie Walsh who killed the woman on Coney Island ten years later?' I said, adding two and two together to the demon drink and getting five.

'A drinking man doesn't always have to be suspect,' Thaddeus became edgy, 'murders are as a rule pre-meditated and carried out in sober senses.'

'They are?' I said.

'Absolutely.'

Thaddeus hadn't planned to kill his wife and was understandably sensitive around the subject of drunken misadventures. By his own admission he'd been 'filthy drunk' the night he walked from the car he'd just crashed, getting clear away before it went up in flames with Hector's mother inside.

'What happened on Coney Island in nineteen sixty-three?' I asked, voice neutral. Thaddeus was even voiced too when he answered me. His eyes were bloodshot.

'The young woman I mentioned earlier, she was about the same age as Shirley Walsh, was found strangled and naked on the steps of a hospital morgue.'

'You said she was Russian...'

Thaddeus waved me to silence. 'Coincidence,' he said, 'no link with your friend's Russian lover. Fact back then was that Uncle

Joe Stalin died in nineteen fifty-three and a fair number of the first wave of the Russians to move out ended up on Coney Island, by all accounts. There's another generation altogether of Russians crossing the world now.'

'Was Ritchie Walsh a suspect?' I asked.

'No, it appears not,' Thaddeus shook his head. 'The police there seemed fairly certain from the beginning that the woman's husband was responsible. He was already known to them, as the saying goes, and couldn't, or wouldn't, account for his whereabouts on the night his wife was murdered.'

'But the *way* it happened,' I persisted, 'strangulation, the morgue door ... surely that wasn't just put down to coincidence?'

'It was put down to Ritchie's never-ending drunken talk about what had happened in Dun Laoghaire,' Thaddeus was sour, 'seems he'd spent the best part of the ten years gabbing to anyone who would listen about the tragedy, about why he'd to leave the old country. The Walshes were friendly with the Borodins so the husband would have heard the story more often than he needed to.'

'Makes a sort of sense...' I said. Sort of; copy-cat murders were common, just as copy-cat suicides were common. 'Did the husband confess?' I asked.

'Murderers don't confess,' Thaddeus said, 'confessing and seeking redemption's the sort of thing normal people do. Murderers aren't normal.'

'I take it the answer's no,' I snapped.

'He didn't confess,' Thaddeus rifled through the newspaper cuttings, 'there's something here on the case...' He lifted and opened a folded paper. When I held out my hand to take it from him he moved it out of reach. 'Doesn't give a lot of information,' he said, 'just that he was convicted and sentenced to death. He did die, I remember that, in the electric chair.'

'There must have been a great interest in it here too, at the time,' I said. I would have been seven years old.

'Not as much as you'd imagine,' Thaddeus shook his head, 'the killing of the American president was the topic of the day. He'd been shot less than a week before. It over-shadowed everything to a powerful degree.' He put the paper back in its pile. 'Now you know,' he said.

'I suppose I do...' I said.

'You do know that the guards will be going back over all of this,' Thaddeus was watching me, 'there's going to be a lot of media talk and speculation, theories and talk about copy-cat murders. Mad talk. Keep away from it, Frances, don't get involved. The gutter press will have a field day and you'll be dragged in and made a part of it if you're not very careful.'

'I already am a part of it,' I reminded him, irritably.

'I'm talking about damage limitation,' Thaddeus said, in his most annoyingly autocratic tone, 'you don't have to be any more involved than you are. I think, in fact, that you should take a holiday, go away for a few weeks until the fuss has died down.' He began packing up the suitcase. 'I'll put these back where they were.'

'I'd like to go through them,' I said. 'Can I borrow the suitcase?'

'There's nothing in there that I haven't already told you,' Thaddeus snapped the suitcase shut, 'any further interest on your part would be unhealthy.'

'I'll make decisions like that for myself, Thaddeus,' I remembered the tear and kept a check on my temper. 'Is there some reason why you don't want me to see the cuttings?'

'Melodrama doesn't suit you, Frances,' he said. 'I've not left these out of my keeping for fifty years and I'm not going to do so now. No...' He held up a silencing hand. 'Don't ask if you may look at them here either. I don't want to be the one responsible for you poring and brooding over such things.' He hesitated, then said again, 'It would be unhealthy.'

'Don't worry about my health, Thaddeus...'

'You're annoyed.' He stood with the suitcase. 'Why don't you lie down in the spare bedroom for a few hours? I'll bring you a cup of sweet tea. You're in shock.'

'The guards will have files on the other murders,' I reminded him, 'I can look at those or search the web.'

'Do those things if you want,' he said stiffly, 'but remember you're a woman alone. It's not safe.'

'What do you mean, it's not safe? This concern for my mental health is...'

I stopped. I was suddenly, if dimly, hearing what he was saying. 'You're afraid something else is going to happen, aren't you, Thaddeus? Do you think the person who killed Alannah might hurt or kill someone again? Is that what you think, Thaddeus?'

'I think the person who did it is mad, which is a perfectly rational view to take,' Thaddeus said. 'I *know*, and so do you, that he's out there somewhere, free to kill again if he thinks he has to.'

'Me reading up on old murders is hardly a reason for him to kill again.'

'Could be, if he felt it would lead you to discover him...'

'What have those old murders to do with this one, Thaddeus?' I demanded. 'What didn't you tell me?'

'I told you everything,' Thaddeus sighed, 'but it would be a foolish man or woman who dismissed what happened last night simply as a copy-cat murder.'

'Why? The other women were murdered fifty and forty years ago,' I said.

'Keeping an eye on what's gone before is only wise. It was Faulkner's view that the past wasn't dead, nor even past.'

'So it *is* the past you're worried about?' I said.

'Don't involve yourself any more, Frances. It's enough that you know what went on.'

'Do you believe the second murder was a copy-cat thing?' I don't know why I asked this question. It seemed to come from an unconscious place in my mind.

'A court of law decided it was,' Thaddeus said.

'Do *you* believe it was?'

'I don't know,' Thaddeus said.

'Do you believe Jimmy Walsh killed his wife in nineteen fifty-three?'

'I don't know whether he did or not,' Thaddeus turned away with the suitcase. 'None of this has anything to do with you, Frances. It was chance made you find that poor child this morning, nothing more. Keep out of it from now on.' He left the room with the suitcase. He was slightly unsteady on his feet.

I was suddenly very, very tired. I called a taxi and went home.

5

I slept for four hours, solid. Then I woke, suddenly, as if someone was calling me. Someone was. Lucifer was alternately barking and whining in the kitchen, a trick of his when he's feeling ignored.

I went down to him. He made it immediately clear he wanted another walk. As far as he was concerned I was home so it must be time for the end-of-day outing.

I'd taken the phone off the hook but the message light was flashing. When I checked there were six; I didn't listen to any of them and turned it on to message only. I'd always loved the stillness of my small house but now I couldn't find it anywhere. I took the mobile and the dog and headed for the west pier and a long, long walk. I felt a serious empathy with the heaving discontent of sea and sky when we got there. Lucifer, chasing gulls, had no such problem. The pier was almost empty and I walked quickly.

We'd used to walk the pier a lot, Hector and I with Emer when she was young. The rot which had set in between us was always easier to bear on the pier; there was always the possibility we would meet someone, that

Hector's boredom would be relieved, that my patience might hold. It was the one thing we did together that sometimes worked.

Sex was the one thing that always worked. Hector was very, very good in the bed department. In the six years since we'd split up there had been precious little to compare with him.

I'd continued walking the pier with Emer, when Hector finally left. When Emer moved out, walking it alone kept me, to some degree, sane. I was aimless for a while after she left, functionless and ridiculously lonely. I became frightened too when I found it hard to get out of bed in the mornings, mainly because I hadn't slept in the night.

My notion of myself had been hung around the framework of motherhood for so long that, with the harness removed, there was hardly anything left of me. Until the coffee shop.

I was more than halfway along the pier when I heard my name being called. I knew the voice and cursed my too-well-known habits as I turned to wait for Hector to catch up with me.

'Bit of a storm coming,' he said when he came close.

'Are you talking about the weather?' I said.

'What else?' he said and fell into step beside me when I started walking again.

'Dog's in good shape,' he said.

'He is,' I said. I wasn't going to help him. I'd spent too many years trying to make life work for him. He didn't need me any more, anyway.

He looked good, in his pale, decadent, indoor way. He always did. He was too thin, of course, but he was always too thin as well. His raincoat was grey, the leather jacket underneath black. His grey trousers were probably Italian, his grey, fine wool jumper ditto. Grey with a touch of black was a sort of uniform with Hector. Women liked the air of weary desperation he cultivated. I thought I spotted a thinning in his hair when the wind lifted it on his head. A balding Hector was somehow unimaginable.

'Emer keeping well?' he said. 'Haven't been speaking to her for about a week.'

'She's fine,' I said. 'She's doing production for a film somewhere in Wicklow.'

'That should keep her out of harm's way,' he said. Out of his way was what he meant; Emer liked to ask questions, Hector hated answering them. Emer called him Dude, as in Cool Dude, a tag not without malice since she thought him an emotional eunuch. She maintained he was scared of life's 'squelchy bits', by which she meant love and fun. Anally retentive was another phrase she used about him. And still they got on, in their own way. Now. Emer was wrong about the fun. He needed lubricating but Hector Shaw had a few laughs in him.

He turned and caught me looking at him.

'Are you okay?' he said. 'You should have called me.'

'There was no need.'

'I'm on the case now anyway, so anything you want to say...' He stopped and stood in my path, waiting.

It's difficult trying for eye contact with someone wearing shades. Difficult to tell someone wearing shades how you feel too.

'It's a bit chilly,' I said, 'we should keep moving.'

He whistled to Lucifer, who came lolloping back to him. We walked on, more quickly. The wind in my face felt cleansing.

'Thaddeus told me you'd left his place. I called to the house and when the car was gone reckoned you'd be here,' he said.

I resisted a cheap crack about his detecting skills. He was actually good at his job, and respected. 'Old habits die hard,' I said, inanely.

'We're putting together a good-sized team,' he said. 'The bastard who did it needs to be brought in quickly. It was an ugly one, and planned.'

'Do you think he'll do it again?'

When Hector didn't immediately answer my precarious calm deserted me and thoughts, racing in sick circles, chased images of another cold, white body on the granite slab of the morgue step.

'If we knew the answer to that we might have some idea why Alannah Casey was murdered,' Hector said. 'As it is we've none. We're questioning the Russian lad but it's looking like he's in the clear. He was working all night, stacking supermarket shelves. Four or five of his co-workers have all vouched for him.'

'That's that then,' I said.

'Might be,' he said. 'Doesn't mean he didn't have something to do with it.'

I wished he would go. I wanted to walk the dog to the end of the pier and back as many times as it took to come to some sort of terms with the revolving images of Alannah Casey's white, drowned body and empty eyes. I walked on, quickly. Hector kept pace with me.

'I know how you must feel...' he began.

'You haven't a fucking clue how I feel, Hector.' I didn't raise my voice but I said what I had to say quickly. 'She was Emer's age, for Christ's sake, give or take a few years. I've been serving her coffee five days a week for months. The last time I saw her, which was yesterday, she smiled when she paid for her coffee and said "see ya". She didn't often smile and I remember feeling grateful, as if she'd given me approval or something. She was just a child, with a thin, child's body. I don't want to talk about it.'

'She was the mother of a two-year-old girl,' Hector said and my heart slid to a stop, then began beating again. I had deliberately not been thinking about her child.

It was looking as if it would rain any minute. Hector would hate it if his clothes got wet.

'I heard about the child,' I said. 'What's her name?'

'Zoë,' Hector said and then, forestalling my next question, went on. 'She's with the dead woman's parents. They all lived together; the child's father was never part of the scene.'

The dead woman. That's what Alannah Casey was to Hector, to the police.

'Where do they live?' I zipped my anorak up past my chin. Hector's leather flapped jauntily.

'Top of the town. You don't need to get involved, Fran. Keep a distance. You'll become too emotional and cut-up otherwise. The post mortem's this afternoon.' He rooted and found cigarettes in a pocket. 'We'll know more after that.'

I walked on while he lit a cigarette. I would have yelled at him otherwise. Concern about my emotional state from a man who'd deliberately frozen his feelings I could do without.

'Did you want to talk to me about something in particular, Hector, and right now?'

I said when he caught up. He'd buttoned the leather jacket. Spray speckled his Ray-Bans but he kept them on. Hector was a creature of the night.

'Just checking how you were,' he dragged on the cigarette, 'and deviously hoping we could go over a few points.'

'You'll have seen my statement, I'm sure. I told them everything I could think of in the station this morning,' I said. We were coming to the end of the pier, and rougher seas.

Hector checked his watch, took my elbow and turned us around. 'You don't have to talk now,' he said. 'Thaddeus is worried about you,' he said.

'I'm worried about him,' I said. 'He's started to drink again.' I wasn't about to bring up the story of the earlier murders. I might betray emotion and we couldn't have that.

Hector took off the shades and rubbed his eyes. They looked more tired than usual; he had trouble sleeping. 'Thaddeus is drinking?' he said. I nodded. 'Jesus Christ,' Hector said. 'That's all I need.'

The dog barked when the first drops of rain fell.

We made it to the bandstand before it began to fall in earnest. We had it to ourselves so we sat at opposite ends and watched the downpour tear in and across the harbour. There's a merciful quality about

71

blinding rain.

'Tell me, Fran,' Hector said, 'you that's so good at the old character analysis, what you thought of Alannah Casey.'

The character-analysis crack was one he could never resist. I'd been studying psychology when we met and hadn't taken my degree because of Emer. Hector was cynical to the point of paranoia about psychoanalysis but did value my gut instincts. I have very good gut instincts.

'I don't think that's appropriate, Hector,' I snapped.

'Don't you? Don't tell me you weren't figuring her out while she was drinking her coffee. Get off the fence, Fran, you might even be of some help.'

I listened to the rain on the roof while Hector waited for me to answer.

'She was full of a discontent,' I said after a while, 'and very aware of the effect she had on men.'

'Not a child then?' He was dry.

'Her sex appeal gave her what confidence she had. She practised a disdain that kept her at a distance from people. My guess is she was a trusting child who, when betrayal came along, took it badly. The father of her child might have been the one who did the damage.' I paused. 'Look, Hector, this is all just guesswork. I really don't know anything at all about her.'

'What about Dimitri Sobchak?' He leaned back against the wall. 'Any views on him?'

'He was older than his years,' I said. 'About four hundred years older. Dimitri Sobchak had seen more than he needed to of life. Nina thought him cold but...'

From nowhere there came an image of Dimitri Sobchak the day before, his eyes on Alannah as she paid for the coffee, the flash of childish, exposed longing in them. 'He cared very much for Alannah Casey,' I said.

'He's a smart lad too,' Hector said. 'He's got himself a Rottweiler of a civil rights solicitor. There's bound to be some racist fall-out.'

'That didn't take him long,' I said, surprised.

'He was got for him by a businessman type into a bit of altruism. There are a few of them about, you know. It's not enough for them to make money, they want to be seen as good guys too. So they weigh in with support for high-profile cases like this one's going to be. No free lunches – improves their image no end.'

I went to the door and held out my hand. When the palm was filled with water I splashed it across my face. Lucifer looked up with mournful impatience.

'Thaddeus told me about the other murders,' I said, slowly. I'd never been any good

73

at keeping my mouth shut around Hector.

'Thaddeus told you about the other murders...' he echoed me.

'The women who were murdered in 1953 and 1963, here and in New York,' I said impatiently. 'Murdered and left in morgue doorways like Alannah Casey.'

'Then you probably know as much about them as I do,' Hector was brisk, 'as much as anyone on the case does at the moment. We were hoping to keep it quiet for a day or two. It's likely to throw up all sorts of red herrings when the public debate opens.' Hector, a luke-warm democrat at best, had no time for public opinion. It muddied the waters for police work, he said.

'There's no way you can keep a thing like that quiet,' I said. 'I'll bet half the town's talking about it already.'

'You're probably right,' he conceded. 'Thaddeus is hardly the only one who remembers. That's part of the problem. The murderer is likely to be some sad bastard who heard about those earlier murders and obsessed about them. At this stage we're inclined to think that if there's any link it's to do with copy-catting.'

'That probably lets Dimitri Sobchak off the hook,' I said. 'He'd hardly have known about them.'

'No reason why not,' said Hector, 'nothing secret about them.'

'But why would anyone want to copy-cat a murder?'

'Why indeed? If we knew that we'd probably have our murderer.'

'I thought copy-catting applied mainly to suicides?'

'Applies to most crimes. Nothing original about the varieties of evil doing, when you come down to it. Pick any murder you like and it'll replicate something done before. The murderous mind's not an original one, by and large.'

'But the detail in this instance, the morgue door?'

'Just means the killer wants attention. We're concerned with getting as many facts together as we can before the speculation starts. The first seventy-two hours are crucial, but you'll know that.'

He joined me in the bandstand opening and we watched as the rain eased off. 'I suppose I should tell you...' Hector hesitated. When he showed no inclination to immediately continue I prompted him.

'Tell me,' I said.

'One of your regular customers was a witness in the nineteen fifty-three trial,' Hector said. I stared at him. He'd taken the shades off and I could see the bloodshot state of his eyes. Late-night poker game most likely.

'Which one?'

'John Rutledge. I don't have the details for

you, as yet. It was something that just came up in the station.' He was being too casual by far.

'So he and Thaddeus *do* have a history,' I said, 'I knew it! Thaddeus admits he knew John Rutledge years ago but they're barely civil to one another.'

'You'll probably find a lot of people their age,' Hector said, 'who were around at the time of the nineteen fifty-three murder, will have opposing views about what did or didn't happen.'

'Thaddeus has kept the newspapers of the time,' I said. 'He knew the murdered woman and her husband and family. So he says.' I didn't mention the photograph. It seemed like a betrayal of Thaddeus, somehow.

'I'm sure he did,' Hector was dismissive. 'Dun Laoghaire was a lot smaller then. A lot of people knew Alannah Casey too.' He turned the collar of his jacket up around his ears. 'This is as dry as it's going to get for a long while,' he said. 'Think we could make a run for it?'

We walked, fast. We talked about Emer, and how I would tell her. Filming in the wilds of Wicklow it was unlikely she'd have heard yet about the murder. Or about my finding the body. I hoped, aloud, that Thaddeus hadn't told her.

'On the subject of Thaddeus,' Hector's tone tightened when he spoke about his

76

father, 'he's going to insist on blundering about this case, Fran. He's already had a go; he's fixated on some link with those earlier murders. And now you tell me he's bloody drinking too. Don't encourage him. I don't have the patience or time to deal with him.'

Deciphered, this meant that if Thaddeus interfered with police work, for whatever reason, there would be almighty rows between father and son. I was being asked to help avoid this.

'That's your problem,' I said, coldly.

'Whatever he knows, we know too,' Hector said, 'we've got cuttings, verbatim witness accounts too, transcripts of the court proceedings, the lot. We don't need his help and if there's a link we'll find it ourselves.'

So Thaddeus had communicated his ambiguity about the 1953 murder to Hector too.

'But you don't think there is a link,' I said.

'A man was convicted. He hanged himself.'

'Yes. I know that.'

'Thaddeus is intent on making this personal,' Hector effortlessly and annoyingly read my mind, 'you should know better than to be drawn in.' He might have been talking to a ten year old.

'What about the Coney Island murder?

The Walsh family were there when that happened.'

'That was an established copy-cat. I'm sure Thaddeus told you as much. A man was convicted, and executed. It was forty years ago, Fran.'

His tone implied I should apply intelligence and logic and stop wasting his time.

'We're in touch with New York,' he said. 'Everything's being covered, the Walsh family's being tracked down. We're keeping an open mind but the likelihood, as I said, is that it's copycat, some sick bastard's idea of a game. Something like that.'

'It's just too bizarre,' I said.

We were coming up to my car so I put Lucifer on his lead. Hector's reliable old Corolla was a couple of hundred yards down the street. Clothes were his thing, he didn't much care what he drove or where he lived.

'The media's going to take the bizarre line too,' he said, 'there's going to be a lot of shit written and said about the earlier murders and their relevance to this one. You'll be hounded for comment but if you've anything to say about it, Fran, I want you to save it for us. For me.'

'Don't bully me, Hector,' I said. I opened the back door of the car for Lucifer, then the front door for myself. Hector's hand on the frame stopped me from getting in.

'Would I do that?' he said.
'You might still try,' I said.
'Take care,' he said.

6

November, 1953. Dun Laoghaire.

Shirley dabs a cut on her daughter's forehead with TCP.

'Her eye could have been put out.' Ritchie Walsh fixes a baleful eye on his brother's wife.

'Could have but didn't,' Shirley says. 'Teach her to look where she's going.' She looks the child in the eye as she fixes a plaster. 'Won't it?'

Stella nods.

'She gave her sister and me a bad fright,' Shirley says, 'losing her temper and screaming and banging her head against the banisters like that. She wouldn't do it if her father was here.'

'It's over,' Ritchie says, 'let the child be, Shirley.'

Shirley glares at him and turns a smile on the boys standing behind Ritchie. 'I've been baking,' she says, 'you two look as if you could do with a feed.'

Ritchie, his sons Bernard and Michael and Shirley's two daughters all follow her to the kitchen.

Shirley is flushed and beautiful when she turns from the heat of the oven to put the bread on the table. The cold ham and tomatoes brought by her brother-in-law are already on a plate in the middle.

'The first slices of hot bread go to my handsome nephews,' Shirley smiles as she begins cutting. The boys smile too, shyly. They are fifteen and sixteen years old. 'Get the water and make the tea,' Shirley says to Melanie, who immediately does as she's bidden.

Six people is a capacity crowd for the small kitchen. Ritchie Walsh and his large sons squeeze themselves into chairs around the table, their tweed trousers steaming in the heat after the rain outside. The girls stand in the scullery corner, by the sink. Shirley opens the back door to let in some air.

'I'm hungry,' Stella says.

'You'll have to wait your turn.' Shirley puts the bread, as well as butter and jam, in front of the boys and their father. Stella watches them, and her mother.

'Jimmy's up the town.' Ritchie Walsh stubs a cigarette in a saucer. 'He's in Doolan's with Thaddeus Shaw.'

'He's getting close then,' Shirley says, with a shrug. She turns a bright smile on the boys. 'I might have time to give you haircuts before he gets here. You look as if you could do with a trim around the back and sides.'

'I'll do as I am, thanks,' Michael says.

'Mine could do with a bit of a cut right enough.' Bernard puts a self-conscious hand to the hair on his neck.

The kettle whistles as it boils and Melanie makes the tea. Shirley sits in a fourth chair by the table and the girls pull up stools. Everyone eats except Shirley, who smokes Ritchie's cigarettes and watches the wall clock.

When they are finished Shirley orders the reluctant girls into their pyjamas. Ritchie, his sons and Shirley begin a game of cards at the table. Shirley opens and shares with Ritchie the bottle of Paddy whiskey she had been saving for her husband's homecoming.

They have it more than half finished at 9.30 p.m. when Jimmy Walsh bangs on the front door and calls a greeting through the letter-box.

He is expansive and beaming, a hunter returned, when Melanie opens the door. Both girls are beside themselves, clinging to him and vying for attention as he moves along the hall to greet Shirley, standing in the kitchen doorway. He gives her a large, wet kiss and sweeps her into the kitchen where he stands with an arm about her and a grin on his tanned face as words pour out of him.

'By Christ but it's good to be home,' he cries, full of beer. 'A man's nothing without his wife and children.' He gives Shirley a squeeze, ruffles his daughters' hair.

'It took you long enough to get home to your wife and children,' Shirley steps away from him, 'Thaddeus Shaw must have had a lot to talk about.'

'The spies were out, were they?' Jimmy's mood changes, just a little.

'Your brother was, anyway.' Shirley lifts her whiskey glass. 'He was the one told me.'

'What did you bring us, Daddy?' Melanie shakes her father's arm. Her father, eyes on his wife, begins to empty sweets and cigarettes from his pockets onto the table.

'I just had the one.' Jimmy Walsh shifts his gaze to his brother. His nephews, who have been sitting on the stairs with the kitchen door open, come to stand behind their father. 'Why didn't you join me, Ritchie?' Jimmy smiles at his brother.

'The likes of Thaddeus Shaw wouldn't be my choice of drinking companion,' Ritchie Walsh says.

'What did he ever do to you?' Jimmy asks, reaching again for his wife.

'It's not what he did to me,' Ritchie says.

'What then?' Jimmy asks. He squeezes his wife's waist. He is still smiling. 'Who's he offended to annoy you so much?'

'Thaddeus Shaw!' Shirley snorts. 'Don't

we have more important things to talk about than him? Give me your coat, Jimmy. It's wet.'

'What else did you bring us?' Stella pulls at her father's sleeve.

'Can we eat the sweets now?' Melanie asks.

'Get out of the kitchen,' their father tells them, 'take the sweets upstairs and eat them there.' He doesn't take his eyes off his brother.

Shirley, without warning, pulls away from him.

'You're four months away from me,' she is tearful, 'and all you want to do when you get home is drink and pick a fight with your brother.' She knocks over a stool getting to a wall cupboard, kicks it out of her way as she comes back with a velvet-covered tin box. 'What were all these about, Jimmy?' She opens the box and scatters letters across the table. 'They're about nothing but lies ... filthy lies...' She gathers up the letters and throws them onto the fire. 'Ashes to ashes,' she says as they blaze and fly up the chimney.

There is silence in the kitchen.

'There was no call to do that,' Ritchie says after the last scrap of the last letter has gone up.

'There's every call,' Shirley shouts, 'and you and your pimply dolts of sons have as much to do with it as Jimmy has...' She hurls the violet tin against a wall. 'I didn't come here to be a mother to the lot of you. I'm old before my time.' She is close to the back door. 'I should never have left my family. My father said I'd rue the day I came to this sewer of a country.' She drags open the door. It scrapes on the linoleum. 'He was right,' she screams, 'he was right and I'm going.'

Shirley's feet in their high-heeled shoes can be heard running around the side of the house and into the street.

'Let her go,' Jimmy says, 'she'll be back.' He sits and cuts himself some bread. 'She knows which side her bread's buttered on,' he grins.

7

March, 2003. Dun Laoghaire.

Emer was waiting for me when I got home. So was Thaddeus. They claimed I'd been missing for two hours.

'I took a walk,' I said, 'on the pier.'

'I thought as much,' Thaddeus said, 'and I said as much to Emer.' He then, wisely, disappeared into the kitchen.

'For Christ's sake, Fran,' Emer said, 'you might have left word where you were going. I was worried. I couldn't get Hector either, but there's nothing new about that.' She'd always called both Hector and me by our given names. I sometimes wondered if it made us less a family.

'He was with me,' I said.

'Oh, right...' She looked at me, doubtfully, checking if this was a good or bad thing. I didn't enlighten her. There are things you shouldn't share with your children. But as we stared at one another, tiredness creeping through me, my daughter did something she'd never done before. She reached out, put her arms about me and held me tight.

'Jesus God, I was so fucking frightened,'

she said into my hair. 'I thought something had happened to you.' She stepped back. 'You look terrible.'

'Thanks,' I said.

She was right, of course. The mirror reflected eyes in shallow graves and ashy skin, my hair a bigger mess than usual. It needed to be cut. I was running my fingers through it when Emer took a hair brush from her bag and stood behind me to gently disentangle it. She'd never done this before either. I wasn't at all ready for this role reversal. Not then, maybe not ever.

'I've seen people in the terminal stages of withdrawal looking better than you do right now,' Emer said. 'Talking of withdrawal, do you know Thaddeus is drinking?' She looked shocked as she said this. But then she looked back at me and said, 'why don't you take a holiday?'

'I'll do my hair myself,' I said, gently, and took the brush from her. 'You heard?' I said and she nodded. Her face, which can be beautiful when she forgets to be intense, was as pale as my own in the mirror. My wonderful daughter who took life so seriously and lived it so energetically.

'On the radio,' she said. 'Just about the body being found, nothing about you being the one who found her. I tried to ring you, in case it was anyone we knew. When I couldn't get you I rang Thaddeus.'

'Sorry you had to hear it like that.' I gave her back the hair brush. She was wearing mud-splattered wellingtons. She was also, I saw almost immediately, more upset than I'd realised.

'I drove like a maniac to get here...' She began to shake. 'Thaddeus was so fucking spooky on the phone.' She wrapped her arms about herself to stop the shaking. 'He was talking about some other murders and how you didn't realise what you'd got yourself into and, oh God, I don't know what else, all sorts of Thaddeus-speak. I told him in the end to shut up and got into the car and drove through miles of county Wicklow shit to get here...'

'There are roads in Wicklow,' I said, hoping to stop the flow, 'you should have used them.'

'When were you going to tell me?' she demanded. 'After I heard it on the news myself? After I read it in the papers?'

'I would have phoned you tonight.' I touched her hair, honey-coloured and with none of my red-brown in it: Hector's hair had been honey-coloured when I first met him.

'I wish you'd told me,' she said, 'I would have come. Why do you always have to keep things to yourself?'

'I don't know,' I said.

It was because, in part, I preferred it that

way. But it was also because whenever I phoned her I interrupted something or caught her at a busy time.

'Even a bloody text message, for God's sake...' She stopped. 'Was it terrible?' she said.

I nodded. 'Awful. She was younger than you. Only nineteen.'

I talked about it then, a bit, sitting side by side on my navy-blue sofa. It didn't help much and I was relieved when Thaddeus came to the kitchen door and said he'd made dinner and that we should eat it *now*.

Dinner was a cooked chicken he'd bought on the way with a salad put together from bits and pieces in my fridge. Emer, a vegetarian, ate the salad. I couldn't eat anything at all. Thaddeus's appetite seemed fine. He didn't serve wine.

'Understandable,' Thaddeus said. 'Only normal that your digestive system would be affected.' He speared himself another piece of chicken breast. 'It's the most vulnerable part of the body, you know.'

'I wonder about that,' Emer said. 'Half of the crew are doing the Dr Atkins thing and swallowing buckets of lard three times a day...'

'Could we please stop talking about bodies,' I said.

'Absolutely,' Thaddeus said, 'nothing so boring as talk of body weight when one is eating. I mentioned the earlier murders to Emer, by the way. It's as well she know the facts too.'

'Hector says there's no need for you to be concerned or involved,' I said, primly.

'I'll be the judge of that,' said Thaddeus. Emer looked from me to Thaddeus. 'I didn't really get it when you spoke to me on the phone,' she told him. 'Give me the story again.'

I excused myself and went to call Nina. I did more than call her, I invited her over. A dose of her hard-headed pragmatism was just what I needed. As well as news of the Now and Again.

'I passed by twice and there were gawkers with their noses pressed into the window,' she told Emer and myself while Thaddeus washed up. I'd asked him to. I couldn't bear seeing him half-drunk. 'There should be a law against that kind of thing.'

'I suppose you'll have to close for a while,' Emer said. 'Either that or become a sort of side show.'

'We will close for the rest of the week only,' Nina was firm, 'as a mark of respect. After that it will be business again. People will find a new sensation. Do you agree, Frances?'

I agreed.

'Do you know that Mr Shaw is outside your house?' Nina said.

'Hector?'

'Hector,' Nina affirmed dryly, 'the other one is in the kitchen, isn't he?'

'Are you sure?' Emer said.

'Go to the window. See for yourself.' Nina was tetchy.

Emer went to the window. 'You're right,' she said. 'He's sitting in a car with a garda in uniform. Putting two and two together it looks as if the house is being put under surveillance. Or protection.'

'He can't do a thing like that without asking me first,' I felt a white rage, 'there's no need for it.'

But there was, according to Hector when he eventually got out of the car and came inside. The guards didn't want me pestered and bothered, I was a valuable witness, I deserved security and privacy. They didn't want anything to happen to me.

'There's nothing very private about having a uniformed garda outside the house,' I said.

'It's for your own protection,' he said.

'Protection from what?' Emer demanded.

'The media, stalkers, crazies,' Hector rattled off his unholy trinity of *bêtes noires* with a shrug.

'She can come and stay with me, she knows that,' Thaddeus said. Hector gave him a cold, close look and was silent.

I wished they wouldn't talk as if I wasn't

there, or had become deaf, or suddenly incapable.

'You have arrested Dimitri Sobchak?' Nina said, abruptly. She had moved to the window and was standing there with her arms folded. I stared past her. The blooms were budding on the magnolia tree in the garden, a neighbour was passing with her children by the hand. I wished my visitors would all go, leave me on my own to find some peace in my house. I would have said it to them if Nina hadn't said, in a voice harsh enough to silence the room, 'You have arrested Dimitri Sobchak for the girl's murder?'

'Is that a question?' Hector said, carefully. He didn't know Nina, not in any real sense. If he had he would have known she was making a statement.

I looked at her, shocked. 'Where did you hear that?' I said.

'It is what everyone is saying,' Nina said in the same harsh tone, 'that the Russian did it. That is what you hear out of every mouth in the street.'

'He's being questioned,' Hector said slowly, 'nothing more. He has a good solicitor, paid for by a fellow called Gerry Fuller who claims to be worried about injustice and racism. I'm surprised Fran hasn't told you this.' He gave me a wearily disappointed look which I ignored. He turned again to Nina. 'It would help,' he said, 'if you could tell me anything you know about Sobchak.'

'I know nothing about Sobchak,' Nina said, 'but that is not unusual. Russians are secretive people. Our history and our culture has made us that way. Russians have spied on Russians for too many years for us to trust one another.' She paused. 'That does not mean that Dimitri Sobchak is a murderer.'

'No. It doesn't,' Hector agreed. 'But it doesn't let him off the hook either. His alibi does that.'

'You're looking in the wrong place.' Thaddeus, an apron around his waist and a damp dish-cloth in his hands, was back in the kitchen door. He stayed there, wary about coming any closer to his son. He didn't seem drunk, exactly. Just a bit off-key. 'I'm telling you now, Hector, and I'll keep on telling you for as long as it takes to get you to listen to me, that the police are going to have to do a bit of lateral thinking on this one. I'll be doing my bit to help.'

'If you know something, Thaddeus, then you'd better tell me now.' Hector sharpened up considerably. 'Withholding information is an offence.'

'As soon as I have anything concrete to report I'll let you have it,' Thaddeus said, 'but in the meantime I'm glad to see you're making arrangements to have Frances protected. You might do the same for your daughter.'

'This is effing ridiculous,' Emer said, 'I wish for once that you two would...'

'Keep out of it, Dad,' Hector said and signalled Emer to be quiet which, amazingly, she did. 'I'll get you for obstruction if you keep this up. We've got people looking into the nineteen fifty-three angle.'

'You'll need all the help you can get,' Thaddeus said, darkly, 'and you dismiss the past at your peril.'

'Jesus, Thaddeus!' Emer exploded. 'Give us all a rest. Keep the melodrama for your mates in AA. *WHEN* you go back to them.'

This was below the belt and if I hadn't seen the picture of Shirley Walsh, heard Thaddeus's story and seen his treasured newspaper collection, I would have told Emer so. As it was I left it to Thaddeus to defend himself. He fell back on pomposity, diluted a bit by the apron.

'Your detachment does you credit, Emer,' he said, 'but you will in time find that life's a murkier and messier business than you imagine. More melodramatic, even. As it happens, I'm off to an AA meeting in a few minutes' time.' He untied the apron. 'We may discuss there what has happened, we may not. But the members will, I'm sure, bring an open mind to the subject.'

'I can well believe it.' Emer was caustic;

the family history had diluted her sympathy for alcoholism.

Thaddeus's word for his own, early drinking days was 'debauched'. Marriage and responsibility had worsened his addiction and Hector's childhood, according to both his own and his father's penitent account, had been a dark hole in which Thaddeus had been cruelly indifferent and his gentle mother lonely and desperate. It had ended with the car accident and her death. Thaddeus had spent two years in prison for manslaughter and sent the sixteen-year-old Hector to boarding school.

Thaddeus, in prison, had discovered Alcoholics Anonymous and a sort of redemption. The eighteen-year-old Hector, in college by the time his father emerged from prison, had been unforgiving and unrelenting in his hatred. He had also, by the time he was twenty, discovered alcohol to be a great number of feelings.

We repeat our parents' mistakes, they say, and Hector certainly did. From being the wild man about college he became the wild man caught in marriage. But I'd learned from *my* mother that you only get one crack at life. It took a while for hope and belief in Hector to die in me, but die it finally did.

Thaddeus the Redeemed, by that time a diligent grandfather and censorious father, gave evidence in the divorce court on my behalf. It was two years after that before Emer saw her dad again. By then he'd stopped drinking, in his own way and on his own terms. He'd never forgiven Thaddeus, for anything.

'Don't let us keep you from your meeting,' Hector said now. 'Looks like you've a bit of confessing to do.'

'I'll make you a mug of coffee first,' said Thaddeus. Domesticity and feeding people were his ballast and crutch. I liked him for it.

'Will you be questioning a lot of Russian people?' asked Nina, not a woman to let things smoulder.

'Some,' Hector admitted. 'Sobchak has applied for nationality but he's got some doubtful friends. They're more likely candidates for murder than someone who's been hanging around for fifty years or more...'

'This half world you talk of,' Nina interrupted, 'are you talking about the Russian mafia, those people we read about in the gutter press who deal in trafficking and prostitution and drugs?'

'Are you saying these things don't exist, Nina?' Hector was quiet. Gentle even.

'No. I know they do,' Nina said. 'Corruption and crime have brought great misery to Russia. I worry that the rest of us will be persecuted here, now, because of this murder.'

'I worry too,' Hector said, unexpectedly. 'I think it would be a good idea to close the café for a few days.'

'That's been decided already,' I said.

Thaddeus, wearing his coat, appeared with a mug of black coffee for Hector. 'I'd be glad of a lift to the meeting,' he said, 'Emer very kindly collected and brought me here so I'm without transport.' He handed Hector the mug and looked from him to Nina. 'I would be most grateful,' he said.

'I'll take you.' I got up. 'If the café is going to be closed for the guts of a week I might as well call by and empty the fridge.'

It was as simple as that, the decision which started a journey that took me on an exploration of the past and into collision with the present.

It had started to rain by the time I dropped Thaddeus at his meeting. It was relentlessly pouring by the time I'd emptied the fridge, locked up the café and was heading across the road for Thaddeus's place.

A half an hour, maybe forty minutes, was all it would take to go through the suitcase of newspapers. Easier than pleading with Hector for a look at the police files, more comprehensive than anything I might find on the internet. The past is not dead, Thaddeus had said, not even past. I wanted to see what he meant. Why he was drinking again. I had my own key to the penthouse and there was no time like the present.

8

I'd never before been in Thaddeus's place when he wasn't there. I stood for a while with my back to the hall door, eye-to-eye with an albatross in flight on a plinth. Thaddeus had given me a key the day he bought the apartment. He said it was in case he ever lost his own but we both knew it was in case he ever became ill, or worse. His blood pressure wasn't great and his heart given to unpredictable flutters.

I felt like a thief. Thaddeus had left the lights on and the curtains open and the silence was deafening. I checked my watch. I had the place to myself for an hour, at most, before he got back.

I found the suitcase in his bedroom. The newspapers, when I took them out, were in two separate piles tied with brown string. The larger pile was dated 1953, the smaller one 1963. I spread the earlier papers across the smooth, green cover on Thaddeus's bed and arched the arm of his reading lamp so as to give myself plenty of light. Then I knelt by the bed and began at the beginning, with the first, headline story about the discovery of Shirley Walsh's body. It was in *The Irish*

Press and the date was 30 November 1953. WOMAN MURDERED IN DUN LAOGHAIRE, it said and, underneath, BODY LEFT TO BE DISCOVERED ON STEPS OF MORGUE. The picture, large and yellowed and taking up most of the rest of the page, was the one Thaddeus kept framed and wrapped in brown paper.

The story told how three young boys, who lived nearby, had discovered the naked body on the morgue steps just before eight in the morning. They were being treated for shock and a man was being held for questioning. Foul play was definitely suspected.

There were few personal details – Shirley had been married to James Walsh, was the mother of two children and a native of Liverpool – and a great many pictures of the morgue, its door and steps.

It was news to me that the morgue, in 1953, had been in a building at the end of a lane leading to the small harbour known as the Coal Harbour. News too that it had been called The Dead House. The father of one of the boys who had found the body was quoted as saying that if his son had gone to school, as he'd been told to, 'he'd have been spared seeing what he saw'. True; but my heart went out to the child.

The reporter had asked the same father if he or his neighbours had seen or heard anything strange on the night of the murder.

'We did not, and even if we did we'd have stayed inside our homes,' he said, 'we stay away from The Dead House for the sake of our health. Only a month ago the decomposed head fell off a body they brought in from the sea. It could be the killer took Mrs Walsh out of the water to prevent the same thing happening to her. He very likely laid her on the steps so's she could be given a proper burial.'

He made it sound like a kindness.

I went through the papers quickly, choosing what to read from headlines. The reporting was restrained, but they had been restrained times. Thaddeus hadn't kept any tabloids. Maybe there hadn't been any to keep.

The Irish Times gave a detailed description of the morgue and environs. The harbour wall was low, it said, the harbour itself a picturesque place where children went swimming in the summer. The lane leading to the morgue was leafy and had dense hedging on either side. Children played there all the time; hiding games mostly. A single lamp lit the top of the lane at night. Not that anyone went there at night since, as the paper said, 'the nature of the business of the morgue ensures that it is severely avoided during the hours of dark'. The murderer would have had the place to himself then.

I wanted to get to reports of the trial, and

conviction, so skipped fairly quickly through the weeks of incidental reporting which passed for news while the garda investigation went on. The guards weren't revealing much and the papers had fallen back on Shirley Walsh's neighbours for news, and views. The picture which emerged said as much about the times as it did about Shirley Walsh and her brutal death.

Shirley Walsh's neighbours were like a Greek chorus in their agreement that she'd 'kept herself to herself'. Her brother-in-law, Richard (Ritchie) Walsh, had called regularly to the house with his sons. So had other, and occasional, male visitors. Friends of her husband's, the neighbours had assumed.

The implication, barely concealed, was that Shirley had kept her decent neighbours out and allowed unknown men in.

One woman, speaking to *The Irish Independent*, said Shirley had 'kept herself nice, even with two daughters to look after'. She was a tart, in other words, putting herself before her children.

A week later, in *The Irish Press*, a paper which gave the story more space than the others, two other neighbours told how they had tried, 'in vain', to get Shirley Walsh to attend the church sodality. Shirley, being Protestant and English, had refused. She didn't go to mass on Sunday either.

The same women said Shirley went to the

pub alone. 'You'd often see her down at the jetty too,' one of them added, 'watching the passengers getting off the ship from Liverpool. Sometimes she took the daughters on the train into Dublin.' She was polite enough, they said, but changeable.

Jimmy Walsh, on the other hand, was reported as a 'decent man and very fond of his wife.' He was away 'a fair bit' but he was a seaman and that was the nature of the job. He was generous, to the neighbours as well as to his wife and children.

Changeable. I hadn't heard the word for years. It was a word my mother had used to mean unbalanced or unstable. It said more about Shirley Walsh than the thousands of other words put together.

Four days after the murder *The Irish Press* reported that the 'man held for questioning', Shirley Walsh's husband James Thomas Walsh, had been charged with her murder and put back for trial.

The trial began at the end of January, 1954. It went on for two weeks and was given acres of newsprint.

Witness after witness testified, again, to the outsider Shirley Walsh had been. Several spoke of her as being 'changeable'.

I read quickly, ignoring preamble, of which there was plenty. I had about forty minutes before Thaddeus got back. I wanted to be gone by then.

Ritchie Walsh, the brother of the accused man, was described in *The Irish Press* as being 'well made, dark haired and speaking in a soft voice'. He wore a brown suit and tie.

In evidence Ritchie Walsh told how there had been a row in the house the night his brother, James (Jimmy) Walsh had arrived home after four months at sea. His sister-in-law, Shirley Walsh, had been drinking while waiting for her husband. Cross-examined he admitted to 'sharing a glass with her'. She was a 'changeable' woman he said, and drink didn't agree with her.

'In what way did it disagree with her?' the prosecution, a Mr Sutton, had asked.

'It made her unpredictable,' Ritchie Walsh explained, 'and inclined her to be short tempered. She was fighting with her daughters when I arrived with my sons. I heard her through the door. My brother, James Walsh, was himself hardly through the door before she started a fight with him. She was mad that he'd called in at the pub on his way home.'

'She had been anticipating his arrival?'

'She was.'

'And he was late?'

'He was a bit overdue.'

'How long overdue?'

'An hour or so.'

'One hour, Mr Walsh, or two or three?'

'Two.'

'I see here,' Mr Sutton consulted documents in his hands, 'that Mr James Walsh's ship came into Dublin Port at thirteen hundred hours. My enquiries tell me he could have reasonably have been expected to be in his Dun Laoghaire home by sixteen hundred hours. What time precisely did he arrive at his home on Malone Terrace?'

'Some time around nine.'

'Twenty-one hundred hours. Five hours late then.'

'She wouldn't have been expecting him to get home until about five or six.'

'Mrs Walsh was used to her husband not coming straight home then? Even after months away from her and his children?'

'It would have been usual for him to have a drink. Any man would have done the same.'

'But Mrs Walsh clearly didn't feel five hours a reasonable delay?'

'She didn't.'

Cross-examined further, Ritchie Walsh admitted that his sister-in-law had prepared a homecoming meal, baked bread and dressed her daughters especially for their father's arrival.

'You told her you'd seen him in Doolan's public house?' Mr Sutton said.

'I thought to prepare her for him being a bit late. I told her he was drinking with a

105

friend of both of them, thinking to soften things a bit.'

'But this news did not soften, or mollify, the dead woman?'

'It seemed to anger her more. She told my brother when he arrived that he could go back to the pub and Thaddeus Shaw if he preferred his company to her own.'

And so, almost incidentally, Thaddeus came into things. Richard Walsh, who gave long hours of evidence, told how Shirley had 'slammed out of the house and into the night' after the row with her husband. His brother, he said, had 'been all for letting her cool her heels', believing she'd be back in no time.

But she hadn't come back and the girls had become fretful and so, at about ten o'clock, it had been decided that Jimmy Walsh would stay with his daughters while Ritchie Walsh and his two sons went searching for his wife. It was raining heavily and they split up and went in different directions.

Ritchie Walsh went to Doolan's pub where he met Thaddeus Shaw. Shaw and the barman, John Rutledge, both told him his sister-in-law had been and gone.

I would have missed the name if I hadn't been reading carefully. John Rutledge, if Ritchie Walsh was telling the truth, had probably served Shirley Walsh her last drink before she died.

'Was Thaddeus Shaw known to you before this meeting?' Mr Sutton asked.

'He was. But he was better known to my brother and his wife. He wasn't what I'd have called a friend.'

'What would you have called him?'

'More of a nodding acquaintance. My brother had more in common with him. They met on the boats.'

Ritchie Walsh told the court he'd had a drink while talking to Thaddeus Shaw, 'half thinking' his sister-in-law might return to the pub. When she didn't he left and went to look around the streets again. He'd even gone into the church. At around half-past-midnight he'd headed back to the house.

His sons were already there but his brother Jimmy was not. The girls couldn't say exactly what time he'd left to go searching for their mother, only that he'd taken the bottle of whiskey in his pocket. Ritchie Walsh sent his sons on home, told his nieces to go to their bed and waited alone for his brother's return. Someone had to stay with the girls.

Jimmy Walsh did not return home until just after six in the morning.

'What was his condition when he arrived?' Mr Sutton asked.

'He was very wet. He was not sober,' Ritchie Walsh said.

'What did he say to you?'

'I asked him where he'd been and where Shirley was and he looked at me, like he wasn't really seeing me. He said he hadn't found her and hadn't a very good memory of where he'd been himself either. He went to his bed and I went home to mine.'

Ritchie Walsh's elder son Bernard, aged 16, was called to the stand. His brother Michael, who was 15, was considered just too young to testify. Bernard, described as earning a living selling fish on the pier, corroborated his father's evidence. Shirley and James Walsh's daughters, Estelle and Melanie, were also too young to be called.

A resumé of the post-mortem results said that an attempt had been made to strangle Shirley Walsh before she'd been drowned in sea water. Material evidence included a muddy, salt-water-sodden scarf and whiskey bottle found in the laneway leading to the morgue. Both belonged to Jimmy Walsh.

On the fourth day of the trial, when I had twenty minutes of my allotted reading time left, Thaddeus was called to give evidence.

9

Shirley is cold and wet and still angry when she pushes open the door of Doolan's pub. She sees Thaddeus Shaw at once, sitting at the bar with a double whiskey in front of him. One of three old men sitting at a table by the wall mutters as Shirley passes. She flashes them a look of pure dislike. There are no other women in the pub.

'Have you no home to go to?' one of them says.

Shirley sits on a high stool beside Thaddeus Shaw. When he doesn't respond she lifts and downs his glass of whiskey. He calls for another, along with a single shot for Shirley. He puts five shillings on the counter.

'Why aren't you in the arms of your husband?' he says. His dark eyes appreciate the way the wet, emerald blouse clings to her breasts. 'Bored already?' He takes a raincoat from the hook by the counter. 'Put this over you,' he says. The old men mutter again, louder this time.

'What were you and Jimmy talking about?'

Shirley demands.

'Nothing you need worry about,' Thaddeus says.

Shirley puts the raincoat around her shoulders before crossing her legs and shaking the rain from her hair. Some of it sprays onto Thaddeus's jacket. When the barman brings Shirley a towel Thaddeus takes it and rubs the pale corduroy of the jacket dry before handing it to her.

'Sure you've finished with it?' Shirley says and, to the barman, 'Thanks, John, you're a gent.' She gives him a grateful, teasing smile as she raises her arms over her head and begins to dry her hair with the towel. Thaddeus and the barman watch her.

'Public bar's no place for a woman,' one of the old men says, loudly. 'You shouldn't let her in here, John, never mind serve her.'

'Mind your manners or I'll have you out on the pavement.' The barman splays his hands on the counter.

'You wouldn't like it out there, in the rain and wet.' Shirley spins on the stool, smiling at the old men, high-heeled foot swinging.

'You should be at home with your children,' another of the men says.

'English whore,' says the third, blessing himself before bringing his empty glass down on the table with a sharp tap. 'God will deal with you.'

'If you three want another round you'd

better mind your manners,' the barman warns them, again.

Shirley spins back to the bar. 'Here's to you,' she raises her glass to the barman who grunts and continues washing glasses.

Shirley, rubbing her wet arms with the towel, turns her attention to Thaddeus Shaw. 'You still haven't told me what you said to Jimmy,' she says, 'I want to know.'

'I told him you were a great woman and that he should take better care of you,' Thaddeus Shaw says and touches her knee.

Shirley swats him with the towel. 'He was with you a long time. I should know, I was waiting at home with his children so don't try my patience, Thaddeus. Tell me what you were really talking about.' She leans forward. Her brows, angrily drawn together, give her face the look of a sharp diamond.

'I wouldn't want to try your patience, my sweet.' Thaddeus leans away from her in mock fear. 'Shirley with her patience tried is no joke.'

'Tell me,' Shirley's teeth grind.

'We talked about the sea and boats,' Thaddeus says, 'and about the price of drink.'

'That's all?' Shirley demands.

'Of course that's all. Do you think I'm mad? Do you think I want my head beaten in?'

'You could do with having your head beaten in but I suppose you're not com-

111

pletely mad,' Shirley says. She downs most of the whiskey in her glass.

'Why do you ask?' Thaddeus orders another for himself.

'Ritchie was trying to stir things up back at the house,' Shirley grins drunkenly, 'said he wouldn't drink with your kind.'

'That's his prerogative,' Thaddeus says. 'Can't say I'd enjoy his company much either.'

'I'm sick to death of it all,' Shirley is suddenly and hissingly explosive. 'I'm sick of looking after them all.'

'So you walked out, into the rain?' Thaddeus says. 'How're the girls?'

'The girls are all right. They're with their father,' Shirley says, sour. She finishes her drink and gives him a sideways glance. 'I'm free for the night.'

'Go home, Shirley,' Thaddeus, sighing, shakes his head.

'That's not what you used to say,' Shirley hisses again, leaning towards him.

'That was then,' Thaddeus says. 'This is now. Your husband's at home waiting for you, Shirley.'

'You've a wife at home. And a baby son. Do they not count, Thaddeus?' Shirley's tone is mocking, her eyes bright with tears and temper.

'They count, Shirley. What happened is finished and done with.'

Shirley slips from the stool and wraps her arms about herself, shivering. 'You've a backbone the colour of canary shit, Thaddeus, do you know that?' She steps closer to him. 'You could have had me for tonight, Thaddeus Shaw,' her breath is whiskey hot in his face, 'we could have been together one more time. I'm not afraid.'

'Go home, Shirley,' he says.

She stands, lost-looking and childish in the way she stares at him. When he starts to say something else she shakes her head and puts a finger over his mouth.

'Too late,' she says, 'the good's gone out of it. You can keep your raincoat too. John,' she calls to the barman, 'any chance I could borrow a raincoat to get me home?'

She slips behind the counter and goes through a door with the barman. When she emerges she's wrapped in an olive-coloured oilcloth.

'Yer like a green madonna in that get-up,' one of the old men comes to life with a snigger. His companions shake with silent laughter.

Shirley, leaving the pub, ignores them. 'Goodbye, Thaddeus,' she says.

Thaddeus Shaw nods and watches her leave in the gilded mirror behind the bar. The barman watches Thaddeus and the old men laugh at another joke.

Outside, Shirley stands for a while in the

doorway, smoking a cigarette.

A hand-painted notice on a wall opposite announces that the Redemptorist mission is in town and that there will be no dance that Saturday.

When the rain shows no sign of easing, Shirley leaves the doorway. She keeps close to the wall, stubbing the cigarette out on the Redemptorists' notice when she comes to it. The night has grown wilder and she is buffeted by the wind. She keeps her head down, clutches the oilcloth to her and keeps going.

When a figure separates itself from the shadow of a wall and begins to follow her she doesn't look round.

10

March, 2003. Dun Laoghaire,

Thaddeus was described in *The Irish Independent* as a ship's engineer. He wore a 'light-coloured' suit for his appearance in court.

Giving evidence Thaddeus said he thought Shirley Walsh 'a bit tipsy' when she arrived in Doolan's pub. She was angry too that her husband hadn't come home directly to her and their daughters. He was a father too, of a six-month-old son, and could understand her being upset.

'As a seaman myself I would have known to go straight home to my wife,' he said, 'or have expected consequences.' When this response drew titters from the court the judge advised 'the dapper Mr Shaw' to stick to the necessary facts when answering.

Asked how well he'd known the dead woman, Thaddeus replied, 'Somewhat better than other customers in Doolan's. It was my local and she came there quite often. Since I knew her husband I would naturally speak to her and buy her a drink.'

'Was it your opinion that she drank an

excess of alcohol?'

'No. She didn't drink a great deal. She would have shandies mostly and sip them slowly. She didn't have a great capacity to hold drink. I believe this is true of many slightly built women...'

'The court will look at such matters without your help, Mr Shaw,' the prosecution said. 'What drink did you buy her on the night she died?'

'A small whiskey. She said she'd already been drinking whiskey.' Pause. 'I could smell it on her breath.'

'She was close to you then?'

'She sat on the stool next to me at the bar.'

Asked about his friendship with Jimmy Walsh, Thaddeus said they'd met when working on the same ship together. Asked if it was usual for a ship's engineer to befriend an able seaman Thaddeus said he already had a nodding acquaintance with James Walsh from Dun Laoghaire. They had discovered, in conversation on board ship, a shared interest in ornithology. This was accepted without question by the court.

'I told Mrs Walsh she should go home, that she'd made her point by leaving the house,' Thaddeus said when questioned further about his conversation with Shirley. 'The barman loaned her a raincoat and she left as she'd arrived, through the back door.'

'Was there a reason for her coming and

going by the rear exit?' the prosecution wanted to know.

'She maintained that the back laneway presented the shorter journey from her home.'

Thaddeus's reply prompted the court reporter to comment that his use of English 'was at all times formal and precise'.

He was still like that, especially when cornered or put on the spot.

'Did you remain in Doolan's public house for any length of time after Mrs Walsh's departure from said establishment?' Mr Sutton's pedantic use of English wasn't commented on.

'Not very long, no,' Thaddeus said, 'I finished my drink and left. By the front door.'

'So you have no idea whether or not anyone might have left Doolan's public house and followed Mrs Walsh?'

'No. It was, in any event, a wet and stormy night. Apart from myself and Mrs Walsh there were only three other customers in the bar. They were regulars and elderly and had pints in front of them. I doubt they followed her.'

'You are not being asked for an opinion, Mr Shaw,' Mr Sutton reminded him.

The elderly regulars, most vocally represented by a Reginald Moore, gave evidence of Shirley Walsh arriving wet and 'the worse for wear', of being 'careless in her manner' and leaving via 'the back way in'. They corroborated everything Thaddeus said.

So did the barman. John Rutledge's age was given as '22 years'. He was from Co Waterford and lived in a room over the pub. He agreed he'd lent Shirley Walsh an oilcloth, said he knew her as a regular customer and 'felt sorry for her, the state she was in'. He hadn't seen her leave because he'd gone to the cellar to check the Guinness pump after giving her the oilcloth. There had been an earlier complaint by Reginald Moore about his pint. This too was corroborated.

John Rutledge was described as dapper and wearing a cravat.

Dapper was another of my mother's words. She'd used it to describe my father, a bookie who one day didn't come home from the racetrack. She'd been carrying me at the time but had always maintained she was better off without him anyway. 'He wasn't the stuff of a husband,' she said when she was dying and putting her affairs in order. 'He was the dapper kind, with his sports coats and silk hankies and cravats.' Dapper, as a consequence, had always seemed to me to be up there with jerk and no-good and rat.

Jimmy Walsh took the stand on the first day of the second week of the trial. He'd been reported as being ill the Friday before and was described in *The Irish Press* as 'a gaunt version of the man arrested for his wife's murder nearly two months ago'. The paper said he was pale and stooped as he stood in the dock, his hands clasped together to keep them from shaking.

He gave evidence against the advice of his counsel. He spoke from notes made in prison and seemed, in newsprint anyway, to have been lucid and clear. His defence, unadorned and bathetic, was that he'd drunk too much to have been in any state to murder his wife and besides, he loved her too much ever to harm her.

He told the court how he'd left the house with the bottle of whiskey and gone searching for his wife in places where they'd spent time together in the early days of their marriage. He'd gone to the People's Park but found it locked up for the night. He'd gone to the West Pier to find it sea-swept, to the jetty in case she was waiting there for an early morning ship to England.

He'd gone to the small harbour known as the Coal Harbour, beside The Dead House, because they'd often gone there in the summertime with the girls and Shirley had liked it. When he didn't find her he'd turned for home but, the rain worsening, had stepped inside the Victorian pagoda to shelter for a while. He'd fallen asleep there. He agreed he'd been drinking since coming ashore almost twelve hours before. He agreed he'd stopped at several public houses, as well as Doolan's, on his way home to his wife and children. He bitterly regretted this. He had loved his wife and he loved his children.

He hadn't killed his wife. The last time he'd seen her she had been running from their house in anger.

Jimmy Walsh swore to the court that he was shocked to find it almost dawn when he woke and emerged from the pagoda. He noted too that it was still raining and admitted he hadn't seen anyone else about at that hour, nor met anyone on his way home.

'So there were no witnesses to your emergence from the pagoda, nor any to vouch for your journey home?' Mr Sutton asked.

'None.'

Jimmy Walsh admitted that he had probably been drunker than at any other time in his life the night his wife was murdered. Too drunk to account for an empty bottle of Paddy, the brand of whiskey he'd been drinking, being found in the laneway leading to the morgue. Too drunk to account for the more damning fact that his scarf, muddy and sodden with what had proven to be sea water, was also found in the lane.

The Irish Times gave autopsy details at some length two days later. I read quickly, an eye on the bedside clock. Thaddeus, if he came straight home from his meeting, would be back in fifteen minutes.

The autopsy reported that Shirley Walsh had had sexual intercourse in the hours before her death, possibly immediately before. It noted the 'marks of an overpowering grip' on her neck, with bruises of a finger-tip kind on the skin and the tissues immediately underneath. There were nail-tearing scratches too, made by the victim as she tried to free herself from the strangling hand.

But it wasn't this overpowering grip which had killed Shirley Walsh. Death, the autopsy report said, had been due to 'cardio-respiratory inhibition brought on by sudden immersion in ice-cold water ... that air and water had been gulped into the oesophagus during the agonal struggle to survive'.

Put simply, as the paper explained to its readers and the coroner to the court, this meant that Shirley Walsh had been breathing when she went into the water and that whoever had killed her had tried to strangle her before drowning her. After she was dead he'd taken her body from the water to the door of the morgue.

The jury took five hours to decide that Shirley Walsh's husband had killed her. The case was put back for sentencing.

The Irish Press, a month later, reported that

121

James Thomas Walsh (32) had been sentenced to hang. Sentencing would be carried out within the month, when Mr Pierrepoint would be available to come from England.

The very last paper in the pile, an *Irish Press* dated three weeks later, said that James Walsh had been found hanged by his own hand in his prison cell.

I had ten minutes to read the second pile of papers. I was speed-reading now, torn between a frenzy to know all there was to know before Thaddeus got back and a recklessness which said let him find me, I'll brazen it out.

But I didn't want him to find me. Not with the papers and in his bedroom anyway. He would have told me if he'd wanted me to know that he'd been one of the last people to see Shirley Walsh alive. What I'd done I'd done on impulse and didn't regret; I very much doubted Thaddeus would understand, however.

Thaddeus had kept three copies of *The Irish Times* from 1963 and a cutting from 1964.

The murder of Liliya Borodin was, briefly, reported on 29 November 1964 and the article said simply that a woman's dead body had been found in Coney Island in circumstances similar to those surrounding the finding of the body of Shirley Walsh, murdered ten years before in Dun Laoghaire. Liliya Borodin (28) was described as a Russian immigrant mother of two who had been living in the US for ten years. The paper said American police were investigating links with members of the Walsh family who had emigrated and were living on Coney Island.

Most of the rest of the paper was given over to details of the aftermath of the assassination of President John Kennedy.

The Irish Times, two days later, reported that Liliya Borodin's husband, Sergei Borodin (42) had been arrested and charged with his wife's murder. I skimmed through a larger space given to the trial in the third paper, picking up just enough to learn that Sergei Borodin had been found guilty of strangling his wife.

And to read where the judge decided that Sergei Borodin had left his wife's body on the steps of the morgue in a cruel imitation of the fate which had befallen a relative of his friend Richard Walsh's ten years before in Dublin, Ireland.

The last cutting was from the spring of 1964 and said that Sergei Borodin had died in the electric chair the day before.

I was putting everything back into the suitcase, pleased with myself and my timing, when I saw the letter. It was inside a flap in the suitcase lid, addressed to Thaddeus and had a Coney Is., New York postmark dated

May 1964.

I saw all of this at a glance, and at precisely the same moment I heard Thaddeus's key in the lock of the hall door.

He who hesitates is lost. I removed the letter and put it into my pocket. I closed the lid of the suitcase and put it back against the wall. I stepped into the hallway, opened the bathroom door opposite and stood as if I'd just come out of there. Thaddeus was a dozen or so feet away, his back to me as he bolted and locked himself in for the night. I'd never before had reason to be grateful for his fastidiousness.

'How was the meeting?' I called to him, not too loudly. I didn't want him having a heart attack. He turned immediately, looking startled. I closed the bathroom door behind me.

'It took longer than I expected to clear things up in the café,' I lied. 'I decided to use my key and come up to have a cup of tea with you before going home.'

'That's nice,' he said, his face blank as he tried to register what was going on. 'That's nice,' he said again.

'I'll make the tea,' I said. He followed me to the kitchen.

'Are you all right?' he said as I plugged in the kettle and he got us two mugs. 'It's not like you to...'

'I slept during the day,' I interrupted him,

'I won't be able to sleep for while. I suppose, if I'm to be honest, that I'm hiding out here. I don't want to go home just yet, face my policeman protector, anyone else who might be around.'

I was doing what all liars do; babbling as I created a fantasy. I wished I hadn't used the word honest.

'I understand,' Thaddeus patted my shoulder, 'relax and let me make the tea.'

'Did you tell them you'd taken drink?' I said.

'I did,' he said.

I sat at the kitchen table, smiling until my jaws ached at his anecdotes about the meeting, dry mouthed because of the letter in my pocket, half wishing I hadn't taken it, knowing full well I wasn't giving it back until I'd read every word of it.

'A woman who hasn't had a drink for forty years came to talk about her cats,' Thaddeus said as he put the inevitable chocolate biscuits in front of me.

'Maybe she's lonely,' I offered.

'Course she's lonely,' Thaddeus said. 'That's probably the reason she became a drinker in the first place. Deserves to be lonely too if she can't broaden her conversation base.' He didn't mention his own drinking again.

He took off his cap, hung it on the beak of a bronze heron on top of the fridge, and went on in some detail about meeting times being changed. I let him go on, but not for long.

'I must go.' I stood, too suddenly for him to protest. 'See you tomorrow,' I said.

He walked me to the door, pillows of petulance set into his cheeks. 'I don't know what your hurry is,' he said, 'first time ever you make an unscheduled visit and now you're running off after a few minutes.'

'Can't seem to stay still,' I said. 'Good night, Thaddeus.'

He opened the door for me and I gave him a Judas kiss. It didn't even occur to me to do the decent thing and give him back his letter. He stood in the door, waving to me as I stepped into the lift opposite. The albatross's eyes stayed with me until the doors closed.

He would miss the letter if he opened the suitcase. But, by his own admission, he hadn't opened it for years before that morning. With any luck it would be a while before he opened it again.

I resisted opening the envelope until I was in bed. There was a single sheet of lined notepaper inside, with cramped writing in blue Biro on both sides. The address read simply Coney Is. New York and it began with a 'Dear Thaddeus'.

I read it slowly; it was the letter of someone not used to writing.

I am writing to share the burden we both carry and because I must make the journey home to see my sister Concepta who lives still in Bray and is not expected to live long. You will no doubt be told I am in the vicinity but there is no point in us meeting. The two of us raking over what happened will not change anything. Best to leave it go.

This is a hard letter to write and it has taken me a long time to compose. You will have read in the papers about the murder of a Russian woman here. It was Shirley all over again, the way it happened. Like things went with Shirley too, the woman's husband was found guilty. He died in the electric chair some weeks ago. I have not been myself since all of this happened. We are destroyed as a family, broken up, my sons and my nieces gone their separate ways. I am left only with the hope that this parting will be a good thing, for all of us, that in the scattering the past will be crushed.

Over the years since arriving here I was forever talking about what happened in Dun Laoghaire in 1953. In this way I kept it alive and in this way too I am to blame and must live with my burden. I will pay the price to my dying breath.

But you have a burden too. You had your doubts about my brother, your friend, and all that happened in Dun Laoghaire ten years ago. As I had. You kept your silence and so did I and

127

Jimmy took his own life. I was wrong, but there is a limit to what a man can or cannot do for his own, how truthful he can be when he has a choice like the one I had to make. It was too much to expect from any man.

You were constrained in your truth-telling too, by your fondness for my sister-in-law and your care for your wife and child. And the thing you thought you maybe knew was too horrible to contemplate, I know that.

Because of all this I had doubts myself about the man they put to death for the murder here. But he had done a great deal of evil in his life and I'd often thought death too good for him. For this reason it was an easier matter for me to keep silent this time.

I remember my mother saying that if things don't go right at the start of a life then those early shadows will fall on everything that comes after. She knew what she was talking about, God rest her. I pray to the God of our innocence and youth that the shadows are at an end for this family.

Writing about the cross we bear has brought me some peace. I will bid you goodbye now and end,

Yours sincerely,
Richard Walsh.

I read the letter again and came to the same conclusion I'd come to the first time. What it said was that both Thaddeus and Ritchie

Walsh had had reason to doubt Jimmy Walsh's guilt and had kept quiet. Maybe even perjured themselves. What it didn't say was why...

It left other questions unanswered too. Did Ritchie Walsh think Sergei Borodin innocent of his wife's death too? And just how 'fond' had Thaddeus's 'fondness' for Shirley Walsh been? It could be, of course, that they suspected one another of the crime; only I didn't see Thaddeus in the role of murderer.

The letter was nearly forty years old and Ritchie Walsh's shadows were surely at rest by now. I put the letter under my pillow and slept on it.

A ringing on my front-door bell woke me at 3 a.m. My garda protector, standing on the step when I opened the door, was apologetic.

There was a fire in my café premises. The fire brigade was dealing with it, the worst was over. He'd be obliged if I could get dressed and come along with him to see the damage. There were formalities and some police work to be dealt with.

11

The next morning, as luck and irony often have it, was a clear and lovely spring day. The sea glittered under cloudless blue and there were warm breezes to thaw the bones. It was particularly warm in and around the 400 sq. ft. which had once housed the Now and Again café.

The entire place had been gutted.

At 9 a.m., when I returned after ragged and futile hours spent watching the fire go out the night before, the blackened shell was still smouldering and the debris of my livelihood, not to mention my *raison d'etre*, still too hot to handle. My cherrywood counter was a charred upright in the middle of it all, the tables and chairs contorted sculptures in the rubble. The scorched air was thick with silence.

The barber and newsagent shops on either side had escaped. Once their owners had dealt with smoke and water damage they would be able to open for business. There were still a few firemen about, as well as a couple of guards and onlookers who were being kept at a distance. I saw John Rutledge among them but he left before I got a chance to speak to him. I was grudgingly allowed past the safety cordon and into the men-dealing-with-things world of the charred remains.

Hector was there too. He joined me on the 'safe' spot I'd been allocated.

'Any ideas about why this might have happened?' He lit a cigarette then put it irritably out when a fireman gave him a quick look.

I noted he'd said *why*, and not *how*.

'No,' I said. 'I'd tell you if I had.' It was his job to find out. 'Are you telling me it wasn't an accident?'

'It definitely wasn't an accident.' Hector looked at the blackened walls of the buildings on either side. 'Miracle was it didn't spread.' He turned and looked up at Thaddeus's windows. 'I suppose some of the credit must go to the old man for getting the boys in the brigade here so quickly.'

'Even insomnia has its upside,' I said.

Thaddeus had been awake and reading by the balcony window when he'd seen the flames. So he said. I wondered if he'd been drinking. He was the one called the fire brigade and the one who'd stood with me in the night while the firemen fought to contain the flames, the proverbial tower of strength. He hadn't uttered a word about old newspapers being disturbed or about missing an old letter. He seemed sober.

'How do you know it wasn't an accident?' I asked Hector.

My ex-husband, who likes to control situations, took his time before telling me what he knew about the cause of the fire. I was too tired to do battle with him so I waited. Lack of sleep was catching up with me; I'd stood with the fire until dawn and a sunrise like scorched sheets came into the sky. I'd gone home then, but couldn't sleep. If I waited long enough, like maybe for another hour or two, exhaustion was bound to knock me out.

Hector began his answer to my question with a question of his own. Typical. 'You didn't notice anything or anyone odd, when you came in the café to sort out the fridge last night?' he said.

'Nothing and nobody.'

I could have but didn't tell him I'd gone across to Thaddeus's place. It didn't seem to me relevant and I didn't want to open that particular can of worms. What I'd found and read was my business, for now. It was going to stay my business too until I'd had a chance to put the letter back and talk to Thaddeus, see what I could worm out of him about Ritchie Walsh and whatever had happened in 1953. I wasn't one bit keen to cause trouble for Thaddeus, rake up a past which might cause him grief or worse, unless there was a very good reason.

'What's really odd though is the sudden way the fire started,' I said. 'In a flash, according to Thaddeus. He was at the window when he saw the dark night outside lighting up. He says that when he looked down it was as if there had been a sudden explosion of flame in the café.'

'He was right,' Hector said, 'and explosion's exactly what happened. Someone threw a Molotov cocktail through your window.'

'Jesus! Why didn't you tell me before now?'

Hector shrugged. 'I wish I didn't have to tell you at all,' he said, 'you've had a fair bit to contend with in the last thirty-six hours. Fact is, a fireman found enough of the remains of a bottle and petrol-soaked cloth to be certain. Fairly primitive stuff, but it did the job.'

'So it was arson?' I said, stupidly.

'Looks that way.'

I swore, under my breath and then out loud, 'Bastards. Rotten little shits. Why would they do a thing like that?'

'Who do you think did it, Fran?'

'Seems to me like the dangerous and infantile thing a gang of teenage boys would do,' I said, wearily. There was a fair amount of adolescent thuggery and mayhem went on in the town.

'We think this one's a bit more complicated than that,' Hector said.

'It would be nice to know what you think happened,' I snapped.

'Simmer down.' Hector was at his most calmly irritating. 'You're understandably upset and this isn't the best place to have this talk. If you hang on for a few minutes we'll have a coffee somewhere and I'll go over things with you.'

I waited on the footpath while he spoke with a colleague, then a fireman. The crowd watching from across the road had grown to include several of my customers. Mrs Crawford was there, leaning on her buggy. Eddie Mulvey and Ronnie Fox were eating baps and drinking take-away coffees. I couldn't decide whether them having their breakfast on the hoof while surveying the charred remains of their usual dining place was an act of loyalty or one of betrayal. Eddie raised his paper coffee cup in salute.

Hector came over and we walked up the road and round the corner to a small hotel. The coffee was adequate.

'You think this has something to do with the murder, don't you?' I said, watching Hector light a cigarette and wishing he wouldn't. For my sake, not his: I'd a craving for smokeless air. 'Or at least with my finding Alannah Casey's body?'

'It could have,' carefully.

'Why?' I felt suddenly tearful. Tiredness, I

told myself but knew it was a sadness. Alannah Casey dying, and in the way she did, was bad enough. That it should have such a cruel and pointless consequence seemed unbearable.

'There are no such things as coincidences...' Hector began.

'If you believe that,' I snapped, 'why are you so certain yesterday's murder had nothing to do with the earlier ones?'

'I didn't say that.' He was reason itself. 'I said I didn't think it related to them, that it was more likely to be a copy-cat job.'

'Semantics,' I said, 'were always a strong part of your artillery.'

He let this pettiness go. All in all, I had to admit, he was being admirably tolerant of my mood.

'The thing about your average murderer, Fran, is that he isn't your average Joe. Usually.' He said this thoughtfully, studying the tip of his cigarette. 'Once he or she has murder in mind they'll begin to inform themselves about ways and means, pick up on related information, listen to things, read every related item they can lay hands on that might be of use. It's rare for a murder to be unique, or original, for someone not to have been killed in the same way somewhere before. Murderers very often want attention too; a copy-cat job ensures plenty.'

'Very interesting,' I said. He was no doubt

right. But he didn't know about Ritchie Walsh's letter.

I could have told him about it there and then. I like to think I might have given in to wisdom and the better part of valour if he hadn't gone straight into telling me that the guards thought the fire in the Now and Again was racist in origin. Life is all about timing.

'Doesn't take great powers of deduction,' he said. 'A Molotov cocktail is a pretty crude missile and the message would seem to be as crude. Molotov equals Russian evil, and it looks to be adding up to there being someone, or some people, who feel strongly enough about Dimitri Sobchak to make their point by burning down the place where he used to meet with Alannah Casey.'

'But the only person that really gets at is me, and Nina since she has no job now,' I said.

'That's right. Your sin was in facilitating him. The human mind's a warped piece of equipment,' he shrugged, 'the less you expect to find logic in this business the more you're inclined to come up with answers.'

'Do you really believe that's what happened?' I stared at him.

'It's a strong possibility.'

'And you've no idea who the person might be?' My head and shoulders might have been supporting tons of wet sand, they felt

136

so heavy.

'Go home, Fran,' Hector said, quietly. 'There's nothing more you can do here and you haven't had much sleep.'

'Sleep isn't what I need.' I looked away from the carefully composed concern on his face. 'I need to know who did this, whether they're coming after me again, if my insurance will cover everything and how long it'll take to rebuild and get me back into business.'

'You're not going to get any of that information here and now,' Hector stood. 'So you might as well go home.'

We walked together to my car, parked a few hundred yards from the smouldering shell of the Now and Again. Hector had left me and I was about to get in and drive away when I saw Thaddeus, unmissable in a silver bomber jacket, crossing the road. I waved to him.

'I've made coffee,' he called loudly as he approached.

'Another time,' I said, 'I'm all coffeed out.'

He stood shaking his head and looking at the night's destruction. 'It'll be a while before you get this place up and going again,' he said. 'You could be facing a fairly long-term closure.' The idea seemed to please him.

Nina had been equally pessimistic when I phoned her earlier. 'We will not be working then for a long time, it looks like,' she'd heaved a sigh as long drawn as a train, 'it's true that troubles never come singly.'

'At least there was no one there at the time,' I said.

'Yes, of course. There is that good point. Will you put up a notice to say we will be back?'

'I suppose so. Yes, I'll do that. As soon as I know when, how long it'll take to rebuild the place.'

'I think you must put a notice in the paper. It is what a proper business would do.'

'No need,' I said, briskly. 'I'm going down there now, to see the worst in daylight. Do you want to come with me?'

'I have seen too many burned-down houses, cafés too. It will be the same as all the others,' Nina said. 'I would prefer to think of a plan for us. I will talk to you later, when I have some ideas.' She hung up.

I relayed some of this conversation now to Thaddeus as we stood by my car. 'How long do you think it would take to rebuild?' I asked.

'It would be quicker and easier to rebuild from scratch than to do a repair job,' he said. 'A new and improved version could be up and running in two to three months.'

'Oh, God,' I said, and then, 'I'm going home to get some sleep.'

Thaddeus shook a doleful head as I got

into my car. 'Hope the guards get their fingers out and catch the bastard who did this.' Without looking at Hector he nodded in his direction. 'He's looking after this too, is he?'

'Seems to be. Helping out anyway. You didn't see anyone last night? No one running away? Anything like that?' I said.

'Just saw a flash and the flames as they sprang up. Told the guards as much. Told Hector too. Go on home, Frances. Nothing you can do here...'

I left. I was getting very tired of people telling me what to do.

It would probably have made sense to feel fearful, or at least worried, about my personal safety but all I felt was a sense of loss, and a void ahead of me which would have been filled by the days running the Now and Again café.

12

November 1953. Dun Laoghaire.

The rain gets heavier, so heavy that it runs down the narrow side streets like a river and splashes Shirley's nylon-clad legs with every step.

Her movements are less certain now too. She finds that she needs to hold onto the wall as she goes, her sureness of step diminished by the amount she has had to drink. She knows that she must head for home, eventually.

But eventually is not now, not just yet. She wants to punish Jimmy for a while longer. He deserves to be punished.

It is very dark too. There have been problems recently with the street lighting and in the back and side streets she has chosen there is none at all that night. She stumbles, breaking a nail and swearing as she scrabbles for balance against a pebble-dashed wall. She goes on. She is still drunk enough to be anaesthetised against the cold, indifferent to the meagre protection offered by the oilcloth, to her increasingly sodden state.

Drunk enough to feel sorry for herself.

She steps into a doorway and sobs. Jimmy is such a bastard, never giving her the love she wants nor the attention she needs. She sobs on, cursing the day she met him, swearing revenge, swearing to herself that she will never again lie with him.

She hopes he is good and sorry for spending so much time in the pub. By now, if he hadn't behaved like a shit, if she hadn't had to leave to teach him a lesson, they would be licking the sweat from one another, ready for a second round...

She gives a small moan and leaves the doorway. She is not sure where she's headed, but is still intent on keeping away from the house, and from Jimmy. The longer she stays away the more worried he will be and the less inclined to beat her when she does turn up. Shirley has welts on her shoulder to remind her why she should be afraid of him.

She rounds a corner to discover she has somehow made her way to within a few hundred yards of the small harbour she and Jimmy used to visit in the early days of their marriage. The girls swim there now, in the summer, sometimes even with Jimmy when he's home. She hasn't been for years herself.

She stands looking across the wider stretches of a bellicose bay, and is consumed with an even intenser self-pity, a greater anger.

Fuck Jimmy, and his entire family and their children too. Fuck this whole, endlessly stupid place and fuck the predicament she's got herself into. She *will* go, leave them all to hell and Dun Laoghaire winters and the watchful eyes of their black devils of priests.

She takes the short cut along the laneway by The Dead House, which is what people call the morgue, to the low wall of the harbour. This is where she is standing when he finds her. He comes up behind her and says, 'Surely you know that everyone's out looking for you.'

She turns. He is as soaked through as she is herself. 'Well…' she looks up at him, 'now you've found me. Clever you.'

'You've been out in the rain long enough. You should come home with me now,' he says.

'Why?' She smiles and shrugs, 'Why should I go home with you? Why should either of us go home? Is home where your heart is?'

'You're wet through,' he says, 'through and through…' He lays a tentative hand on her hair, moves it slowly to her shoulder.

'Through to the skin,' Shirley says, softly, smiling at him. 'Nothing to be done but go the whole hog now…'

She catches the hand on her arm and holds it, tightly, for a minute. Then she puts his fingers to her mouth and runs her tongue over their tips. She keeps her eyes on his all of the time.

'You're very good looking, you know.' Her breath is warm on his fingertips. She is experienced enough to read in his face the desire to know how sweetly her breath tastes too. 'The whole hog...' she murmurs, almost to herself. She seems to have forgotten the cold, to be glowing all over. She is excited, drunk again, full again of a rampaging desire for revenge.

'What do you mean by that, Shirley?' His voice is a croak. 'What's the whole hog?' He is unable to remove his hand from hers. Unlike her he is shivering.

'I mean we might as well strip to our skins, get into the water and have a swim,' she laughs, loudly, 'wash away our sins, like at the river of Jordan. You'd like that, wouldn't you?' She puts his hand through the opening in the oilcloth, lays it at the warm base of her neck. 'The rain is our friend. It's keeping everyone indoors. We're alone. No one to see us. Why are we wasting time? You know you want to. I know you want to...'

'It's November, Shirley,' his voice is no longer croaking, just shaky. 'We'd die of the cold...'

'Are you afraid?' Her tone is incredulous. 'Is that it? Are you afraid of what people might say?' She steps right up, until she is touching him, until his hand, still in her grasp, has been moved lower and is covering the swelling responsiveness of her breasts. 'They're small people. You know they are, you agreed with me once, when I said that. Small people who don't matter. We don't care about them, you and I, we don't care.' She pauses, raises herself on tiptoe, catches his bottom lip between her teeth, moistens her own lips with her tongue, and whispers, 'Do we?' with her mouth against his. Her tongue flickers against his teeth. His hand moves deeper into her bra and finds a nipple.

'We don't care,' he has to clear his throat to get the words out, 'it's just that the cold...'

'Am I not worth catching your death for?'

She moves away from him and lets the oilcloth fall to the ground. Then she begins opening the buttons of her blouse. The hand which had felt her breast falls to his side. He doesn't answer and he doesn't try to stop her.

'The water is warmed by the rain falling on it,' she has opened the blouse and is standing with her white, satin slip exposed. 'Bet you didn't even notice what I was wearing earlier.' She puts a coquettish head to one side, raises an eyebrow.

'I did,' he says, 'I saw everything. Your skirt's getting all wet now...' he reaches out his hand '...and your underwear...'

144

With a laugh, wild and worrying, she catches the end of the blouse and pulls it over her head and off. The white satin slip darkens as the rain falls on it. She shakes her head and her sodden, golden curls throw rivulets of rain onto her shoulders and chest.

The rain continues to fall and the moon, drifting momentarily into a break in the cloud, turns her into an alabaster goddess.

'The water is warmed by rain falling on it,' she says for the second time, wrapping herself in her arms. 'What are you afraid of? Is it the water or is it ... me?'

'I'm not afraid.'

'Prove it.' She unzips her skirt and lets it fall.

13

April, 2003. Dun Laoghaire.

Nothing, it seemed, was going to be easy.

The insurance company said things could not be rushed. The boyish agent they sent to see me talked a lot about investigators' reports, liability, indemnity, loss adjustments. He seemed to think I was joking when I said I would like to get the place up and running again in a few months.

I rang a small building contractor I knew. He said he couldn't go near the place until the insurance people had finished their investigations. As soon as I got the okay he'd make a start, he said. That, all things being equal, would be in three to four weeks time. I should, he said, take a holiday in the meantime, get away from it all to the sun. I told him I didn't want to take a holiday. He said I sounded as if I needed one. I realised I'd been roaring down the phone at him.

Three days after the fire Nina called to the house and told me what she'd been planning for us.

'You must learn to be like the snail,' she said.

'That's a great help, Nina. I'll try it,' I said and handed her a glass of orange juice. She doesn't touch coffee. Sarcasm is also wasted on Nina.

'The snail goes to the mountain carrying his home on his back.' She sipped the juice. She was perfectly serious. Her hair was newly washed and she looked delicate and wistful. She was neither.

'And gets there, eventually,' I said, trying to be helpful.

'The location of his house does not matter to the snail,' Nina went on, 'he is always prepared to move, to do what he must to live wherever he can...'

I was in no mood to listen to fables or the wisdoms of nature. I cut her short. 'Wonderful creature, the snail,' I agreed, 'except that he's squashed and destroyed along with his home on a regular basis.'

Nina gave me a sadly disappointed look and put down the orange juice. 'You must open your mind, Fran,' she shook her head, 'the Now and Again Café can exist in another place.'

'I know that,' I said. I'd briefly thought about setting up elsewhere, then dismissed the idea. Maybe two heads were better than one on the subject. 'Tell me what you've been thinking,' I said.

'You must go to the mountain, Fran. If you make breakfast for the men on the site where they are building you will make more money, and so will I. You must rent a van, or caravan, and cook big breakfasts and serve them where they work. It is nearly summer-time. The men will not mind the outdoors.' She leaned forward. 'Their boss will be glad to have them all the time under his eye.'

'True,' I said, 'except that a site caravan is not a coffee shop.'

It would be something else altogether. 'Of course not. It would be a big fry-up van serving giant Irish breakfasts with,' she counted on her fingers, 'beans, bacon, eggs, mugs of tea and coffee. We will have plenty of hard work. You must give the men what they want. We will be there, ready to start frying for them, at seven in the mornings. They will be grateful. The boss will be grateful. It will not be so comfortable and the work will be harder but I have worked out the costs and you will make a lot of money while the café is being rebuilt. And you will pay me more.'

She was right. Nina Lisekyo, survivor and entrepreneur, was right. I would do it.

'I'll make you a partner,' I said.

'I don't want to be a partner,' Nina said, 'I just want more money.'

'We'll see how it goes,' I said and then, because it was on my mind, added, 'do you ever wonder about those other murders? The women who were left on morgue steps here and in New York?'

'I have thought about them a little bit,' she said. Her tone wasn't encouraging. Nina most definitely believes the past is dead.

'I think about them a lot,' I said.

'Why?'

'I'm not sure,' I lied. 'Maybe because Thaddeus knew the woman who was murdered in Dun Laoghaire...'

'Then let Thaddeus think about what happened,' she was brisk, 'you must put your mind to our plans. It is enough for you to think about at the moment.'

It wasn't until I went to the building site, spoke to the foreman, met my former customers and agreed to set up a canteen-on-wheels in the middle of the mud, cement and building bricks of the site that I realised, like J. Alfred Prufrock, I'd been measuring out my life with coffee spoons for a long time.

Derek Moran showed the enthusiasm Nina had predicted he would. Or at least he was encouraging. 'You'll be out of the way here,' he said, showing me a rubble-filled corner. 'We'll clean it up a bit before you arrive. When do you think that'll be?' His eyes fixed on Greg Slattery, hovering to have a word with me.

'Soon as I get a suitable catering van and suppliers set up,' I said efficiently, 'two weeks, say?'

'Make it sooner if you can,' he glared at Greg, 'there's too much time being wasted with the lads going off-site. I'll bid you good day.'

He said something sharpish to Greg as he passed him but, sheepish as a scolded schoolboy, he approached me anyway as I was leaving.

'Sorry to hear about your troubles,' he said. 'Any word on who it was burnt you out?'

'Only that it was deliberate,' I said. 'They found the remains of a bottle with petrol and a rag.'

'The lads here are saying the Russian's behind it,' Greg said, 'the feeling is he's too smart for his own good, with his civil rights solicitor and rich do-gooder to pay the bills.' He was wearing a helmet. With his red curls hidden, his face was harder and older looking. He shifted a lump hammer he was holding from one hand to the other as he spoke.

'They didn't know him,' I said. 'None of us knew him, really.'

'That's right. He'd been drinking coffee beside us for the best part of three months and none of us knew him.' Greg's eyes were pellets of anger. 'He was a cold little shite and he probably did for her.' The words were torrenting out of him. 'Nothing to do with him being a Russian. I've worked with Russians. They're all right, as people go. Sobchak isn't all right.'

'If you know something...' I began.

'I don't know anything,' Greg interrupted. 'Like I said, he was a secretive bastard.'

Derek Moran appeared out of nowhere. 'You're wanted on block B,' he said to Greg, 'I want you to get over there. Now.'

He kept his eyes on his back as Greg Slattery walked away. I felt them on my own back as I left the site.

I had Thaddeus's letter from Ritchie Walsh in my bag. It was time to get it back to where I'd taken it from, though not before I made a photocopy for myself.

Brady's Newsagent's was back in business, Jack Brady milking the whiff of smoke in the air for all it was worth. The barber's was up and running too. I copied the letter on Jack's photocopier, the envelope too for good measure. I bought both *The Irish Times* and *The Irish Independent* as well as chocolates for Thaddeus and crossed the road to his apartment.

He met me as I got out of the lift, cross-looking in a red dressing gown with a hood. 'You're not using your key today then,' he said.

Was I being paranoid or was the look he gave me a suspicious one?

'No,' I said. 'I've brought you chocolates

151

though, and the papers. You look as if you haven't gone outside all day. Are you feeling okay?' He'd been drinking.

'I'm feeling fine.' He didn't sound it. He padded ahead of me to the kitchen in a pair of ancient flip-flops. I was seriously uncomfortable by now. 'I've been giving the place a bit of a clean up. Needed it badly ... things are all over the place...'

He was muttering and distracted as he plugged in the coffee-maker. The place looked distracted too, in an untypical mess. Drawers had been left open and letters and bills scattered across the work-top.

He'd missed Ritchie Walsh's letter then, and he'd been looking for it. There was no other explanation.

'I'll have a glass of water,' I said, 'but I need to use your bathroom first. Back in a minute.'

He watched me as I crossed the living room. He was still looking when I opened the door to the hallway, where the bathroom was.

'Anything wrong?' I said.

He shook his head and turned away slowly. He knew, or suspected, but was probably befuddled enough with drink to doubt himself. What, or why, was he hiding that he couldn't talk about? He was elderly, of course, something one was inclined to over-look about Thaddeus. He looked it too, that day, an old man in a ludicrous red dressing gown with blue-veined feet, fastidiously matching cups to saucers, saucers to plates.

'Won't be a minute,' I called and closed the door behind me before crossing the hall to his bedroom.

It was in complete chaos. The bed was unmade, the rugs rolled back, the wardrobe shelves empty and their contents on the floor. His search had been frantic. The suitcase with the cuttings was in a corner, some of them stacked beside it, others inside.

I slipped Ritchie Walsh's letter under the suitcase. He might, just might, think it had been stuck to its underside all the time. It would create a doubt in his drink fuddled mind, at least. In the bathroom I perfumed myself and slicked on some red lipstick. By the time I got back Thaddeus had made the tea and tidied the kitchen.

'Nice scent,' he said. He was a man who appreciated what other men didn't even notice. It was one of the many nice things about him.

'Why are you drinking, Thaddeus?' I said.

'Decided it didn't much matter any more,' he said, 'not at my age.' He was lying. We both knew it.

I sat on a high stool and he shoved a plate of the Florentines I loved my way. I was feeling pretty bad about deceiving him when I said, 'Any chance I could have a look at those old newspapers now, Thaddeus?'

'I'll give them to you another day.' He didn't miss a beat.

But neither did he look at me as he poured himself a coffee, helped himself to a biscuit and leaned against the work-top to deliver me a lecture. He wasn't offering drink today, I noticed.

'You've been through enough the last few days. Give yourself a rest, Fran. Plenty of time to read them next week. Your problem is that you don't know when enough is enough. You really do need that holiday. Just say the word and I'll sign the cheque. Go wherever you want. Australia if you like.' He smiled suddenly, pleased with himself. 'Now that's a good idea. Go to Australia. Lovely time of year down under.'

'I don't feel like a holiday, Thaddeus.' It took great restraint to keep my voice even. He'd refused to let me see the cuttings, was clearly trying to get me out of the way. 'Hector will let me see the file on those years in the garda station,' I said. 'They've probably got a more complete set anyway.'

'Please yourself,' Thaddeus said, 'you are too stubborn by half.'

Takes one to know one, as they say.

Hector phoned that evening with the official post-mortem results. Alannah Casey had died by strangulation. By hand. He also told me that, thanks to a 'gap in the schedule', the coroner's inquest would take place the following week, much quicker than usual.

'She was pregnant,' he said, quietly, when I thought I'd heard it all.

'Oh, God,' I said.

'We'll be bringing Dimitri Sobchak in again,' Hector said, 'though without much hope of getting anything out of him. This doesn't prove he'd anything to do with the death. Doesn't even increase suspicion.'

'I suppose not,' I said. There were other things the forensic people could be sure of, however. 'How can they be certain she was strangled by hand?' I said.

'Because,' Hector said, 'there were thumb marks on each side and to the front of her neck, with the marks of counter pressure from fingers over the back of her neck. That means, Fran, that she was strangled from the front.' He paused. 'She probably knew her murderer.'

'That should be a help in finding him,' I said, as evenly as I could.

'We hope so. I've to go now,' Hector said.

'Don't go,' I shouted, panicking, 'I've got a favour to ask you.'

'Yes?' He was cool, and very, very cautious.

'Could you arrange for me to come down to the station and look through the papers on the 1953 and 1963 murders? I need to make some sense of all of this.'

'Don't see how that would help...'

'It *would* help, believe me, Hector, it would. I'm at a loose end. Too much time on my hands.' I abandoned pleading. 'I could apply through the Freedom of Information Act but that seems a bit extreme when you and I might more easily, and with less public fuss, come to an agreement.'

'Don't threaten me, Fran.' He was curt.

'Don't refuse me then,' I said.

'Find something else to do with yourself, Fran,' Hector said. 'Walk the dog.'

'Nice of you to worry about me, Hector, and about Lucifer, but I've already done something about occupying my time. I'm working on a stop-gap business venture until the Now and Again's rebuilt. But that won't happen for a few weeks.'

'What're you planning?' Hector demanded and I told him, in outline, about the catering van.

'Sounds a reasonable enough idea,' he said, surprising me. Put-downs came more normally to Hector. Perhaps he hadn't been really listening. 'Maybe you should take a holiday first,' he said. I pretended I hadn't heard him.

'I've got to get a catering licence,' I said, 'rent the van, contact suppliers – but I've free time in between too.' I cleared my throat and adopted an apologetic tone. 'I suppose I shouldn't have asked you, Hector, you're far too busy. I'll put in an official request. Probably better to go through your superiors anyway.'

'Come into the station tonight,' Hector said, resigned. 'I'll free up a room for you, and a computer. About eight.'

He hung up without saying goodbye.

Once I'd officially seen the cuttings I could talk to Thaddeus about what had happened.

I could ask him for answers to some of the questions spinning in my head; like how well he'd known Shirley Walsh and what she'd really been like, whether Ritchie Walsh had ever come back to Dun Laoghaire and, if he had, whether Thaddeus had met him.

I also wanted to know where Ritchie Walsh was now. The US cops might have given the guards an answer to that one.

14

A chance meeting with John Rutledge answered one of my questions.

I'd been to see Ted Cullen in the hopes that he would continue to work for me, collecting and delivering bacon, eggs, bread and sausages to the catering van at the crack of dawn. I'd gone on impulse and he hadn't been all that pleased to see me. He was sorry for my troubles, he said, but he was too busy to oblige. He didn't invite me in, just stood in the doorway of his small house, ignoring a yell from within telling him to close the door. I'd got on well with him before and was surprised.

'I thought you'd be out of business for a long time,' he said, interpreting my look, 'so I decided to retire.' He bent down to pat Lucifer as the yell became more strident. He looked me in the eye as he straightened up. 'I'm too old,' he said, 'I want a rest from it all. And all the grief... I want an end to it.' He started to shut the door.

'Did you know Shirley Walsh?' I stopped the door with my hand. 'Is that why you're upset?'

He was past retiring age, as he'd often

enough told me. He might have known her, just. Also, he liked to talk.

He looked at my hand, as if he wanted to forcibly remove it. 'I was talking about the business, about work,' he said. 'It's time to hang up my gloves. In a manner of speaking.'

'Did you know her?' I insisted. No point pretending to believe him.

'I did...' He turned as an inner door slammed, then quickly closed the door and stepped outside to join me on the narrow footpath. 'I'll talk to you for a couple of minutes,' he said, 'but I won't deliver again, so there's no good asking me. I didn't know Shirley Walsh in the way most people thought, the way a lot of other young men of the time did...'

He traced the outline of his moustache with a bandaged hand before standing with his arms folded above his stomach. He stared into the middle distance, like a soldier on parade. A lace curtain in the front window twitched behind him.

'She was a troubled woman. Very good to look at and all of that but troubled. I could see that and I was only a teenager at the time. There would have been help for her today but,' he shrugged, 'there was none back then. It was fifty years ago. Fifty years...' He stopped and I waited. There was a loneliness about him, the way he stood there on the footpath. 'They'd have given her pills today, or had her talking to one of those therapy people.'

'What was wrong with her?' I risked a question when he stopped again.

'How do I know what was wrong with her? All I know is that she had to be on the go all the time. Had to be forever moving. And she was changeable. Always ready to explode. She'd be very kind and then she'd be very cruel and she wanted to be in the company of men all the time. I was a married man then, I was married to May on my eighteenth birthday.' He jerked his head at the window. 'I was thin and I was fit, you can believe that or not as you like. I did butcher deliveries on a bike. Shirley Walsh asked me in one day when I went there with a pound of minced beef. She was wearing nothing but her slip. She didn't care who I was or my situation. I was nineteen years of age by then and the father of a five-month-old child. She said that she was alone and that she was lonely.'

'You didn't go in?'

'I left the mince on the doorstep. I was afraid to hand it to her in case she grabbed a hold of me. I told her I'd be back. I only said it because I was sorry for her but it was the wrong thing to do. She was like a child, standing there in the doorway with hardly any clothes on her on a cold day. A child that needed a mother and father to care for her. She wasn't strong enough in her head to be left alone. She had no one, only a husband who was no use to her at all.' His short laugh dismissed Jimmy Walsh. 'Even when he was at home. But they were a handsome couple, I'll say that for them.'

'What did she do when you put down the meat?' I said.

'She kicked it back out onto the footpath and told me she'd give me the same treatment if ever I came near the place again.' Ted unfolded his arms and shoved his hands into his pockets. His stomach gave a gentle roll and rounded itself out again. 'She was drowned less than a week later but that day was the last time I saw her. I told the guards as much at the time and I told them again the other day.'

'They spoke to you about it?'

My small yelp of surprise sharpened him up. He became disapproving; much more the Ted I knew than the revealing loneliness of minutes before.

'I thought it my duty to go in and talk to them about what had happened,' he said, 'in case it might be of interest or use to them. They told me they had the matter in hand. But I've done my bit and I've said as much as I'm going to about the subject.' He held out his hand. 'I wish you luck with your venture. It was an unfortunate thing happened to you but with the grace of God it's all over and done with now.'

'Do you think Alannah Casey's death had anything to do with what happened then?' I said.

'That's for the guards to find out and the rest of us to keep clear of,' he took his hand back, 'no good came to anyone who was involved then and no good will come to anyone involves themselves with it now either.'

I was getting into the car, when he called out, 'You'd be better off going away some place until they find who did it.' He rang the doorbell as I stared at him. 'You're too caught up in it as it is, what with Thaddeus in the family and John Rutledge a big customer.'

The door opened and I caught a glimpse of a blue wool jumper in the hallway before he called, 'Good day to you now', and stepped inside and shut it behind him. I stared at the door, a green expanse with a shining brass knocker. When it didn't open again I drove away.

And so, when I saw John Rutledge coming out of a pub later in the day I made a point of stopping him. He was wearing a red and white spotted tie.

'If you've the time I'd like to buy you a coffee,' I said.

'I know what you're after,' he treated me

to a narrow-eyed look, 'you're a decent enough woman and I don't begrudge you a half an hour's question and answer session. But I'll have no truck with anyone else, in your family. If Thaddeus Shaw is anywhere in your shadow you'd be better off telling me now.'

'I've no idea where Thaddeus is.' I moved closer; his breath came at me in a gust of whiskey fumes. Another man bothered by memories. 'Will we go back inside?'

He found us a seat near the window. He disliked being too far from the light he said; dark interiors were for rats and other nocturnals and not suitable for humans. I bought him a whiskey along with the cup of coffee. I got myself one too. I needed it.

'You've been looking things up, of course,' John Rutledge said when I sat down.

'What makes you say that?'

'You're the kind would.' He lifted the whiskey.

'What kind is that?'

'Busy and restless,' he shrugged, 'a poor combination.' He downed half the whiskey. He made me sound like Shirley Walsh.

'Well, you're right,' I conceded. Anything to keep him mellow and talkative. 'I had a look at some cuttings and came across your evidence at the trial. You served her in a pub the night she died. It must have been hard for you, recounting what happened.'

He took a while to answer, looking meditatively into the whiskey glass, swirling it about, the corrugated folds on his face blank of all expression.

'It was harder for your father-in-law,' he spoke eventually, slowly and without looking up at me. 'He was closer to her than I was. I felt sorry for her and served her drink and that was all. I kept my distance. To do anything else would have been to take advantage of her. Many did.' He paused. 'I wasn't that way inclined,' he said.

'Is that why you and Thaddeus don't speak? Because you feel he took advantage of her?'

'He did take advantage of her, that's what happened and that's how it was. It's not a case of it just being a feeling I have; Thaddeus Shaw took advantage of Shirley Walsh. So did others but your father-in-law was more to be blamed than most of them because he was a so-called educated man and knew her husband and her situation. He may blame the drink but the flesh has to be willing,' he finished the whiskey, 'as well as the spirit.' He shrugged as he signalled for another. 'I'm no lily-white myself but my conscience is clear on this one,' he said.

'Are you saying that Thaddeus has a guilty conscience?' I said.

'I'm saying it's a cap might fit him,' he said.

'Is that what you told the guards?'

'It is. Then and now. I'm not saying he had anything to do with her death, although...' He stopped, frowning and looked out the window. His long nose met the curl of his top lip. 'Ask him himself,' he said, curtly.

'I was talking to Ted Cullen this morning,' I said casually as the barman brought the second whiskey. 'I went to ask him if he'd do deliveries for me again, to a temporary place I'll be opening. He said no. He doesn't want to work for me, said he doesn't want to be caught up in anything that might involve the past.'

'He wouldn't. Ted's soft. Always was. That's how he came to marry that harridan of a May Gorman. Anyone else would have seen her coming. He was a lovely lad, and a good-looking one and it's sad to see what that woman and the years have done to him. He's soft and foolish outside as well as inside these days.'

The barman waited to be paid and John Rutledge waited for me to do the honours. I paid and said, 'The newspapers said nothing about him giving evidence in court.' I was hesitant, as if aware I might have missed something.

'That's because he'd no evidence to give,' John was short, 'he kept out of her way for fear of his scold of a wife. There was nothing to show he was anywhere near her the night she died. He was always the innocent, our Ted, always.' He trailed into silence, took a sip of his coffee and pulled a face. 'Not a patch on what you used to make,' he said with something of his old gallantry.

'It's cold,' I said. 'I hope you'll be a customer when I re-open. Or you might even drop up to the catering van I'm setting up on site down the road.'

'You're setting up on the site?' He raised his eyebrows. 'That's good thinking. I might well drop along for the occasional cup. Fine body of men working there. I pass by regularly.'

He smiled, still holding the coffee cup. With his pinky delicately poised and his eyes mistily mischievous he looked oddly appealing. He also looked anything but one of life's innocents.

'See you soon then.' I stood up.

'When do you open for business?' he asked.

'Hopefully in a couple of weeks,' I said.

'Good,' he said, 'very good...' His face folded into its usual discontent as his mind drifted on to something else. 'Ted Cullen...'

He said the name loudly, making sure he got my full attention. Which he did. I waited as he carefully positioned the cup in its saucer and leaned back in his chair, hugely sighing.

'Ted Cullen...' I prompted.

'Our Ted isn't quite the harmless citizen he makes out to be,' he said. 'But that's enough on the subject for now. You can be on your way now, m'dear.'

There was a degree of malice in his eye now. John Rutledge wasn't harmless either. I went on my way, straight to the garda station to read through the cuttings and on-line data on the earlier murders.

Hector, as promised, had set aside a room for me. It was windowless, had a door which didn't shut, a PC on a table and a stack of files alongside it. A guard brought me a chair to sit on, along with one for himself.

'I'll keep you company,' he said and sat on his own inside the door, foot tapping and not even pretending to be happy about what he'd been asked to do.

The newspaper cuttings weren't as comprehensive as Thaddeus's had been. They were mostly from *The Irish Press* and gave an outline of events which lacked the broader scope and finer detail of Thaddeus's three-paper version. I learned nothing new.

The paper-file on the Coney Island murder of 1963 consisted of half a dozen cuttings. A couple told the story of Liliya Borodin's drowning, a couple more gave summaries of the court case and Sergei Borodin's conviction for the murder of his wife. There was a full, feature-length article on Coney Island and the unfortunate break-up of the Borodin and Walsh families following the murder. The Borodin children, a ten-year-old girl called Sofia and thirteen-year-old boy called Alexander, had been sent to separate care homes. Richard Walsh remained in Coney Island, his sons and nieces had all left. Only Michael Walsh, now aged twenty-five, had spoken about it.

'We want to put the past behind us,' he said, 'it seems if we stay together it just follows us.'

The garda on his chair cleared his throat and asked if I was 'anywhere near finished?' I promised I was 'getting there' and went quickly through the last cutting on the file, a brief report of the execution of Sergei Borodin.

Hector had also left a web site address which, when I looked into it, told me what was happening with the US police follow-up on the Walsh and Borodin families. Not much, was the answer.

Ritchie Walsh was in a home, paid for out of an account presumably set up by his sons and nieces. He'd been there for several years. His sons and nieces were scattered across the States and hadn't yet been tracked down. There was a page too on the fate of the Borodin children but by the time I got that far the guard's impatience was a force in the room so I jotted down the web address and left.

Thaddeus was in the house when I got back, along with Emer. Emer had invited herself for a bite to eat. Thaddeus was a surprise; I was beginning to feel under siege and didn't like it.

Emer opened the door as I was going through my usual doorstep search for the key.

'Jesus, Fran, where the hell were you?' She stepped outside, pulled the door shut and continued in a hissing whisper, 'I've had Thaddeus for more than an hour and I swear he gets worse with age. He's been cooking and giving me a lecture, a *lecture*, on how to plug in the friggin' electric kettle. The man's a major control freak. He's totally done my head in...' She sat on the cold granite step and produced a packet of cigarettes. 'He's drinking too. It's weird...'

'Thought you'd given them up,' I said.

'I had. How're things with you?' she said.

'Fine,' I said, 'fine.'

'I've been thinking...' she eyed me, cautiously, through a screen of smoke, '...that you should expand your horizons a bit. Taking a holiday would be a beginning.'

'Maybe I will,' I said, and meant it.

With so many people telling me to get away it was inevitable that I should think about it. The result was that a half-baked idea, which had raised its head while I was going through the cuttings in the station, was fermenting fast. A few phone calls would make it a hard plan.

'I've been thinking I should visit Alannah Casey's parents,' I said, changing the subject to talk about something else which had been on my mind.

'I wondered about that,' Emer said, 'do you think they would want to see you?'

'Don't know,' I said, 'I'll give them another day or two, then maybe just go round to the house.'

Emer was watching me still, not half so covertly as she thought either. 'How was your day?' she said.

'I had a look through the files on the earlier murders,' I said, 'there are more people around than you'd imagine who were involved at the time.'

'Yes?' She sounded interested.

'Could we go inside?' I said. 'I'd like to tell Thaddeus what I came across too.'

'Oh, God, I suppose so...' Emer said and stubbed out her cigarette.

Thaddeus had taken over the kitchen, again, and prepared pork chops, potatoes and salad. I sat in my usual place at the table and Emer sat where she'd sat for years resisting the balanced diet I prepared for her.

'Plain food's best,' Thaddeus intoned as he served us, 'can't beat it for nutrients.'

'I won't have a chop,' Emer said.

'I'll eat yours myself then,' Thaddeus said, not without petulance.

I cut to the chase. 'I had a look at the police files on the 1953 and 1963 murders,' I said. 'You didn't tell me, Thaddeus, that you gave evidence at James Walsh's trial.'

'I didn't?' Thaddeus took his place at the table, two chops on his plate. 'I'm sure I mentioned that I knew his wife, the murdered woman?' He began to eat. 'I showed you a picture of her.'

'Yes, you did,' I said. 'But I didn't know until I read the reports that you and John Rutledge were among the last people to see her alive. Nor that you'd both given evidence.'

'Is that so important?' Thaddeus said. He was antagonistic.

'It's interesting,' Emer said.

'I gave you as much information as I thought necessary,' Thaddeus said, frowning and irritated, 'Emer too. I didn't, and don't, want either of you becoming caught up in the gutter-press version of things. You know the full story now, Frances, so there's no need to concern yourself any further about it.'

'Very protective of you, Thaddeus, I'm sure,' Emer drawled, 'but we're all in this together, whether you want it that way or not.'

We were not all in this together, not by a long shot. Thaddeus was in it alone, upset enough to start drinking again, keeping to himself whatever it was bound him and Ritchie Walsh to the past. He'd told me, and then Emer, as much as he needed about 1953 to keep us at bay. He'd probably played the guards the same way. An easy enough thing to do given Hector's antagonism to his father's involvement.

'You're not "in" it at all,' Thaddeus snapped, 'it's over and done with.'

'Only in a manner of speaking,' Emer said. 'You're still with us. So is mother's Mr Rutledge. How did he come into it?' She turned to me.

'He was the barman who served her in the pub the night she died,' I said. 'Thaddeus was in the pub too.'

'As were several other regulars,' Thaddeus snapped.

'The brother, Richard Walsh, was given quite a grilling in the witness box,' I said, casually, tones even.

'He was,' said Thaddeus, tone curt.

'Did anyone ever hear from him after he left the country?' I said.

'Not that I know of,' Thaddeus said.

'Surely he had other family, friends...'

'I believe he made a clean break,' Thaddeus said, 'best thing in the circumstances.'

I took a deep breath. 'Odd that he didn't

make contact after the 1963 murder on Coney Island,' I said.

'Why should he?' Thaddeus looked at me across the table. I stared at him. He looked me right in the eye. 'He'd been gone ten years at that stage,' he said.

'You're the one told me the past is never dead,' I reminded him.

'I was speaking figuratively.' Thaddeus didn't move his gaze from mine. His eyes had never seemed so darkly unknown. I couldn't read a thing in them.

'Speaking figuratively...' I echoed his lie.

He'd been speaking before he knew I'd read the letter, and he'd been speaking truthfully. The past was not dead, not as far as Thaddeus was concerned.

Nor as far as Ritchie Walsh was concerned either.

15

November 1953. Dun Laoghaire.

Shirley Walsh drops the straps of the slip and wriggles it to the ground at her feet before stepping smartly out of it. She is wearing black suspenders on her nylons. She takes off her brassiere and stands with her hands on her hips. Her breasts are large. When he moves towards her she holds up a staying hand.

'Now you,' she says.

He hesitates for seconds only before taking off his bulky jacket. He hesitates again before taking off the jumper he's wearing underneath and the short-sleeved vest under that. He comes to a full-stop when he gets to his trousers.

'Never thought you'd be so gutless when it came to an adventure,' she says, 'you're too timid for your own good.'

She picks the oilcloth from the ground, spreads it on the wall and sits on it, crossing her legs as she does so and swinging one of the emerald high-heels on a toe.

'Go on,' she laughingly encourages him, beginning to open a suspender. She is rolling down a nylon stocking when he kicks himself free of his trousers and comes towards her.

She moves to the other nylon, smiling to herself as he runs his hands over her back, caresses her thighs, tries to hold her breasts. Free of the nylons and green shoes she leans back to give him access to whatever parts of her body he wishes to explore. She is smiling, still, her eyes closed.

'Open your eyes.' It is the first time he has spoken for several minutes and his voice is thick and commanding. Shirley opens her eyes. He is standing over her, naked.

'My, oh my,' she says and laughs, loud and delightedly. 'Aren't you a big fellow! Now that's what I call a first-class whanger. One of the best I've seen...' her laugh becomes shrill '...for a long time.'

'Hold it,' he says, his voice hoarse, 'take it in your hand.'

'I'll do better than that.' Without taking her eyes off him she removes her black satin panties, opens her legs and sits with them spread wide.

'Do it to me,' her voice is harsh, commanding, 'get it in there and give it to me, hard.'

'Not like that...'

'You can't – is that it?' She is suddenly sneering. She keeps her legs open. He looks at the darkly inviting place between them, at

175

the rim of pink flesh in the dark hair.

'Not like that...' he repeats and lunges, grabbing her by the shoulders with his big hands, lifting her from the wall, pulling her hard against him while he smothers her mouth with his.

She struggles but he is too strong for her. He stifles her mouth with his when he carries her body to the ground beneath his own, when he forces her legs open with his knee, when he enters her quickly and far too violently.

It is over in a minute. Spent, he lies on top of her. She is very still.

He raises himself on his hands and looks down at her. A tear rolls from the corner of her eye into her hairline. It is followed by another.

'You wanted it,' he says, perplexed. She is silent, her head turned away. 'You got what you wanted,' he says again and gets up, leaving her there, gathering his clothes.

He is totally unprepared when she leaps on him from behind, sobbing and making small, animal-like sounds and tearing at the flesh of his back with her nails.

'Get off!' He spins, round and round, but she clings like a leech, digging her teeth into him like a leech would too. He bends, then straightens suddenly and viciously and she falls off, onto her back into the gravelly, muddy ground. She curls into a ball and turns on her side, whimpering.

'I'll get you,' she says, 'I'll get you for what you did to me. I'll tell them how you raped me.'

'You wanted it.' He is perplexed again, standing with his trousers in his hand, the rain beating the rest of his clothes into the same gravelly mud in which Shirley lies, curled up still and weeping. 'No one will believe you,' he says. The idea seems to comfort him.

'They'll believe me all right.' Shirley raises her head. Her eyes are stones of cold, calculating sobriety. 'You'll be sorry, I promise you.'

'But why? What did I do?'

He watches as she sits up and pushes her dripping hair back from her face. She looks down at her mud-splattered body and begins to weep anew.

'You raped me,' she sobs, 'that wasn't what I wanted. That wasn't the way I wanted it.' She hauls herself back onto the harbour wall and begins to rub the mud from her body with her slip.

'We should go for a swim, like you said.' He looks beyond her, into the dark waters of the small harbour. 'It would wash us clean.'

'It would wash away the evidence,' she says, narrowing her eyes as she looks at him, 'but maybe that's what you want. The bible tells us we must work out our own salvation. I suppose even a moron like you knows that...'

'Don't call me a moron,' he interrupts, 'I'm not a moron. I love you.' He is calm.

'Moron, moron, moron, moron...'

Shirley sets up a chant, saying the word over and over as she gathers her clothes to her, separates her brassiere from the mess and starts to put it on.

Because she has taken her eyes off him she is completely unprepared when he lunges, clasps his hands around her neck. He is squeezing hard when he pushes her over the wall into the harbour waters and jumps in after her.

Shirley goes right down, under the water and into an inky, choking black. She instinctively closes her mouth, just as instinctively kicks her legs to make for the surface. But she is prevented when his arms encircle her, pulling her back down, holding her tight against him.

She kicks out wildly but is unable to move her arms, which he has pinned to her sides. Her legs thrash with a savage and futile panic. She feels as if her chest, her head, her lungs are all about to explode even as a great weight compresses her. Behind her eyes everything is turning a dark red.

Part of her is still thinking, calculating her survival. He will have to break for the surface, unless he wants to drown with her. Maybe he wants to do that. Maybe she took things too far and he sees no way back, nor any way forward either. She wishes she could talk to him, tell him she didn't mean it, that there will be no telling anyone about what happened, that it will stay between the two of them, forever their secret.

She opens her mouth and the water rushes in. She is unconscious when, seconds later, he breaks the surface of the water with her still in his arms.

He treads water, supporting the limp Shirley, preventing her from sinking while he looks about and catches his breath in gasping gulps. This he does for several minutes, until he quite calm and quite sure there is no one about. Then he bends his head, looks gently and bemusedly at the insensible face of the woman in his arms. He sighs and, as he does, she gives a shudder, her head jerks forward and water spews from her mouth. He sighs again, letting the breath out as he pushes her head under the water and holds it there until her body goes into a few last, feeble spasms.

When he sure she is dead he swims with her body to the stone steps he has often used on brighter, more hopeful occasions. He carries her through the opening in the hedging around The Dead House, across the gravelled front to the steps at the front entrance where, very carefully, he lays her down.

For several minutes he looks at her lying there, white and oddly graceful, before bending down and folding her arms across her chest. He walks away then, without looking back once.

This time, crossing the gravel, he feels the discomfort of the stones under his bare feet. He curses softly to himself and runs for the opening in the hedge.

His clothes are in a sorry state so he takes them, along with everything belonging to the dead woman, and sits on the stone harbour steps, rinsing the lot of them until the mud has been washed clean and lost in the changing waters of the harbour.

When he puts his clothes back on he is once again and simply a man wet through from the rain. He bundles those belonging to Shirley Walsh under his arm and walks back up the laneway, stopping only once on his way home.

16

When a picture of Alannah Casey's parents appeared in *The Irish Independent* next morning I was shocked to discover I knew her mother. Not very well, but I knew her. She worked on the supermarket check-out; a smiling, efficient, dark-haired woman whose queue generally moved more quickly than the others.

Nuala Casey wasn't smiling in the newspaper picture. She had Alannah's bones and dark hair and had lost weight since last I'd seen her in the supermarket. Her drawn face was expressionless.

She was pictured sitting on a chintzy couch in their home with Alannah's father, whose name was Malachy. Alannah's daughter Zoë sat between her grandparents. She had blond curls and was smiling into the camera.

Malachy Casey was quoted as saying that they had agreed to the picture appearing in the paper so as to keep their daughter's death alive in people's minds, remind them that her murderer hadn't yet been caught.

A killer was on the loose, Malachy Casey

said, and they wanted him caught and brought to justice. It would be a small return for what they'd lost, for the mother Zoë would grow up not knowing, for the terrible destruction of innocence and trust.

The last reference, at first glance, seemed to refer to little Zoë. On closer reading it became clear Malachy Casey was referring to what he thought was his daughter's naïve belief in Dimitri Sobchak.

'We knew she was meeting him,' he told the reporter, 'but what nineteen year old ever listened to her parents?' He'd a lot more to say on the subject of who might have been responsible for his daughter's death, he said, but had been told to 'button his lip' by the law and lawyers. 'I'll have my day in court,' he promised, 'no matter how long it takes the guards to get the case together and someone into the dock. And I'll have a thing or two to say when I get there.' His wife had refused to speak to the reporter.

It was time I paid them a visit.

The house was an artisan red-brick, about the same size as my own but older and opening directly onto the street. I stood at the door, exposed to the glares of passing neighbours for fully five minutes, before a lock was pulled back and the door opened by Nuala Casey. She was as tall as her daughter had been; the weight loss meant I just about recognised her as the woman from the supermarket. She stared at me.

'My name is...' I began.

'I know who you are,' she said, 'you're Frances Shaw. You were pointed out to me one day in the street. What can I do for you?'

'I'm sorry not to have called before now...'

She interrupted me again, face as expressionless as it had been in the newspaper picture. 'There was no obligation on you to come calling on us,' she said. 'But you're here now so you might as well come in.' She opened the door wider and stepped back to allow me inside.

The hallway was dark and narrow, the floor littered with children's toys. When I toppled over a miniature pram I grabbed her shoulder to stop from falling.

'Sorry...' I steadied myself with her help.

'Alannah was forever complaining that the hallway was too dark,' she said, 'always wanting us to put in a glass front door. But the one that's there was good enough for my grandmother and mother. So I never listened to her.'

She led the way into a small sitting room. Alannah Casey's daughter Zoë, Dresden-doll pretty in a lilac dress, sat watching cartoons on a 25 inch TV screen. A picture of Alannah with the child in her arms covered most of the chimney breast. Nuala Casey turned off the TV and lifted her grandchild into her arms. 'Time for a snooze,' she said.

Zoë, with a remarkable lack of protest, allowed herself to be carried from the room. 'Sit down,' Nuala Casey commanded me as she went, 'I'll be back with a cup of tea.'

I avoided the couch on which the Caseys had had their picture taken for the newspaper and sat into an armchair. Alannah was in frames everywhere: in her school uniform aged eight or so, in dungarees with front teeth missing, in her mother's arms at Zoë's age, standing with her father as a tall teenager, everywhere laughing, everywhere living.

Nuala Casey came back with a blue tray on which there was a blue teapot and mugs, a blue jug and a blue plate of biscuits. She brought her husband with her too. They sat together on the couch.

'We'd have preferred a bit of notice,' Malachy Casey said, 'but you're welcome for all that.'

Nuala Casey, who was several inches taller than her husband, poured the tea. Her hand shook. 'We were going to contact you anyway when we were a bit more adjusted to things,' she said, handing me the tea.

'I could come back another time, whenever you like,' I said.

'No. We had to meet sometime so maybe it's God's will you're here today,' Nuala

Casey said, 'stay, please.'

'We don't want to know how she was when you found her,' Malachy Casey sat cracking his knuckles, 'just something about that Russian bastard and their meetings in your place. Was she afraid of him, would you say?'

'No,' I said, 'no, she wasn't afraid of him. If anything he was afraid of her. Or at least wary.'

Nuala Casey, turning a mug of tea slowly in her hands, sighed. She didn't seem to notice when tears began in a slow track down her face.

'My own daughter's just a little older than Alannah,' I said, 'I'm so sorry. So very sorry.'

'I know,' Nuala Casey said. 'I know you are.'

'Dimitri Sobchak was shorter than she was,' I said.

'Finding lads her own height was always a problem,' Nuala Casey said, wearily.

'He saw her for what she was,' Malachy Casey spoke with a low intensity, 'a soft touch, easy prey for a foreign bastard like him. His kind moves in like a bloodsucker once they spot a victim. Anyone could see what he was up to. He should have been stopped.'

'Frances couldn't have done anything, Malachy,' Nuala Casey said, 'Alannah thought she loved him. She'd made her mind up and there was nothing could be done about it. You know that.' She looked at me. 'It's hard not to lay blame,' she said, 'very hard.'

'Yes,' I said, 'yes. It must be hard.'

'There is blame to be laid.' Malachy Casey was defensive and very, very angry. He shook off his wife's hand when she tried to placate him. 'I'll see that bastard drown in his own blood if I ever get my hands on him...'

He stopped and began to weep. It was terrible to see, the sounds he made terrible to hear. His wife held him until he was able to stop.

'Any tea in that pot?' he said then and lit a cigarette. 'I'd given them up.' He took a drag which burned away half of the cigarette. When he took the tea from his wife their hands touched, briefly.

'The Russian's rights are better looked after than my daughter's were,' he said, his anger slightly muted, for now, 'she had a right to be safe from harm on the streets of the town she was born in and reared. His rights are all we hear about, civil and legal. Where's the money to defend him coming from? Answer me that.'

'Some businessman...' I began.

'Business*man* my arse,' Malachy Casey snorted, 'there's a gang of so-called business-men behind the front guy, you mark my

186

words. They've all got Russians and the like working for them. They get them cheap and they don't want them thrown out of the country, or their companions stopped from coming in. The more cheap labour the better and to hell with the consequences. What these great human rights benefactors want are their slave labourers protected, and grateful. That's the great new Ireland for you, run on slavery and corruption.'

'Do the guards know this?' I said.

'Malachy doesn't know all of this for a fact himself.' Nuala Casey reached for her husband's hand. He gave it to her like a child would. 'It doesn't stop him believing it though.' She looked at him, holding his hand in both of hers. 'Give us a rest from it for now, Mal, will you?' She fixed him with a tired look.

'Zoë's a beautiful child,' I said. Uselessly.

'She is,' Nuala Casey agreed, listlessly.

'We'll be moving,' Alannah's father announced, loudly, 'we'll be leaving this place behind us as soon as we can.'

'We'll be doing no such thing,' his wife said, calmly, 'this house has seen a lot. It'll be Zoë's when we're gone. She'll have that at least.'

'It's not right that she should grow up where her mother died,' her husband said. 'We should take her away from here.'

'This is where she belongs and it's where

we belong.' Nuala Casey looked at me and said, without apology, 'This is all the two of us can talk about, over and over. He says we should go, I'm for staying. I won't be chased out. There was enough of that in the past.'

'The child will be pointed out in the street and tormented in the schoolyard and gibed at as a teenager,' Malachy Casey insisted. 'That's what's in front of her, all we've to offer her if we stay. The Walshes knew that and they left.'

'And what good did it do them?' Nuala Casey's patience snapped. 'Whatever curse was on them followed them,' she was acid, 'they took what happened to them with them and never let go of it, talking about it until the idea planted itself in the head of another madman looking for a way to murder his wife. That's all the good running away did the Walshes.' She turned to me. 'You know what I'm talking about, I suppose?' she said.

'Yes,' I said, 'I know what you're talking about.'

'Malachy doesn't come from the town,' she ignored her husband's attempts to say something, 'he only heard the story late in life, after he met me. I grew up with my mother and grandmother talking about it. When I was a teenager they told me the whole story, as a warning against what they called "loose behaviour" with boys.'

'You've never lived anywhere but this house?' I said.

She nodded. 'I was an only child. When my mother died, too young, I got the house. Alannah was *our* only child.'

Her husband stood. 'Just because you've never known anything else doesn't mean our grandchild has to follow...'

Malachy Casey's outburst ended when his wife, still and icy, lifted her head and said, 'As God is my judge, Malachy, I'll have you out on the street if you don't shut up. You'd be making the greatest mistake of your life to think I don't mean it.' She was chewing hard on the inside of her lip.

Malachy Casey was silent, and so was I, waiting for her to go on.

'What my grandmother said,' she said, 'when the woman was murdered in America, was that the Walshes took their cross with them to America and held it up for all to see and gave it life in another's head. I believe that: You have to let a thing go, get on with life. Otherwise the evil poisons everything.' She took a breath and closed her eyes. 'What I'm afraid of, Malachy, is that you will carry this thing to the grave, your own or somebody else's it doesn't matter. You're not letting go of it,' her voice rose, 'maybe you never will...'

'She's eight days dead,' Malachy Casey said, 'eight days. In the name of Christ

Almighty, woman, what do you expect from me?'

'I want you to think about Zoë,' Nuala Casey said, 'I want us to pray together for Alannah, to leave the guards to get on with finding whoever did it. I don't want us to be like the Walshes, poisoned and sick like that mad sister in Bray, carrying the thing on and on.' She put our empty mugs and the teapot carefully onto the tray. 'She's like a malignancy, that Concepta Walsh, spreading infection. She keeps the past alive with her spells and potions and fortune telling. I blame her for the way Alannah was...' she lifted the teapot '...left on the morgue steps. Will I make more tea for anyone?'

I shook my head. 'No, thanks,' I said.

Malachy Casey put an arm about his wife. 'We'll be all right, Nuala,' he said, 'we'll be all right, love. It's early days yet. Early days.'

'I know it is,' she said, 'I know that...' She turned to me. 'You're a mother,' she said, 'and you knew my child. You were one of the last to see her alive and the first, after the animal who killed her, to see her dead. You're a part of all this, through no fault of your own. You'll be at the funeral? She's to be buried tomorrow.'

'I know,' I said.

Four words of all those she'd said hammered in my brain. Mad. Sister. Concepta. Bray.

Did they mean Ritchie Walsh's dying sister hadn't died, after all? Mad. Sister. Concepta. Bray.

'I forget sometimes, for a second, or two,' Nuala Casey seemed to be talking to herself, 'and then I remember and it's like a great, black cave opening in front of me again, as bad as the first time they told me, and I'm walking into the endless blackness of knowing she's never coming back and of what happened to her all over again.'

She took lipstick and mirror from a bag beside her. 'It's best to put a face on things, for Zoë's sake,' she painted hot, red colour onto her mouth, 'lipstick's the refuge of sinners,' she gave a wan smile, 'and of the bereft. My mother used to say that.'

'I might go out for a pint,' Malachy said.

'Go then,' his wife said, gently.

'Tell me what they were like together,' she said to me when he'd gone.

'Like any pair of youngsters who think they've found love,' I said. 'They sat at the same table every time, by the window.'

'We didn't approve so she stopped talking to us about him. She was just gone sixteen when Zoë's father left her with child. He was no good to her and we worried she was going down the same road again. We wanted better for her. Maybe we were wrong. She said he loved her.' She paused. 'Did it look to you as if he loved her?'

'It looked to me,' I spoke slowly, 'as if they were besotted with one another.'

'Her being pregnant would've suited him,' she sighed. 'The baby would've meant he could stay here, get his papers no problem. There was no reason for him to...' She closed her eyes. 'Do you think he's the one...?'

'I don't know,' I said.

'He might have been jealous,' Nuala Casey said, 'he might have thought there was someone else.' She shrugged. 'I've been thinking too that she might well have told him about the drowning of Shirley Walsh in 1953. He being a newcomer to the town she might have given him a history lesson. It was the sort of thing she'd have done. She'd heard her grandmother referring to it often enough, as a warning to keep herself pure and away from boys.'

'He has an alibi,' I said. She didn't seem to hear.

'I shouldn't have let my mother talk to her like that,' she said.

There was a creaking sound in the room overhead.

'That's Zoë, turning in her sleep,' Nuala Casey said. 'We were told we couldn't have children, myself and Malachy, and then we had Alannah.' She put her head into her hands. 'Malachy's real fear is that we'll rear Zoë and that something will happen to her too.'

'Why would it happen again?'

'Why did it happen now?' Nuala Casey said.

I left soon after that.

'Things might be easier after tomorrow,' Alannah's mother said as we said goodbye, 'after the funeral.'

'They might,' I said.

I went home and got out the phone book and looked for a Concepta Walsh in Bray. She wasn't listed. There were quite a few entries for C. Walsh, however.

I phoned a friend in Bray with a vast network of alternative lifestyle mates and a fine-tuned ear to the ground. She'd heard of, but didn't know, Concepta Walsh.

'Mad old bat, by all accounts,' my friend said, 'jury's out on whether she's a white or black witch. I've never met her, so I can't help you much, really. Don't know how legit she is, whether she has a genuine gift or not. She's fairly old now but still reads the tarot cards and turns a few other tricks.'

'Do you know where she lives?'

'I do. This awful business hasn't got you looking for psychic answers, has it?'

'Nothing like that,' I lied.

She gave me an address for Concepta Walsh.

17

I went to Alannah Casey's funeral with Thaddeus, who turned up at the house offering me a lift, and with Emer, who'd arrived as we were leaving. The rain was steady, and it was heavy. The crowd was still arriving in the graveyard and Emer and I were standing back from the grave, sharing an umbrella, when Hector joined us. He had no brolly and Thaddeus, beside us under the shelter of a discreet black number, didn't offer to share.

'Miserable enough day for it,' Hector said by way of greeting.

'Are you official?' Thaddeus barked.

'Unfortunately,' Hector said, 'but personal too.' He stepped, uninvited, under Thaddeus's umbrella. Thaddeus looked steadily and gloomily in the direction of the grave. The priest began the prayers, the huddled crowd responded.

'Only the good die young,' Thaddeus said.

Hector moved away to talk to a colleague.

The family clung together around the open grave, Nuala and Malachy Casey in the middle of them holding one another tightly. I moved closer, with Emer and Thaddeus, as the priest began an eulogy. He was a young man, thin fair hair plastered wet across a high forehead. He had prepared carefully what he wanted to say.

'Pale Death, as we know,' he paused and looked around his listeners before going on, 'knocks with impartial foot at poor men's hovels and kings' palaces. Too often, in the world we live in today, it enters the bright world of the hopeful young. Alannah was part of our collective hope for the future and her death is one more horrific example of the kind of Ireland our recent wealth and the abandonment of moral boundaries has created. Alannah Casey's unique and special life has been forfeited at the altar of the heinous daily violence we are forced to live with. We must pray today that the person or persons responsible for cruelly and mercilessly taking her life will be brought to justice. And for a better way forward.'

'That's telling them,' Thaddeus said.

The prayers were said, including an entire rosary led by the priest. It was hard not to worry that mourners might not catch their own deaths in the cold and rain.

I could find no sign nor sighting of Dimitri Sobchak. I asked Hector, on the way out of the graveyard, if he'd been asked to stay away.

'He's not a fool,' he said. 'The decision not to be here was his own.'

I left Thaddeus to his apartment and Emer

195

to the DART station and headed for Bray.

It wasn't hard to find Concepta Walsh. The first person I asked in the warren of small houses knew immediately who I was looking for and where she lived. When I parked and got out of the car a group of ten or eleven year olds asked if I'd come to have 'Cepta tell my fortune. When they asked for money to look after my car I gave them five euro. Always wise if you value your tyres.

'She's a mad auld cow,' one of them yelled as I opened the gate, 'better not put her in a bad mood or she'll put a spell on you.'

A blackthorn tree in the small, overgrown front garden was a mass of the white flowers you're supposed never to bring inside the house. Bad luck will follow, it's said. There was a holly tree too, and a wilderness of bushes. The house, behind them, had a dark, neglected look.

Concepta Walsh was an unremarkable elderly woman by comparison. She was small and blue-rinsed and peered through wire-framed specs at my appearance on her doorstep.

'What do you want?' she said. Her eyes went over every feature on my face without once meeting my eyes.

'My name is Frances Shaw. I'd like to talk to you about…'

'You're the one who found the body,' she

interrupted me. 'If you want to talk to me you'd better come inside.'

'Inside' was a front room with the curtains closed and a twenty-five-watt bulb in the centre of the ceiling. Incense burned in a purple bowl and a couple of straight-backed chairs faced each other across a small table. The walls were hung with a purple embossed wallpaper and the wallpaper in turn was hung with pictures of sunbursts and unearthly animals. It was oppressive and quite awful.

Concepta Walsh turned on a lamp behind one of the chairs and sat down. It highlighted her blue-rinsed hair and gave her the look of a blue-tit, small and compact with her clearly marked head, yellowish cardigan and greeny/blue dress underneath. Like the blue tit too she was quick and businesslike.

'Sit opposite me, if you please,' she said.

I took off my coat and sat with it on my knee. 'I came to talk about your brother Richard,' I said. She may have sighed, I couldn't be sure. She certainly didn't speak. 'I'm told he's being cared for in a home,' I added.

'Why would you be told that?' she said. 'What business is it of yours where my brother is, or how he is?'

This seemed to me a fair enough question and I decided to give it the straight answer it deserved.

'Thaddeus Shaw, whom you may remember from years ago, is my father-in-law. Your brother wrote to him in nineteen sixty-four to say he was coming home to visit. I wondered if he'd in fact ever come home?'

'Why?' she said.

'Because...' I paused. Concepta Walsh wasn't a fool but I was in danger of making one of myself. 'Thaddeus has been talking about the earlier murders,' I said. 'I feel ... involved. Because of Alannah Casey's death.' I hesitated, then told her the truth – or at least put my half-baked plan into words. 'I thought I might, somehow, talk to your brother about what happened in nineteen fifty-three and in nineteen sixty-three.'

'Did you have something to do with the death of the young Casey woman?'

'Of course not.' I was startled.

'Well then, you were an instrument of fate in what happened, nothing more. You don't have to concern yourself at all, except that you're the type who can't leave well enough alone.' She drummed the fingers of one hand on the table. 'You're here because you want to know about Thaddeus Shaw. *What* do you want to know?' Businesslike she might be, in the way of the blue tit, but she ambushed fast and low like the sparrowhawk. I sharpened my wits for direct confrontation.

'Did you know Thaddeus when you and he were younger?'

'You mean did I know him in nineteen fifty-three when my brother's wife was drowned and my brother Jimmy forced to kill himself?'

'Yes,' I said, 'that's what I mean.'

'Why should I answer your questions?'

'Because I need to know. Because...' the phrase came unbidden '...the past may not be past at all.'

She thought about this for a minute, sitting still and silent, watching me. Then she began to speak. 'I'm acquainted with Thaddeus Shaw,' she said. 'I was living in Wexford when our family's tragedy struck and met him after the event. He was a Jack-the-Lad with notions about himself and I wasn't pretty enough young woman for him to waste time on. He concerned himself only with women like my dead brother's wife. By the time I met him and knew all that it was too late anyway.'

'Too late for what?'

'Too late to save my brother Jimmy. Too late to prevent what happened happening. My brother didn't drown his wife. It wasn't my brother laid her body across the stone slab at the morgue door. He hadn't it in him, not Jimmy. He was the good one, the loved and lucky one.'

'He loved his wife,' I said, 'and she loved him. According to reports of the trial anyway.'

She gave a short, hard laugh. 'You've informed yourself from the newspapers, have you? Did they also report that he might not have been the father of both of the Englishwoman's children?'

'No. There was nothing about children.'

'You can't believe everything you read in newspapers,' she said.

'Are you telling me he wasn't the father of both girls?' I said. 'Was there proof?'

She leaned forward slightly. 'Proof? Where was the proof Jimmy drowned his wife? Did the laboratory tests prove he did? There was no proper proof and they convicted him and he died. So why do you need proof to say who fathered her children?'

'Did the guards look for another man?'

'There were too many other men. The guards decided who killed her the day her body was found. If you're so interested in all of this why didn't you ask Mr Thaddeus Shaw yourself?'

'We've talked about it,' I said.

'You're not a complete fool.' She was thoughtful, as if thinking out loud. 'You've found out enough to be doubtful about your father-in-law. You're wondering if he was the one murdered her, aren't you?'

'No. That never occurred to me. Why should it?'

'There's no proof he didn't do it, is there? No test to say he wasn't the one held her

200

under the water? He was a drinking man, but you know that. You don't want to think about him doing it but can't be certain sure, can you?' She gave another short laugh. 'That's the thing about life. Nothing's certain and nothing's sure. You're here because you're worried. You think what happened fifty years ago has come full circle and that he might have something to do with what happened two weeks ago.'

'No, I don't think he had anything to do with Alannah Casey's death,' I said. 'I think he's worried and hiding something about the past, that's all.'

'That's all?'

The silence filled up with her insinuations. I didn't believe he'd had anything to do with Shirley Walsh's murder; I absolutely believed he could have had an affair with her. Whether, and if, this changed any of the facts I'd no idea.

'You were very ill in 1964,' I said, 'Ritchie came to visit...'

'I've never been sick in my life,' she said. 'And Ritchie hasn't been next nor near me or this country since he left in 1954 with the young people.'

So – Ritchie Walsh had been lying. Or his sister had been lying when she wrote to him. Or maybe she never wrote to him at all.

I couldn't decide because I simply didn't trust Concepta Walsh.

'I was misinformed,' I said.

'Who *informed* you?' she asked.

'It came up.' I was dismissive as she had been moments earlier. 'There's been so much talk about the earlier murders in the last ten days. All sorts of people are half remembering things.'

'Strange that someone would remember something that *didn't* happen forty years ago.'

'Not so strange. People misremember things that happened yesterday.' I was *not* going to tell her about reading the letter, not so long as I couldn't trust her. 'Much easier to get it wrong about that far back.'

'Could have been, of course,' she was watching me carefully, 'that your informant came across letters between Ritchie and Thaddeus Shaw. Your brother-in-law came to see me that year. He said he'd had a letter from Ritchie.'

'But why would your brother write saying you were ill when you weren't?' I was cool reason itself.

'Only the great and lesser Gods know the answer to that.' She was moved to shrug.

'Why did Thaddeus come to see you?' I asked.

As I asked the question an answer came to me. Thaddeus could very well have called to see Concepta when he got the letter, discovered she wasn't ill and sent word to Ritchie.

Maybe.

Concepta Walsh might be creating confusion just for the hell of it, or to hide some truth she didn't want known. I'd no way of knowing.

'Thaddeus Shaw was no friend of Ritchie's,' she said, so suddenly I straightened to attention. 'He was a friend of Jimmy's but he betrayed him when he was alive and took up with Ritchie after he was dead.'

'I knew he was a friend of Jimmy's,' I said. 'On the boats.'

'You have a daughter,' she said.

'Her name is Emer,' I said.

She nodded her head. 'Listen hard to what I have to say,' she said, 'because I'm not going to do your thinking for you when I finish. Thaddeus Shaw came to see me that year out of guilt. He'd changed in the eleven years since nineteen fifty-three. He was putting a new face to the world and he wasn't drinking. But he was the same Thaddeus Shaw inside; self-interested and self-serving. His son, your husband, was just a boy and Thaddeus knew he was marked for life, because of the mother's death in the car. The shadows of a thing like that will fall over a whole life. Boys need a mother, I'm sure you'll agree.'

'They do,' I said.

'A good mother,' she seemed to be talking

to herself, her head nodding, 'not a bad mother.'

'Obviously,' I said.

Concepta Walsh went on nodding. For the first time since she'd opened the door she seemed to me an old woman. Then she straightened and spoke again. 'Ritchie wasn't my favoured brother but I don't fault him for not coming to see me,' she said. 'He had his reasons for staying away, I know that. I don't blame his boys for not coming either, or Jimmy's girls. They had bad and sad memories of their mothers, all of them, so why would they come back? They wanted it all behind them.'

'Do you know where they are now?' I said, lightly.

'They made their lives, and their beds, but I've no idea where,' she said.

'And Ritchie? Where is he?'

'He took to the drink. Neither his sons nor his nieces wanted him. How would I know where he is?'

I put my idea into words. 'I'm planning a trip to New York,' I said, 'I could visit him for you, if you could remember where he is.'

She put her hands palms up on the table and looked directly into my eyes. 'I suppose, since your place was burnt out, you've got time on your hands. Too much of it, maybe. That's why you're here and it's why you're going to America. I can't stop you. There's no one else can stop you either. I can't tell you where my brother is either but I can tell you whether going will be a good thing or not...' She tapped the backs of her fingers impatiently on the table. 'Give me your right hand...' she said.

I'd had my palm read before and been unimpressed. On the other hand...

I turned up my palm and reached it across the table to Concepta Walsh. She held and studied it. She felt and rubbed it, fingering the lines in my palm.

'Saturn's not up to much. You could be wiser than you are...' She looked up at me. 'But you know that. Don't interrupt while I'm reading.' She bent over my palm again. 'Life line's long enough but there's a thinning, warning sign that. Could be an illness, could be an anguished time awaiting you. You'll see it coming. Be careful. The line of the heart's got too much sensitivity. Hopeless. You'll be got there too, no escaping it. Could be that's your anguish, the damage on your life line.' She rubbed the side of my palm. 'You've courage, after a fashion. You're in love with war too. These two could lead you where you shouldn't go and bring tragedy to another...' She looked up again. 'Left alone the past will die a natural death, in its time, in its season.' She gave a final look at my palm before letting go. 'You could be wiser than you are,' she said again.

'Couldn't we all,' I said.

She turned off the lamp and closed her eyes. 'Thaddeus Shaw came here to see me some days ago,' she said. 'I let him go, didn't answer the door to him. Now you can go too. I've had enough of you. You know where the door is.'

My car had 'Fuck You' written across the dust of the bonnet. About as subtle a piece of graffiti as Concepta Walsh's warning to stay out of her family's affairs and an old murder.

18

I stared across the Coroner's Court at Dimitri Sobchak for a long time before I finally got him to look at me. He was sullen and brooding, his hair in need of a cut and his face in need of a shave.

Either that or he was melancholic and so desolate he was indifferent to how he looked. It was hard to tell.

Either way he'd aged. Either way, despite the guards having released him without charge and the dogs in the street knowing that he had a watertight alibi, he was the focus of a frustration and anger in the well of the court. The mob will always need a scapegoat and Alannah Casey had been too young, too lovely and too cruelly murdered not to have a mob following.

I got to the courthouse early. Hector was there before me, sniffling and blowing a delicately red-rimmed nose while he waited outside for a colleague. He was using a large, pale blue handkerchief. There is no one capable of more self-pity than Hector when he has a cold.

'You okay for what's ahead?' he said, meaning about my giving evidence. His voice was hoarse.

'I'm fine,' I said.

If obsessed was fine then I was fine. I'd woken in the night from a dream in which Alannah Casey and Shirley Walsh sat at a round table relentlessly reading my palm, which had no body attached to it and which they kept passing to one another. I was resolutely *not* interpreting this.

'You were seen in Bray,' Hector said.

'Was I seen in Dublin too?' I snapped. 'I was there for two hours this morning. Am I being followed, Hector?'

'You're being kept an eye on, yes. Yesterday we were just making sure your arsonist friend wasn't at the funeral and didn't follow you afterwards. I don't know why you felt a need to see Concepta Walsh.' He was irritated, and not trying to hide it. 'You're not helping anyone.'

'I'm not trying to help *anyone*,' I said, 'I need to know for myself.'

'I can't stop you,' Hector said. 'But Concepta Walsh is an eccentric and unreliable. She wasn't around when Shirley Walsh was murdered in fifty-three and plays the crazy woman when it suits her. She's wasted a lot of garda time in the past.'

'What past would that be?'

'Jesus Christ, Fran, why can't you just let the thing go?'

'Because I can't. Tell me.'

208

Hector swore, under his breath, but told me what I wanted to know.

'Files show she was called in for interview in nineteen sixty-three, to answer some questions the US police had about the family. Her statement is all over the place and includes accusations against the guards present of everything from kidnapping to rape. She claimed the family was being deliberately persecuted on both sides of the Atlantic.'

'Persecuted by whom?'

'God knows,' he was impatient. 'Back off, Fran. We're following a line of enquiry...'

'What line of enquiry were you following when my livelihood was burned down?'

'That's not altogether fair, Fran.'

'No, it's not. I'm sorry.'

'Having time on your hands doesn't suit you. Take a holiday.'

I looked from the grey skies to his red-rimmed nostrils and smiled sweetly. 'You know, Hector,' I said, 'I might just, and for once, take your advice.'

In the courtroom I sat on a bench against the wall. Everyone had come early as well as me, not just family and witnesses but neighbours, friends and gawpers. There was a battalion of guards in place by the time the Caseys arrived.

Thaddeus stayed away but Ted Cullen was there and so was John Rutledge, sitting just inside the door in an unsuitable summer-weight beige suit. Nina pushed her way into a seat close to me.

Dimitri Sobchak's timing had to be his solicitor's. He came through the door just before the coroner, his solicitor straight-backed by his side with just a touch of righteous steel about him.

I began eyeballing Dimitri as soon as he took a seat and nodded when he finally looked at me. He nodded back. Then the court arose.

We were not gathered for a trial, the Coroner reminded the court, nor to decide who had killed her or why Alannah Casey died. The inquest was an enquiry into the cause of death and into matters of fact.

Expert medical and forensic witnesses gave details of the port-mortem results I'd already heard from Hector, and her pregnancy. Alannah's parents, separately, gave witness about her character, state of mind, hopes for the future – and told about when they'd last seen her alive.

Alannah Casey had fed her daughter, put her to bed and left the family home about nine o'clock on the evening of the night she died. She hadn't said where she was going, just that she would be back before midnight. They hadn't pressed her about where she was going; she wouldn't have told them anyway. Nuala and Malachy Casey had checked on Zoë, who slept in her mother's room, and gone to bed themselves about eleven-thirty.

They didn't know their daughter hadn't come home until the police called about nine o'clock the next morning to tell them she was dead.

I was called to describe how I found her and how she'd looked.

Then Dimitri Sobchak was called.

He looked only at the judge and he stood very straight. He said he'd spent the afternoon of the evening she died with Alannah Casey in the bedsit room he shared with a fellow immigrant, also Russian. They didn't often have the place to themselves but his room-mate was working that afternoon. He had met Alannah earlier in the Now and Again café, their regular meeting place.

She had left his room to go home at about six o'clock, to be with her daughter. That had been the last time he'd seen her alive. He had gone to work at eight o'clock and worked a ten-hour shift through the night, stacking shelves.

He delivered all of this without emotion, stolid and matter-of-fact even in the way he stood. Nuala and Malachy Casey looked equally unmoved. I could have wept myself.

I left immediately it was over. But not quickly enough. Behind me, as I reached the door, mutterings in the court room grew to a rumble and Dimitri and his solicitor, surrounded by guards and ahead of an angry group, were propelled out the door and into the street on my heels.

The driver of a waiting car got out immediately and opened the rear door. I recognised Dimitri's benefactor from the pictures in the paper – a businessman in suit and glasses who fitted like a clone with his solicitor. Dimitri Sobchak slid into the back of the car and pulled the door shut. His companions stood talking while the Caseys came out of court and were driven away in a taxi.

'Your ex-husband is coming,' Nina said, 'I have decided he is a nice man, maybe a good one too but I don't know.' She gave Hector a rare smile as he came up to us.

As he joined us Hector nodded to the men standing by the car. 'Things going all right for you, Donnacha?' he said.

The solicitor answered. 'No complaints so far,' he said. 'A stronger statement from the guards would be appreciated though. One that made it absolutely clear my client was released without charge *or* need for further questioning. The point doesn't seem to have got home.'

'We *may* need to question him further,' Hector said, 'but he's not a suspect so that point can be made again.'

'Have you met Gerry Fuller?' the solicitor asked. Hector had and reluctantly, and because there seemed no polite way out of it, introduced the businessman to Nina and myself. He kept his hands in his pocket and smiled, the solicitor shook hands with us. Nina tapped on the window beside Dimitri Sobchak's pale face but he ignored her, staring straight ahead. She made a disgusted, clicking sound. Gerry Fuller looked at his watch and cleared his throat.

'How's the investigation going?' he asked Hector.

'Moving along,' Hector said. 'The bad weather on the night meant there weren't too many people about but we're confident, very confident.'

'You will of course keep Donnacha, Mr Ryan that is, informed?' said Gerry Fuller.

Hector said he would and turned pointedly away.

'Emer's not here?' he said to me. I told him no, she'd felt there was no point her attending. He said she was probably right, sniffing miserably.

'I can make you a herb infusion which will help your cold get better.' Nina was smiling again. 'I can bring it to the station if you like.'

Hector, looking startled, said, 'Thanks, but don't trouble yourself, please.'

'It will be no trouble,' Nina said and added, 'what have the police discovered so far?'

Weary in tone, and in bone too from the look and attitude of him, Hector gave her as succinct a run-down as I'd heard him give so far. 'All I can tell you is that we've questioned her friends and anyone else who might have known her or with whom she came in contact. We've questioned the father of her child, who hadn't seen his ex-girlfriend or their child for three months. We've talked to the Now and Again customers and we've brought in a bunch of the usual suspects and had them account for what they were up to on the night in question. We haven't found even a scrap of her clothing, the rain washed away footprints or anything else helpful from around the morgue door. We've gone over and over the town, anywhere she might possibly have been.' He stopped to produce and use the blue hanky. 'It's as if she became invisible once she left her parents' house.' He gave a rattling cough. He really didn't look well but it had always been hard to tell with Hector where his natural pallor and storm-tossed look ended and genuine illness began.

'Are you taking anything?' I said, briskly.

'Cough mixture. I've been wet every day for an effing week,' Hector grumbled, morosely irritated.

'I will bring my infusion to the station,' Nina said, firmly, 'today.' She ignored the look I gave her.

'It's very likely that whoever killed Alannah Casey was someone she knew,' Hector said as he walked with Nina and me to my car. 'Certainly it was someone she was very careful to keep secret. Another lover, perhaps.'

I invited Nina home with me for a bite to eat and thought about what Hector had said as we drove. He was wrong. Alannah Casey had cared very much for Dimitri Sobchak. I couldn't believe that she would have cheated on him.

'Hector's wrong about her having another lover,' I said.

'He would have killed her, or had her killed, if she had,' Nina said, 'but I don't believe she had another lover either.' She paused, then said casually, 'Did your husband have lovers when you were married?'

'I don't know,' I said, which was true. Hector may have had had alcoholic dalliances but never anyone, as far as I knew, who could have been called a lover. 'Why do you ask?' I said. Nina had never shown much interest in Hector before, but then she'd seen very little of him before.

'Because he is interesting and I think he is nice,' said Nina.

'Do you?' I said, and nothing else. Which was remarkably restrained because I could have given her a thousand reasons to stop thinking he was nice.

We were waiting for the food to heat in the oven when I remembered the website address I'd picked up in the garda station and decided to look up the Borodin family.

My timing, for once, couldn't have been better. One thing led to another and a half-hour later I'd made a life-changing decision without the slightest idea that this was what I'd done.

Nina was more than ever dismissive of what she called my 'normal but unwise' interest in 'the old murders' but sat looking at the website with me anyway. It was pretty perfunctory stuff. The Borodin children had been taken into care, no relatives coming forth to claim or foster them. They had been separated but allowed to spend 'vacation times' together. Probably because they had roots and were born in the area they hadn't fled seeking anonymity in the way of the young Walshes. They both still lived in New York.

'They could help me find Ritchie Walsh,' I said to Nina.

'Ritchie Walsh?' She looked blank.

'I told you,' I said, and I had, though I'd been aware at the time she hadn't been listening. Nina had an enviable cut-off point. 'He's the brother of the man who was convicted of murdering Shirley Walsh in nineteen fifty-three. He's still alive, in a home in New York somewhere.'

'In New York somewhere?' She wasn't looking blank any more. She was looking very sharp in fact. And suspicious. 'How can you talk to him there?'

'Ring on the doorbell and ask to see him,' I said.

'You would go to New York...'

'I need a holiday, everyone seems to think so. I've never been to New York. It'll be a couple of weeks before we move onto the site. Flights are cheaper than ever they were...'

Her look clearly said she thought me irresponsible, capricious and out of my mind. 'You are mad,' she said, flatly. 'It will do no good, it will not be a holiday and you will spend money unnecessarily.' She paused. 'Also, there is work to be done here.'

'Nothing you can't look after,' I said. 'Look, why don't I do a search for the Borodins? If I come up with anything that shows they're not both hopeless druggies, or dead, then it might be worth going to talk with them...'

'Worth what?' She seemed mystified.

'My time,' I snapped and went into the Google search engine.

I hadn't told Nina about Ritchie Walsh's letter. Nor about the extent of Thaddeus's involvement nor about Concepta Walsh. It had all happened so quickly, and telling her would have been a betrayal of Thaddeus. I would come clean with her, and with Emer and Hector, as soon as I'd put the whole story together. Or an even half-satisfactory version of it anyway.

I wanted to know what Thaddeus was hiding, what Ritchie found so impossible to live with, what Concepta had been inferring.

The Borodins were alive, still living in New York too. Alexander Borodin's name came up in relation to events in 1963 and as the author of a book entitled *Childhood Trauma and Worst Fears*, published in 1988. He was a teacher, it said, in a public school in New York City and involved with the federal No Child Left Behind Law. The only contact seemed to be through his publisher, who was not one I'd ever heard of.

'Sounds like a man who's turned his life story to some use,' I said.

'Or maybe become locked in his own trauma,' Nina said.

Sofia L. Borodin's name came up too; third listing on the first page. I was betting it was the right woman because her name was given as Sofia L. in all of the entries about events in 1963.

Sofia L. was a partner in a New York legal firm. Medina & Borodin specialised in family and property law. Elliott Medina looked after the property side of things, Sofia L. was the family law specialist. They had a staff of ten, an address in Manhattan, and were established 'a healthy and progressive fifteen years' – it was not a modest web site. Ms Borodin could be contacted by e-mail. On the basis that an e-mail would be too easy to reject, and far too difficult to write, I decided to ring her at Medina & Borodin.

I told Nina what I proposed doing.

'You have made up your mind,' she said, 'so do it. It does not matter to you that I think you crazy.'

'The timing's perfect,' I said, 'it's about 9.30 a.m. in New York, the beginning of the day. She's likely to be in her office about now...'

'I'm going into the garden to talk to Lucifer,' Nina said.

Ms Borodin was busy right now, a professionally friendly voice told me, but if I gave my number she would get back to me. I did.

Sofia Borodin returned my call within minutes. She was the Borodin I was looking for and she would be glad to meet with me in New York. She'd heard about the murder in Ireland.

I went on line about flights, and hotels, and things fell cheaply and miraculously into place – providing I was prepared to leave early the next morning. I booked myself a week in New York.

It was as simple, and irresistible, as that.

Nina wasn't happy.

'But it is, of course, your life to do as you wish,' she said. I agreed that it was, told her I didn't want the same lectures as she'd given me from Emer and Thaddeus. I gave her the hotel address and asked her to keep quiet about my departure until after I'd gone. She promised, eventually.

'And your ex-husband?' she said.

'You can tell him too,' I said, 'though it's really none of his business.'

'I will tell him anyway,' she said. She looked quite pleased at the prospect.

19

November, 1963. Coney Island.

He is fishing. He likes to fish because it reminds him of home. He is fishing alone, from a sheltered spot he likes on the board-walk. It's the sort of afternoon in which only the hardy would venture to cast a line. Hardy or lonely, all the same to him.

He hauls in a frostfish. He's already landed a couple of tomcod. He'll gut and bring the lot with him to dinner tonight. Liliya will be glad of them.

He's walking back along the boardwalk when he hears Sergei Borodin's voice. Liliya's husband is coming out of a shooting gallery, yelling at its owner that he needs to sharpen up his act. Borodin's mood is not good, it rarely is.

They nod to one another as they come close. It's acknowledgement enough. Neither likes the other. Sometimes, around Liliya, they make an effort to be more civil. They work the same capers, compete for the grifts. There isn't room for the two of them on Coney, least of all on the Boardwalk.

Neither of them bothers to say anything

about the fact that they'll be eating Thanksgiving dinner together that evening.

His father and cousins are ready to leave when he gets home with the fish. His brother is rarely home these days. Even for Thanksgiving.

His cousin Mel sniffs and twitches her ugly face at him. He should give her a slap but can't be bothered.

'Clean yourself up,' his father says to him, 'we'll go on ahead so as not to be late.' His father is grateful to be asked to dinner, is always trying to please. Especially Liliya Borodin.

When his father, brother and cousins leave the apartment he cleans himself up and downs a couple of glasses of the Irish he keeps hidden for himself and follows them.

'You're very kind,' Liliya says to him when he gets there and gives her the fish. 'If you like, while we wait for Sergei, I can fry up a little of the frostfish. Fresh fish are so special.'

'Thank you,' he says, pleased, liking the idea of her cooking the fish especially for him.

'The rest we will have tomorrow,' she says as she goes to the kitchen with his catch. He sits watching her cook through the open door.

'She's made a fine dinner already,' his father says, uneasy that their hostess is putting herself to such extra work. 'The Thanksgiving food would have done you fine.'

His father feels beholden, grateful that he and his sons and nieces are included in this family dinner. Good food and a fine woman looking after them all is how he sees the night. His father is craven, always was.

He knows that Liliya Borodin feels sorry for his father, with his never-ending tale of why they left Ireland and his drunken, whining homesickness.

The girl, Sofia, eyes him when he sits at the table. The boy, Alexander, ignores him. Liliya thinks her children are a wonder to the world but he sees Sergei Borodin in them, and Liliya in bed with Borodin making them, and wishes they didn't exist.

He himself has often wondered what it would be like to be with Liliya Borodin. He has wondered about this for a long, long time now. He's often thought too that if the right time and right place happened he might have her.

It's crowded in the small, apartment with everyone there – the five Walshes and three Borodins.

It is even more crowded when Sergei Borodin arrives home. He has been drinking so it becomes a lot noisier too.

20

May, 2003. New York.

The weather, for the first week of May in New York, was unseasonably cold and cloudy. The worst for years, people said at the airport. The worst ever and no change in sight, according to the gloomy desk clerk in my hotel.

For this I had left a dreary Dun Laoghaire; I cursed my own and sod's luck.

The lift to my room on the fourteenth floor in the Jameson Hotel, between fifth and Madison Ave., was a shuddering three foot square with a gap through which you could see the shaft's bottomless plunge to ground level. An Hispanic hotel employee reassured me this was 'okay'.

'I done a job on her yesterday,' he said. 'I work on her all the time.'

'What about the shaft?' I said. 'Couldn't you cover it in, or something?'

'Means nothing,' he assured, 'seeing the shaft's nothin'.'

'I believe you,' I said.

My room was small and it would have taken spotlights in the four corners to brighten the gloom of mustard wallpaper and intimate views of the grey, next-door skyscraper. Twenty or so floors above, at the point where the two buildings shot into the sky, there was a scrap of blue.

The air conditioning was turned off and the room had a smell of dead cabbage like one found in Irish small town hotels of the 1960s. I turned the air conditioning to full and lay on the bed trying, and failing, to catch a glimpse of the patch of blue.

Jet lag was not a problem but a wakeful night and a crack-of-dawn flight had tired me and I slept. I dreamed about Sofia Borodin, black-haired and with Nina's face, and woke with my second telephone conversation with her echoing in my head.

She'd struck me, even on the end of a telephone line, as someone used to deciding for others. She decided, when I rang back to say I would be in New York within 24 hours, that Monday was 'good for a meeting', that this would happen at lunchtime, in Manhattan where she worked, in a restaurant she designated. She didn't know the Jameson Hotel, but the location was okay, she said. Sasha would meet me too, she said; Sasha was her pet name for her brother. It would be interesting for all three of us to meet and talk about 'this new murder in Ireland'. She'd heard about Alannah Casey's murder, she told me again.

She'd heard about it when the police had called for corroboration of some 1963 details. There had been a couple of paragraphs in the papers too which hadn't, she said, 'grown into anything. I must admit I put it down to the crime of a dysfunctional surfer, someone who came across my mother's death and allowed the details play on his diseased mind. It was quite a while ago now.'

'The police here might agree with you on that,' I said.

She was businesslike and did most of the talking. The entire conversation lasted about five minutes. I said nothing about wanting to see Ritchie Walsh but did tell her I'd been the one to find the body.

'Have you taken counselling, talked to anyone about it?' She was sharpish, not unsympathetic, and insistent.

'I was upset but not traumatised,' I said.

'You don't know that,' she said, 'and prevention's better than cure.'

She said we should meet at noon on Monday. She had a one-thirty meeting but ninety-minutes would give us plenty of time.

'I'll book the table. They know me. The name of the place is Montazzi's. You'll like it.'

The weekend, two whole days of freedom and abandon, stretched ahead. I put on my favourite, flat Italian leather boots and sallied forth. I left my mobile, switched off, in the hotel.

My hotel room might have been a killer, the lift a death trap, the lobby a faded testament to the place's Art Nouveau origins but everything else in New York, everything, gave me a rush of blood to the head.

I walked, for the entire weekend, until my heels blistered. I had tourist written all over me and was treated with pity, indifference and courtesy. No one shoved me under cars for the hell of it, no one wept their life story onto my shoulder and the coffee was as good, in some places, as any I'd ever made myself.

I mingled with jugglers and lovers in Central Park, with dogs of every description by the Hudson river. I talked to a woman as old as God Himself on the Staten Island Ferry. She was facing Manhattan's towers with her chin forward, like a cliff at the end of a bony, made-up face.

'There are one and a half million dogs, four million cats and an unknown number of alligators and performing bears kept as pets in New York,' she said.

'I've got a dog myself,' I said, 'he's called Lucifer.'

'You didn't do him any favours, did you?' She glared. One eye was a cataract cloud, the other a piercing blue with the rim of a contact lens visible. 'You be careful in New York,' she said, 'very careful. This city's full of anguish.'

I wished she hadn't used the word anguish. Concepta Walsh had used it too.

I bought earrings on Broadway. They were blue and swung when I walked. I bought trainers and plaster for my heels. I slept the sleep of the righteously exhausted.

I still had blisters on my heels on Monday morning and had to wear the trainers, and plasters, with jeans and my red leather jacket, to meet Sofia Borodin. The alternative was a longish skirt which looked great with the boots and terrible with the trainers. I wore the earrings too.

She was tall and X-ray thin in unstructured, impeccably cut charcoal. She had fine fair hair, pale cared-for skin and black pearl studs in her ears. I'd seen versions of her all over Manhattan on my walking tour but few that were as fine boned and elegant.

As I shook her hand the Broadway earrings felt too long and much too bright. The rest of me I didn't want to think about.

'I hope you're enjoying your trip.' She laser-eyed me before raising an eyebrow at a waiter in a taupe apron. 'Pity the weather's so unseasonal.'

The waiter led us to a window table set for three.

'My brother will join us eventually,' Sofia

Borodin said as she sat. 'He has trouble with time-keeping.' She waved away the waiter with the menu. 'I can recommend the grilled calamari and octopus. Or if you prefer it the John Dory with porcini mushrooms and clams is usually quite good. Avoid the gnocchi. I got a soggy mess last time I was here.'

'Perhaps the calamari...' I began.

'Think I'll try the cavatelli.' She gave a delicate frown. 'It's seasonal and fresh. I can of course ask them to put together some alternative if there's nothing you like on the menu.' She signalled the waiter.

A queue had formed in the ante-room inside the door. We were indeed lucky to have a table.

'I'll have a side salad with the calamari,' I said, firmly.

'You're sure?' She looked disappointed.

'Positive.' I smiled at the hovering waiter. 'It's good of you and your brother to meet me.'

'It's our pleasure,' Sofia Borodin said, 'I speak for Sasha too.'

The maitre d' arrived to kiss her hand. The whole performance – Sofia Borodin's imperious air, her long-nosed disdain for the passing crowds, the maitre d's effusive concern for our comfort, the waiter's resentful attentiveness, the covert looks from the waiting unfed – all made me feel uncomfortably like a minnow in a fish bowl. I had to hope her brother was more earth bound.

'Would you like wine?' Sofia eyed the trapezoidal wine rack on the far wall. 'I'll have water but they do a Chablis I can recommend.'

I decided to take some control. 'Lunch is on me,' I said, firmly so as to get her attention, 'since I'm the one wanted to meet you.'

'Of course it is.' She smiled with perfect teeth. 'Do you like this place?' The smile embraced the room.

'It's charming,' I assured, her, 'a good choice. Do they have a decent Chardonnay...?'

'Absolutely.' She had a hand in the air before I finished.

I could only hope that Alex Borodin, if he ever arrived, would help me finish the expensive bottle she ordered.

'I've been thinking about your phone call,' she said as we waited for the water and wine, 'and have to say that in your place I would do exactly as you're doing. I would want to know what had happened before, especially since there are the links with the local family. It makes complete and rational sense to me. I must warn you, however, that my brother Sasha disagrees. He thinks it very odd that you have come here.'

'I wouldn't altogether disagree with him,'

I said, 'and I'm not so sure how rational I'm being.'

'Any woman would do what you've done,' she was brisk, 'or if she didn't would want to. You're merely braver than most. That's what I told Sasha. I salute you, Frances Shaw,' she raised her glass of water, 'for your courage in satisfying your curiosity.'

Taking the piss seemed beyond her so I acknowledged the compliment with a modest smile. The waiter arrived.

'Thank you,' I lifted my glass after he'd poured, 'it took courage on your part to come and meet me too, to agree to open up the past again.'

She shrugged. 'Not really. A lifetime of therapy has some benefits. I've no problem talking about it and I was curious to meet you.'

The wine was good. I sipped for a minute before putting the success of her therapy to the test.

'You were ten when your mother died?' I said, gently. This made her fifty now. She didn't so much not look it as appear ageless.

'I was ten,' she said, with just a trace of irritability, 'and I remember everything I haven't decided to forget. I made up my mind a long time ago that sanity lay in remembering what I choose to remember.' She paused. 'I've proven myself right.'

'What was she like?' I asked.

Sofia Borodin took a long drink of water and, almost as if reciting, gave a resume of her family story. She sipped throughout. 'She was twenty-nine years old when she died, dark-haired and pretty. My father was forty-two. A hard-working man. They came to this country in nineteen fifty-three, the year Stalin died. In the confusion and chaos of the time my father managed to get them out of Russia, to New York and then to Coney Island. He got an apartment to rent there, in sight of the sea.' She paused, briefly, when our food arrived. 'My mother thought she had arrived in heaven. My father was never the kind of man to say what he thought but it is my belief he found America a kind of hell. He adored my mother, obviously.'

I waited until the waiter had gone before I said, 'Why do you think your father found America hell?'

'He lost his sense of worth.' She was quite absolute in the way she said this, as if it was a truth she'd discovered and was not for turning on it. 'The only work he could get was in shooting galleries and penny arcades and the occasional freak show. He said it was like looking after the mechanical gadgets of the devil and it soured him. In time, like many immigrants before and after him, he turned on the system and tried to exploit it for his family.'

As the water level went down she frowned, lifted her glass and studied the contents critically. 'They've given me a different water,' she said. 'They *know* what I like. It's not good enough...'

'I'm not sure what you mean by exploiting the system,' I rushed in to dam a discussion about the kind of water she preferred.

'He would appropriate some of the greedy gains of the amusement owners and stalls,' she said, 'took what he felt was his fair share.'

'He stole?'

'That is a very black and white view of things,' she smiled faintly, 'and it's also the view the police took. I don't mean to condone what he did, but I do understand.'

'They were hard times,' I said, inanely. Thieving is thieving – but compassion is understanding.

Sofia Borodin, encouraged, went on with more passion. 'God, but he hated the steaming summer crowds,' she said, 'the rides, the frenzied bathing, the food stalls, the noise, the smells, the drinking establishments. He told me once he liked the yellow of the sand when it was empty of people. Nothing else.' She shrugged. 'My mother loved everything about Coney Island. Most of all she loved going to the movies.'

'Maybe she found the reality hard to take,' I said, 'maybe those things were an escape for her.' The calamari were good, so was the Chardonnay. Sofia Borodin hadn't touched her cavatelli. 'She was very young when she came here, after all.'

'Perhaps,' said Sofia Borodin. 'Whatever the truth she was coming home from a movie the night she died. *High Noon* with Gary Cooper. She'd gone alone and when it got late my father told my brother and me to stay where we were and went out to search for her. He went along the boardwalk, because she often went there, but didn't find her. A hospital worker found her on the morgue steps at a quarter to six next morning. Long before that I remember knowing in my heart that she wasn't coming back.'

'And your father?'

She examined the food on her plate and didn't answer immediately. I wondered if she was married. Or divorced. Or, as I watched a couple of women walk by the window holding hands, if she was gay. Or simply asexual. There was an untouched quality about her that was quite shivery.

'My father was arrested later in the day.' She pushed the plate to one side and picked at her salad. Her busy tones had become frigid. 'Their case was that he'd found my mother on the boardwalk, put his hands about her neck, panicked when she lost consciousness, carried her to the morgue steps rather than leave her to a grave in the sea.'

'Do you believe that's what happened?'

'Of course not. My father didn't kill my mother. He adored her. He would have forgiven her anything.' She ate a piece of tomato, slowly.

'Was there something to forgive?' I said.

'I don't know,' she said, 'he certainly worried she might have had a lover. The police didn't really look for someone else so we'll never know. Not now anyway. It's too long ago and most of the people involved are dead.'

'Do *you* believe he put her body on the morgue steps in some sort of imitation of what had happened in Ireland ten years before?'

'I don't think he put her body there at all,' she said, sharply. 'I thought I'd made it clear that I do *not* believe my father murdered my mother.'

'You did,' I said, hurriedly craven, 'you certainly did. Please let me rephrase – do you think the person responsible put your mother's body on the steps for that reason?'

'Hundreds, if not thousands of people, heard Walsh tell his story over the years in Coney's drinking establishments.' She spoke with her eyes on the passing crowd. 'It was all he could talk about when drunk, which was often. Jokes were made about it...' She lifted a hand, suddenly, in a tired greeting. 'My brother is here,' she said.

235

Apart from a long, angular look Alexander Borodin was nothing like his sister. His eyes were dark, his hair a gunmetal grey and his raincoat a lively brick colour. He looked older than 53, which was his age, and grinned in friendly fashion as he slumped into the third chair and took my hand.

'Alex Borodin,' he said, 'nice to meet you.'

His impressive grip and friendly grin were automatic. They might even have been sincere.

'Frances Shaw,' I said, smiling too, 'but I prefer Fran.'

'What're you people eating?' He took a menu from the immediately attentive waiter. 'You're paying, Sofia, right?'

'I don't know why you would assume that,' Sofia Borodin said, 'this lunch wasn't my idea.'

'Cheapskate,' her brother wagged a finger, 'Fran is a visitor to our enlightened city. You chose the restaurant, didn't you?' He looked around. 'It's your kind of place and your price range. You're not expecting our visitor to pay, are you?'

'This is vulgar, Sasha.' Sofia Borodin looked down her fine nose with considerable elegance. 'Money is not an issue here.'

'Oh, but it is, Sofia. It always is with you.' Alex Borodin's smile widened. The waiter hovered. So did the maitre d', watching from the side of the room. What was happening had happened before. 'Prove it's not an issue,' he said, 'pay that the three of us may leave here happy and well fed...' he gave a small shrug '...let's leave that at well fed.'

'You're an embarrassment, Sasha, to yourself, to me and to our guest,' Sofia said. She didn't look in the least embarrassed.

Alex Borodin ordered a braised beef polpettine, the first thing on the menu.

'Wine?' I held the bottle over his glass.

'Don't mind if I join you,' he said. I filled his glass and refilled my own.

'We've covered quite a bit of ground,' Sofia said. 'I've told Frances what I remember of things surrounding Mother's death and Father's conviction in 1963.'

'What do you expect to discover here?' Alex Borodin was blunt, sitting back while he waited for an answer.

'I'm not sure,' I said.

'Sofia tells me you found the body of the recently murdered young woman in Ireland?'

'Yes.'

'So you've become a self-appointed sleuth?'

'Something like that.'

'But why?'

'Just accept, Sasha darling, that this is a woman thing,' Sofia said. '*I* can understand. Any woman finding the body of another dead woman would want to know what had happened. Just accept.'

'You're hardly a barometer for other women,' her brother said dryly. He looked at me, waiting again for my answer.

'I knew the dead woman,' I said, carefully, 'the police believe it's a copy-cat murder...' I paused, searching for a way to say things, trying not to resent his putting me on the spot. He had every right to know why I wanted his memories of his parents. 'A lot of people, some of them close to me, remember the woman who was murdered in 1953 and the circumstances. The police haven't arrested anybody for the recent murder and there's a lot of frustrated anger about the place. I wanted to get away from it for a while, hopefully get a broader picture of things.'

'How well did you know the victim?' he said.

'Not well. I run a coffee shop and she was a customer. The shop was burned down a few nights ago. There are racial undertones – the murdered woman was involved with a Russian immigrant.' I paused. I'd started to push back the cuticles of my thumbs, a nervous habit I'd abandoned years before. 'I had time on my hands.' I stopped. I'd told enough half-lies and whole truths.

'Time on your hands I understand,' Alex Borodin. He seasoned his meal and ate hungrily.

In a prolonged silence I finished my own lunch. Sofia's uneaten food was taken away. For dessert the waiter suggested passion-fruit soufflé with blueberries and a shot glass of chocolate cream on the side. I decided to try it, so did Alex Borodin.

'I've got ten minutes.' Sofia flashed a platinum timepiece. 'I've got a case against an on-line file-sharing system to work on. There's a piracy thing going on that's costing a client's husband millions of dollars.' She took a long drink of water. There was new life and animation about her. She stood.

'You were very kind to give me your time.' I stood too. She was leaving, the waiter on hand with her coat.

'I'm so very glad we met today, Frances.' Her handshake was fragile and cool. 'We got to cover a deal of ground and I think I've been of help to you. Do let me know what happens in Ireland.' She let my hand go and looked down at her brother. 'I'm taking Frances to the door with me. There's something I forgot to tell her. Don't go away.'

I looked back as we got to the edge of the room. Alex Borodin, when he caught my gaze, didn't smile.

Sofia, wrapped now in tailored cashmere, led me outside, into the street.

'I should prepare you for what Sasha will now tell you,' she said. It was nippy, my coat was inside, I wished she didn't sound so proprietorial. Her smile was detached and she didn't in the least notice my discomfiture. 'I love my brother but he will give you a whole other angle on this thing. His response to our parents' deaths is still, unfortunately, a too emotional one.'

'Hard not to be, I suppose,' I said.

'The hard facts are these, Frances.' Her eyes, in the daylight, were a passionless green. 'My father loved me. He loved me more than he loved my brother. I was a much-wanted child, Sasha was not. This obviously affected our responses to what happened.'

'Obviously.'

'Sasha lost a father he'd never known and a mother he'd never been close to. I lost a much-loved set of parents. Our childhood views of them were different as a consequence.'

She went on talking as she waved down a cruising cab.

'The one thing Sasha and I have never agreed on is about our mother's murderer. I know that our father did not kill our mother. Sasha is equally certain that he did...'

She stepped quickly from under the awning. I followed and, as she opened the cab door, I said, 'Are you married?'

She turned and said, without surprise, 'No.

Not any more. I tried it, a couple of times, but without lasting success. My brother isn't married either. Never was. And nor, between us, do we have any children.'

She got into the cab then, leaning forward immediately to give directions to the driver. She didn't look back as the car disappeared into the traffic.

21

Alex Borodin was standing by the counter holding my jacket when I went back into Montazzi's. He'd also paid the bill. Our window table was already taken.

'I've had enough of this place and we've finished the wine,' he helped me on with my jacket, 'I'm going to take you somewhere that serves real coffee. Since you run a coffee shop you should have the best.'

We stood together while a downpour beat on the restaurant canopy.

'Thought I'd left this sort of weather behind me,' I said. The windows of the skyscrapers wept rain. 'I'm finding New York oddly intimate. Not aloof at all.'

'It can be like that,' he said, 'at times. It's a trick. It'll move back and leave you exposed if you don't keep on your toes.' He waved down a cab. 'It's not a city for the unwary.'

'So I've heard.'

Something of Hector in him made me *very* wary.

I climbed ahead of him into the cab. I sat back while he directed the driver. He sat back beside me.

'You haven't asked where we're going,' he said.

'I want to be surprised,' I said and he laughed. The laugh brought another warning.

We drove through the rain, out of the wide streets into narrower ones. By the time we stopped, outside a small place called The Street Café so had the rain.

'Best coffee I know, and I know it well. I live just a block from here,' Alex Borodin said.

The café window had pyramids of buttermilk biscuits and muffins, terraced piles of all manner of tartlets. I wished I'd forgone dessert.

'Where's here?' I said. We might have been in New Jersey, for all I knew.

'Tribeca, Ms Shaw,' he grinned. 'Comes from TRIangle BElow CAnal street – put together the first syllables in each word and you've got it. Best neighbourhood in town until nine-eleven and making its way back. We edge onto the World Trade Center area so we took the worst of the blast and subsequent misery. We're still feeling the pain in real as well as unimaginable ways. So's everyone else, of course.'

Alex Borodin held the door open for me, his easy smile still in place.

'The rest of us wonder, watching in our far-away ignorance, how this city does it,' I said.

'Come inside.' Alex Borodin took my arm.

Inside had red brick walls and red-gingham-covered tables in dark-wood booths. There were a lot of raised voices by the counter, all of them male.

'I'll have a double espresso,' I said.

I sat into one of the booths and he went to the counter. A wizened customer in a hat threw an arm about him, a red-shirted waiter eyed me openly and the huge man who served him glanced my way and spoke out of the side of his mouth to Alex Borodin. And New York called itself a city; I might have been in a pub in the west of Ireland. I concentrated on examining a Madonna figure holding a candle on the table.

'I eat breakfast here most mornings,' Alex Borodin said as he slid onto the bench opposite with our drinks, 'sometimes lunch too, coffee all the time.'

I stirred my espresso. 'Sofia says she never married and nor did you,' I said. Maybe I'd read the bar language wrongly, maybe he was gay. I didn't think so but wasn't infallible on such matters. Just pretty acute.

'Never wed, never fathered a child,' he was terse. 'I'd have made a bad father.'

'Most men have no idea the kind of father they'll make until they become one,' I said.

'You think I should have tried it?' His expression didn't change.

'I don't know you well enough for that,' I

said, backing off as discretion became the better part of valour.

'I teach,' he said, 'in a public school. Have done more or less since I left college. It's given me more than enough children to deal with and I do it fairly well.' He shrugged. 'Maybe because I can also walk away.'

'I didn't mean to pry,' I said.

'I'm a fairly open book,' he was off-hand, 'I've avoided replicating myself so as to avoid bringing a child who might grow to be my father into the world. I didn't want a child of mine to grow up either in the shadow of a grandfather convicted and electrocuted for murder.'

'I suppose those sort of fears are why the Walsh family scattered and changed their names,' I said.

'Living somewhere else with a different name doesn't change the reality,' he said. 'I teach kids whose fathers are locked up, whose mothers are addicts. It's hard on them, impossible sometimes, a lot of them don't make it. I've no regrets.'

'Why did you choose teaching?'

'Enough,' he said. 'I've a few questions of my own to ask.'

It had been a long, long time since a man I didn't know had asked me to account for myself. 'What do you want to know?' I said, uneasily.

He studied me for a minute or two. His expression gave absolutely nothing away; a talent borne of long years in front of classrooms, no doubt.

'You're here and we've met because my father may have murdered my mother,' he said at last. 'Odd, when you think about it.'

Bizarre and sad fitted the situation too but I didn't say so. The bizarre bit was that I found him attractive. 'Very odd,' I said.

A monkey-faced man brought us two complimentary cassatas. Good manners made me accept, common sense told me I'd find myself in the street if I didn't. The waiter handed us a red-checked napkin each, laid spoons and dessert forks on the side, said 'Hope you like it,' to me and nothing at all to Alex.

'He's curious about you,' Alex said, 'and annoyed I didn't ask him to sit with us.'

'Why didn't you?'

'Because I want you to myself,' he said.

Good, I thought, so far so good. 'Is he the owner?' I said.

'The owner and only begetter of the place,' Alex said, 'his name's Dino. Now – my questions. Do you have children?'

'I've got a daughter of twenty-three,' I said. 'Her name's Emer. And I've a dog. Name of Lucifer. He was the one found the body of the dead girl. He was ahead of me and started barking...'

'Are you divorced?' he cut across me. 'Or widowed?'

'Divorced,' I said.

'In a relationship?' he said. He picked at the candied peel in his ice cream with the fork.

'No.' I lifted my spoon and wondered where to begin with my own cassata. It seemed a shame to deface it, so perfectly square in its pool of red coulis.

'I didn't think so.' He ate the peel. I tasted the coulis.

'Did you indeed?' I said. 'And why is that?'

'Nothing clairvoyant,' he grinned. 'Just you being here alone, dealing with the heebie-jeebies of what happened in this way.'

'Is that what you think I'm doing here?' I was annoyed. 'All I want is to get some understanding of what happened on Coney Island forty years ago so that, hopefully, it might throw light on what happened in Dun Laoghaire ten years before that.' I paused. 'And on today's murder too, of course.'

'Aha,' he gave a long sigh, separated out some more of the peel from his ice-cream. 'The wheel is come full circle. Would you like to tell me what, or who, has got you so worried about the first murder in nineteen fifty-three?' he said.

I would, as it happened, like to tell him. A part of the story anyway. If and when I found and spoke with Ritchie Walsh, would be time enough to give him the full details. Depending on what Ritchie Walsh had to say.

'My father-in-law's both the what and the who,' I said. 'I'm fond of him. He's what I suppose you'd call a character. He's a decent man who was more of a father to my daughter than her father was for many years.'

'What was your ex-husband's problem?' he said.

'He was a drinker,' I said.

I took a spoonful of my cassata, now a pinky-white soup with floating ice-bergs. Then I took another. It was sweet and comforting. The monkey-faced owner, leaning on his counter reading the paper, nodded approvingly.

'Tell me about the grandfather,' Alex Borodin said, quite gently.

'His name's Thaddeus,' I said. 'He knew Shirley Walsh, the first woman who was murdered, and her husband, Jimmy. He knew Ritchie Walsh too, whom you would have known, and his sons and nieces.' I paused, and then I lied. 'He's been talking a lot about Ritchie Walsh, implying Ritchie knew something about Shirley Walsh's murder that he should have told the police.'

'Is he saying this something could have changed the outcome of the trial?'

'I'm not sure. Yes. Maybe.'

'Is he saying this something might also

have been a factor on Coney Island in nineteen sixty-three.'

'I think so ... maybe.'

'But you think so, don't you? You think this something might mean all three murders are linked?' He spoke carefully.

'It's a possibility,' I said, just as carefully.

'So Ritchie Walsh is the real reason you came to New York?'

'Well, yes.'

'Wish you'd said so in the first place, Fran. I thought you might have an agenda, that there had to be more to your trip than what my sister chose to see as womanly curiosity.' He shrugged. Not happily. 'In a way I'm relieved. Shows you're more than a ghoul.'

'You thought I was a ghoul?' I said.

'Before I met you, yes. Sofia persuaded me to meet you anyway. When we met I thought no, this woman's all right, this woman's not a sensation seeker.'

'Why would you think I was in the first place?'

'Why? I suppose because it was my life you were coming to poke around, Fran. Mine and Sofia's. Even a less suspicious guy than me might think your mission was one of plain voyeurism, that you were tying in a trip to New York with a look at the survivors of an earlier, body-in-the-doorway murder. It would certainly make for dinner-party conversation when you get home at the end of the week.'

I was angry, and knew I'd no right to be – why wouldn't he, why shouldn't he, think like this? I looked at him, and then looked away, chasing what was left of my ice-cream around the dish with a spoon.

The brunt of what I'd done, the weight of my intrusion, was in his face. He'd been prepared to give me the benefit of the doubt and now hated the fact that he'd been lied to, even by omission and because I'd told a half-truth. He'd met me, against his better instincts. Now he was waiting for me to have the decency to explain what I was really doing in New York.

'I'm sorry.' I looked at him. 'I should have been more upfront from the beginning.' He stared back, giving me no help. 'Could I have another espresso, please?' I said.

'Be my guest,' he said and ordered. There was no irony that I could detect in his voice. I took a breath and put the truth together for him, in as much as I could.

'Alannah Casey's murder opened a can of worms as far as my family is concerned,' I said. 'Thaddeus is upset and secretive about nineteen fifty-three. Whatever's haunting him haunts Ritchie Walsh too. Ritchie wrote to Thaddeus in nineteen sixty-four. I read the letter.' I paused. 'I stole the letter to read it, in fact. It's been difficult, as a result, for me to talk to Thaddeus about its contents...'

I told him then about the letter, about its emphasis on the burden shared by the two men. He listened, and was noncommittal. I told him about going to see Concepta Walsh, about her implication that Thaddeus was the father of one of Shirley Walsh's daughters. He committed himself enough to grunt. I told him about the newspaper cuttings and photograph of Shirley Walsh, about John Rutledge, Ted Cullen, Dimitri Sobchak and, even, Nina's pragmatic view of things. I told him about Hector, and a little of Emer. I spoke quickly but he was a good listener.

'I want to know what Thaddeus's involvement was,' I said, 'and to do that I need to find and talk with Ritchie Walsh.'

'You think he'll have the answer?'

'He's bound to know something,' I said. 'It was in the letter...'

'They might both have been in love with Shirley Walsh,' he said, 'or have been involved in a cheating threesome. The story about your Thaddeus being the father of one of the girls might be true. My memory is of them being pretty unalike as children. Who knows where his guilt comes from?'

'Thaddeus would have had to be a teenager, about eighteen, when he fathered Shirley's child,' I said, 'it doesn't seem right. Or even possible.'

'It's certainly not right for an eighteen year old to father a child,' he smiled, 'possible's

251

another matter. Your father-in-law's guilt, as you describe it, has to come from somewhere.'

'I suppose so,' I said. I hadn't thought of this. He could be right. I was feeling jumpy, and it wasn't the coffee. Alexander Borodin didn't know Thaddeus. He didn't know how the recent murder had shaken him, that he'd gone back to drinking after years on the dry. 'I still want to know.'

'Take it easy,' Alex Borodin said, 'just relax, Fran, okay?'

'Could you help me find Ritchie Walsh?' I said.

'First I want to know why you've taken this on yourself,' he said.

'Because there are questions I want to ask Thaddeus and can't without proof, or at the very least without more knowledge. Because I *do* believe there's a link between the three murders. But there's a fifty-year-time span involved, for God's sake.'

'Life is one tenth here and now, nine tenths a history lesson,' Alex Borodin smiled, 'not original but true, up to a point.'

'Thaddeus says the past is not dead, nor even past,' I was wry, 'not original either. Faulkner said it first.'

'He said that?'

'He did. You should know,' I said, 'that Ritchie Walsh wrote about your father in his letter.'

'Yeah?' He put his elbows on the table and leaned across. 'Tell me.' When I hesitated he took my hand in his and looked me in the eye. 'We're on the same side, Fran,' he said.

I hadn't expected this but it was good to know. I left my hand where it was.

'Ritchie wrote that your father had done things and deserved to be punished for them,' I said, 'even if he hadn't murdered your mother.'

'He was right,' said Alex Borodin, 'my father was a proven asshole who did more than his share of wrongdoing.'

'And you think he killed your mother?'

'A jury thought he did. I've always been inclined to agree with them.'

Inclined. Alexander Borodin didn't sound anything like as certain as his sister had said he was about his father killing his mother.

'But you're not certain?' I prodded.

He let my hand go and looked away, towards the glass door to the street, to the life and bustle outside. He was restless. I understood that too.

'What's there to be certain about in life?' he said. 'They say in this country that death and taxes are the only things we can be sure about.' He signalled the owner. 'Dino keeps a bottle of family red for special occasions. You can join me if you like.'

Dino, expression melancholy, appeared with a bottle of Chianti and two glasses.

'Drink,' he put one in front of me and poured, 'we don't know what's going to happen next, not any of us. None of us knew about September eleven on September ten so why would we know today what's gonna happen tomorrow? So drink up. Make the most of it.'

I saluted him with the glass. 'Your health,' I said.

He nodded and filled Alex Borodin's glass. He left the bottle and lit the candle in its Madonna holder before he left.

'Does everyone think like that these days?' I said.

'Not everyone. Just a good proportion of folks.'

We touched glasses and drank. Going down on top of the Chardonnay it tasted as if one glass would be enough.

'Did Ritchie Walsh drink?' I asked.

'I was thirteen when my mother died.' His tone asked me to be reasonable. 'Ritchie Walsh was an adult figure, a friend of my father's.'

'But did he drink?'

'I remember him drinking with my father. I don't know if he drank in the quantities you want to think he did.'

'I don't...'

'You may not know it but you've a theory somewhere in there,' he tapped the side of my head with a gentle forefinger, 'and you want to make it fit the facts. I think you want Ritchie Walsh to be the murderer of both my mother and his brother's wife. It would get your Thaddeus off the hook. Ritchie's a pretty old man now...' he ran a thoughtful hand through his hair and left a wing of it standing above his ear, '...he'd be eighty years, by my reckoning.'

'He might want to talk before he dies,' I said. 'I've been over all the things he might have meant by a burden. I thought at first it was a coded way of him saying he and Thaddeus suspected one another. Then I thought it might be that they both suspected John Rutledge, the barman in the pub on the night. He's gay but hadn't come out at the time. I wondered if maybe they'd both taunted him and suspected he'd tried to prove himself a man with a drunken Shirley.'

The café was almost empty now. Alex Borodin stretched his legs outside the booth and redirected the conversation. 'Anything's possible,' he said. 'Who do *you* think did it?'

I'd been waiting for him to ask this. 'I'm probably wrong,' I said.

'You could be right,' he said, and waited.

'Well ... I have wondered, off and on, whether one of Ritchie's sons could have been responsible...' I hesitated. 'You knew them. What do you think?'

He didn't answer directly. He hedged his

255

bets instead with a picture of the young Walshes he'd known.

'Ben and Mike Walsh were in their twenties when we were neighbours,' he said. 'They worked the fairgrounds and to my thirteen-year-old eyes they looked big, strong men. They'd have known my mother, yes. But not very well. When their aunt died in Dublin they were young teenagers.'

'It just seemed to me a possibility,' I said.

Bernard Walsh was sixteen in 1953, his brother Michael fifteen. They'd been described in the papers as being tall, both of them, and uncomfortable in 'suits for the occasion' when they appeared in court. They'd gone out that last night searching for Shirley. I told Alex Borodin all of this. He took a while to answer and, when he did, he sounded puzzled.

'You're prepared to entertain the notion that a teenage boy could have violently killed his aunt but not the idea that another teenage boy, your father-in-law, made love to the same woman and fathered her child.' He paused. 'Why is it easier to impute violence to a young man than love?'

'Because it is,' I said, 'or was in Ireland in the fifties where there was so much that was dark and so much that was hidden. Abusive sex seems to have been far more everyday than loving sex. Some people knew it then and did nothing. Everyone knows it now,

256

now that the adult children have spoken.'

'I see,' he said, quietly. And that was all he said, even though I waited.

Nightfall was still a couple of hours away but tightly packed cloud and falling rain had made it dark outside. It looked a bit like a doomsday scenario and I didn't really want to go out into it. Dino had disappeared and we had the place to ourselves.

'I've got something to do. I must go,' Alex Borodin said. He got up and stepped out of the booth. 'Wait here. I'll hail you a cab.'

I stood inside the glass of the door and waited there while he tried to stop a cab. It took him one minute and forty seconds. Timing it occupied me, stopped me agonising about why he'd ended the afternoon so suddenly. Stopped me wondering who he'd got waiting for him.

A cab pulled savagely in and alongside the kerb. Alex Borodin had opened the passenger door by the time I got there.

'I'll call you,' he said as I climbed in.

The cab became part of the headlong traffic before I could answer, ask when this might happen. I couldn't see him anywhere either when I looked back.

22

November, 1963. Coney Island.

'Now we will begin.' Liliya Borodin comes in from the kitchen when she hears her husband arrive. She fusses and worries, putting her son out of his place at the table so his father can sit there. The boy wordlessly finds himself a stool and squeezes into a space at the end of the table.

'We're starting with borscht?' Sergei Borodin looks at the plate of soup his wife puts in front of him. 'Thought I smelled fish?'

'I have fish too,' Liliya says, 'Ben has brought us a gift of fish, plenty of it.'

She brings what she has cooked to the table and puts it in front of her husband. She doesn't look at Ben when she does this, nor while Sergei Borodin silently eats the fish. To compound the injury she sits to eat her own soup and forgets she has not yet given any to Bernard.

So he must sit with nothing to eat while Sergei Borodin enjoys the fish he, Ben, has caught that day on the boardwalk.

'This is a fine soup,' his father says, 'a very fine soup. Nice for a change. Russian, is it?

They eat this in Russia?'

Ritchie is afraid of Sergei Borodin and Sergei Borodin likes it that way. It keeps Ritchie in his place and makes him safe and watchful company for Liliya.

'Yes. It is made with beetroot,' Liliya says, quietly. She too is afraid of Sergei, who is picking at a bone between his teeth.

'Ling's a great fish for the brain, they say,' he grins. He knows well the fish was cooked for Bernard.

'It's a frostfish,' Bernard corrects him and sees his father cringe.

'Tastes like ling to me,' Sergei Borodin says.

'I caught it and it's frostfish,' Bernard says.

Sergei Borodin pushes his empty plate away. A glass crashes to the floor. 'Are you telling me, in my own home, that I don't know what kind of fish I've just eaten?'

'I'm telling you that I caught it and it was a frostfish,' Ben says.

'What sort of fish would *you* say it was?' Sergei Borodin turns to his pale wife. 'What was it you cooked with such care for your husband?'

'Ling. It was a ling,' Liliya says, desperation and pleading in her voice as she turns to Bernard for understanding.

'Frostfish,' Ben says. She has betrayed him.

Sergei Borodin stands and lifts his son's

bowl of soup and smashes it onto the table.

'It's what I say it is in my home,' he roars.

'We'll be going now,' Ritchie Walsh slides from the table, 'we're grateful to you, Mrs Borodin, for a lovely dinner. And to yourself, Sergei, for having us.' He urges his nieces, Melanie and Stella, ahead of him and scuttles from the room. Ben rises, slowly, from the table.

'Thank you, Liliya,' he says, softly, full of a white and searing anger. She has betrayed him to agree with a husband for whom, Ben knows, she does not care.

'Don't come back here, ever,' Sergei Borodin shouts at him, 'not to eat, not to visit, not for anything.' He stabs his knife in Ben's direction. 'My family doesn't want your fish.'

Ben is not afraid of him. 'I hope you enjoy the rest of the fish, Liliya,' he smiles at Borodin's wife.

'Get out,' Borodin roars.

Ben leaves, slowly. He hears Sergei Borodin shout and Liliya cry out and the youngsters plead as he closes the door and walks to the elevator.

By betraying him Liliya has proven she is no different to other women. No different to his mother, who hated him and did terrible things to him and then left him. No different to Shirley, who taunted and shamed him.

His father is drunk when he gets home, and whining in his bed in the room they share.

'You could have kept your mouth shut, for once,' Ritchie Walsh says.

'I could have crawled on my belly too, like you,' Ben says.

'She has a hard enough time of it,' Ritchie says, 'without you adding to it.'

Ritchie Walsh is old before his time. He has teeth missing and is wearing his clothes as he lies in the bed. The room reeks of booze.

The girls have gone to a friend's place for the night. There is nothing here for Ben. He kicks the end of his father's bed and leaves the room. His father is snoring as he closes the outer door.

23

May, 2003. New York.

The hotel, when I got back to it, was less claustrophobic, less rancid, more welcoming and very, very familiar. I'd adjusted.

I was also woozy from the several glasses of wine. Someone had turned off the air conditioning so I turned it on again and lay on the bed and thought about Sofia Borodin and what she'd said, and not said, over lunch. Sofia didn't occupy my thoughts half as much as her brother did, however.

I thought about the mobility of his face, his fleeting smile, his sweet dark eyes. I fell asleep thinking about him, still with my clothes on, wishing the phone would ring. My mobile was turned off and at the bottom of my bag. Nina would only ring or give the hotel number out in an emergency. I could fairly confidently expect any call to be from Alex Borodin.

The rattle of the lift woke me twelve hours later, just before six a.m. I got off the bed, checked out my patch of sky and found it clear and blue. I was filled with an indecent energy and impatience.

Ridiculous to expect a phone call at that hour, just as ridiculous to hang around waiting for one. I showered and dressed and did my face, hoping I looked better in the flesh than I did in the yellowy murk of the bathroom mirror.

Breakfast was coffee in dispensers and muffins in a corner of the lobby. The only people sharing the early hour with me were a trio of healthy Australians who pulled up a chair for me to sit beside them. They talked and I dallied, passing a whole half hour with them. I suggested they visit Ireland. They said they'd heard it was a violent and dangerous place. I felt in no position to disagree with them.

Alex Borodin was unlikely to ring before eight so I wandered out and killed some more time along a bright Fifth Avenue. I bought the *New York Post* and sat at the counter in a bagel café and had yet another coffee. The paper's headline screamed 'Momster' and the story told of a mother who had delivered and killed her baby during Christmas dinner.

I looked up Coney Island in my guide book. It advised going there by tram, taking the Q line over Manhattan Bridge to Stillwell Avenue. The views and the experience were second to few in the city, it said, and there was a flea market run by Russians.

'She had to be some sort of depraved cunt

to do a thing like that,' the man beside me said, stabbing a finger at the paper. He was eating a pancake with red jelly, bacon, ham and sausage. I gave him the paper and headed back to the hotel.

I would go to Coney Island. I would take the Q line and have an experience second to few for myself, by myself. I was too old and far, far too wise to wait in for a phone call from a man. I was not going to have what I would do with my day decided by Alex Borodin either.

It was just after 8.30 a.m. and the phone's message light was flashing when I opened the bedroom door. I stood looking at it for several minutes, practising restraint, before I grabbed the receiver and punched the respond button.

Alex Borodin gave his number and asked if I would call him, preferably before 8.30 a.m. since he would be gone for the day after that. He hoped I'd enjoyed New York by night.

When I rang he picked the phone up immediately.

'I was afraid you'd have left,' I said.

'I was hoping you'd ring,' he said.

So far so good. He asked how I was and I said fine, that I'd slept well. 'So well I'm fairly bursting with energy,' I said, 'and thinking of taking myself to Coney Island for the day.' Thinking? What did I mean thinking? I was *going* to Coney Island for the day. 'I'm taking the Q line to Stillwell Avenue. Sounds like a great trip and only about an hour long.'

'I'll drive us there,' he said when I took a breath.

'I like the sound of the train journey,' I said, surprised, ungracious and, immediately, panicking. 'But I would of course love you to come with me.'

'Fine by me,' he said, easily, 'we'll go together on the Q line if that's what you want.' He made it sound as if he wanted it too. I of course had to question my good fortune.

'Don't you have school today?' I said.

'I don't now,' he said. 'I'm due days and this is going to be one of them. I'll meet you at your hotel in an hour. And, by the way, I've got some news for you.'

'News?' I said.

'I did some ferreting around. Ritchie Walsh is in a nursing home in Southampton, out on Long Island. A couple of hours' drive would get us there.'

'He is?' I said. 'A couple of hours?'

'Maybe a bit longer,' he amended. 'We could go tomorrow,' he paused, 'if you wanted to.'

'That sounds ... great,' I said, and laughed nervously, 'I'll have to get used to the idea that I'm actually going to meet him. How did you find out?'

'In a job like mine you build up a lot of useful contacts,' he said. 'A guy in the police force tracked Ritchie down for me. He's in a private home called Parson's Retreat in Southampton. I made a call. They're expecting us about three o'clock.'

'That's it? It was that easy?'

'It was never going to be very difficult, Fran,' he said.

'And you don't mind taking me there?'

'I want to. See you in a while.'

I spent the time waiting for him trying both of the skirts I'd brought with all of the T-shirts. I wore jeans in the end, with a black T-shirt and, again, my red leather jacket. When in doubt go for the reliables. I worked on my face but left my hair as it was, loose and frizzed a bit from the damp. Hair was something I'd found didn't change with age; it was as reliably difficult as it had always been.

Alex Borodin arrived on time wearing the same brick-coloured raincoat and trainers. 'You look good,' he said and took my arm and walked me out the door.

'Tell me about Ritchie Walsh,' I said.

'Let's save it for later,' he said, 'for this evening.' I had no problem with that. We didn't talk much on the way to the station, or on the train either. The silence felt companionable. For my part.

Waiting for the train I saw a sign which read, 'Stand clear of falling trees, mad dogs and closing train doors.' He laughed with me and that felt good too, especially since he'd probably seen it ten thousand times before. He shared my macabre delight in the Q-line train, in the graffiti in the stations we passed through, in the truly epic body piercings of our fellow travellers.

Crossing Manhattan Bridge we craned together for views of the tossing waters of the Hudson River and the serried ranks of 'scrapers pushing back from its banks, a sublime city-kingdom looking as if it had just grown there.

'What a sight,' I said.

'Yes,' he said, modestly proud, as if he were responsible somehow. I'd always thought it was only Dubliners went in for that sort of chauvinism.

The Stillwell Avenue terminus station was messily under repair. Coney Island, by comparison and when we emerged, looked to be falling down. The promised blue day had disappeared into bleak grey.

Surf Avenue, the main drag, had all the appearance of a war zone and smelled of tar and the sea. Furrows were being drilled in the road. Flea-market Russians were strung sadly along one side, the other had tired, low buildings with gaps between. There were a few blocks of brown apartments, several fast-food joints, deserted gaming halls, empty booths, dead mechanical gadgets, lifeless amusement arcades. People moved as if life had been bleached out of them.

There was no magic, nothing of the great myth. It was just a wasteland with a fabled past.

'I didn't know it was being pulled down,' I said.

'Coney needs the sun to shine on it,' Alex said. 'There's life here in the summertime, still.'

I could have told him it *was* the summertime but hadn't the heart. I was glad, later. It was the one, and only, time I heard Alex Borodin defend Coney Island. The one and only trace of sentimentality I would hear about his childhood place, and years.

'Why did it die?' I asked. Giving me his potted version of the place I could see the teacher in him.

'The usual reasons,' he said, 'greed and changing times mostly. Owners wouldn't pay for the upkeep of rides as they got older, wouldn't pay minimum wage levels when those got higher either. The clientele, in its heyday, was mainly Irish-American and Jewish Brooklyn, poor and not able to afford anywhere else for day trips and vacations. They moved up in the world and out to the suburbs. The big attractions closed. I haven't been back for twenty years.'

'What's left?' I said.

'The unyielding,' he said in tones of resigned amusement, 'and the invincible. The Atlantic, the beach, the boardwalk, the Parachute Jump, the Cyclone – and Nathan's.' He pointed. A sign, across the road from where we stood, loudly announced that Nathan's had been selling hot-dogs since 1916.

'I skipped breakfast,' he said, 'come on.'

I'm no connoisseur but the hot-dog he bought me tasted good.

'Have two,' Alex said, 'we're going to walk. A lot.'

'Tell me what it was like growing up here,' I said when we were walking along the lethargic Surf Avenue.

'I was thirteen years old when I left Coney,' he reminded.

'Tell me about those thirteen years,' I said, relentless.

'Most of the time it was a terrifying place,' he said. 'The rides and penny arcades and even the beaches were full of my father's associates. There wasn't any place I could go without bumping into him either. I was convinced, until I was about six or seven, that my father owned Coney Island.'

He was silent for a while. I thought about dropping the subject but he started talking again, unprompted.

'My father began his criminal life about here,' he said. Here was a tattered kiosk with the legend 'Ma's Speciality Grill' across the top. 'He started as a pitchman and put up his pitch, a sort of collapsible stand, right there.'

'A pitchman?'

'Guy who sells gimcrack goods, balloons, small mechanical toys, novelties. Whatever he'd been able to rob or otherwise lay hands on.'

'It must have been hard for him,' I said, trying to understand, 'leaving Stalin's Russia in the fifties...'

'Don't,' he said, gently enough, 'don't try to vindicate him. He moved on to receiving stolen goods, then to extortion. He was impressively terrifying, my old man. He could freeze a man at ten feet with a stare.' He shrugged. 'He could captivate a woman from any distance.'

'A charmer, then?'

'When charm was useful.'

'And you knew all this as a child?'

'In the beginning I only knew the fear. As I grew older I began to know why and what I was afraid of.'

'Did you ever get on with him?'

'No.'

'Sofia did though...'

'Sofia didn't get on with him either,' he said.

'She sounds as if she did,' I said.

'My sister finds it easier to lie to herself

about most things,' he said, 'it helps get her through. She's never really got over what life took from her. To deal with it she completely reinvented herself.'

'It seems to work for her,' I said.

'I suppose,' he shrugged, 'who're we to judge?'

We stopped by a stall selling blown-up plastic animals, odd-looking green dogs beside long, sad, brown crocodiles. He put his arm around me. It had been a long time since a man I liked had done anything so unbearably intimate.

'Tell me about where you grew up,' he said.

'Later,' I said, 'later.' I was so sure, even then, that there would be a later. 'I want to know more about your father, and about your mother.'

We got out of the way of a black woman wheeling a supermarket trolley filled with clothes and papers and moved on.

'My father liked to say he hated America,' Alex said, 'but he didn't, not at all. He became American very quickly. Spoke English within months. A shrink would say it was himself he hated.'

'Did he involve you in his criminality?' I said.

Alex shook his head. 'No. Another of his cravings was respectability for his family. Sofia was his pride and joy and our mother

271

the young woman he'd seduced to give him a family and immortality. He was very afraid of death.'

'Why do you think that was?' I asked. He didn't answer.

'He kept us out of it,' he said instead, 'and in a sort of prison. He controlled everything we did and everywhere we went.'

Paper flew about our ankles, and cardboard boxes. A sign on an empty clapperboard building said 'For Sale' and another read 'No Smoking'. Both seemed equally pointless. I'd wanted to know about the Walshes – but now I wanted even more to know about Liliya Borodin.

'What was your mother like?' I said.

'To look at she was like Sofia, only dark haired. The papers at the time of the trial said she was lovely but they were wrong. She was beautiful.'

He kept me moving, his arm still around me, past the garages housing the Russian flea market, past wheel chairs and old mirrors, dolls, communion and wedding dresses, shoes, pots, pans, irons, hats, electricals, cameras, radios.

'As a person she was an escapist,' he said. 'She lived for the movies. She was braver than any woman I've ever known in her risk-taking to get to the movies.'

'Did she go alone?'

'Mostly. Sometimes she took me with her,

sometimes Sofia. Other times she took Ritchie Walsh.'

'Ritchie Walsh?' This was a surprise. He smiled.

'She was ruthless when it came to getting out to a movie theatre and our father thought Ritchie harmless, a useful fool.'

He dropped his arm and stepped away from me. He was looking skywards, his expression wry. I followed his gaze to the heights of an ancient roller-coaster, uncertain and crude against the grey clouds.

'That's the Cyclone,' he said. 'Eighty-five feet high, two thousand six hundred and forty feet long, made of wood in nineteen twenty-seven. My once and only own getaway place. Guy who ran it used to give me free rides.'

'It was younger then,' I said. I didn't like the way he was eyeing it now.

'It's still operational. Like to try it?' he said, predictably. He also expected me to say no.

'Love to,' I said.

The Cyclone looked even older close up. We paid $5 each to an attendant who looked older still. We climbed into a wooden car and with an anguished rattle of wood on wood were set free.

The wind howled as we came out into the air and the wood rattled to fever pitch in the rush into the first figure of eight. When we dipped down I felt as if I'd left my stomach on the roaring tracks, when we climbed again, to a sign which said 'No Standing', I thought as if, as if, and clung to Alex Borodin. My limbs, all four of them, were jelly-like as we climbed out.

'Like to try again?' Alex Borodin said. I suggested he do it alone and he grinned. He put an arm about me again as we came out onto Surf Avenue. 'Rain's coming,' he said. I hadn't noticed.

It was beating hard on the pavement by the time we got ourselves a window table in an eatery with a yellow awning which was full of shouting Russians. A sad young woman with bad English brought us coffee. It was truly terrible.

'It's not great,' Alex Borodin agreed, drinking his.

'Tell me about your mother and Ritchie Walsh and the movies.' I pushed mine away.

'Ritchie was a sort of lost soul,' he shrugged, 'his heart in the old country and all that, hiding behind the simple man façade. Ritchie always seemed to me to be hiding, and afraid. God knows what of...'

He stopped. I watched him watch an elderly Russian man, walking in front of the slow traffic on the road in dungarees and a baseball cap. Whatever memories the sight evoked brought a bleakness to his face. I wanted to put my hand out and turn his face to mine. After a few minutes he turned back to me anyway.

'He was locked in the past, I suppose,' he said. 'I liked him,' he hesitated, 'or at least I wasn't afraid of him.'

'And he never went home,' I said. It was half a question.

'Not that I know of. He liked my mother. Everyone liked her. He would drop by the apartment with his nieces, sometimes his sons too, with small treats and to talk to her. My father was rarely there in the evenings but she'd of course make dinner, expecting him, and we'd all eat together. Ritchie liked that, he said it reminded him of being at home.'

'I suppose it did,' I said.

I supposed it reminded him of the last night of Shirley Walsh's life. That had been a family occasion too.

'Sometimes, if there was a movie she was desperate to see, she'd ask Ritchie to go with her. She would leave us with Mel and Stella and we'd play cards for the couple of hours it took. Sometime she went on her own. That was really high risk. She went on her own the last night. Just left to go to the movies and was never seen alive again.'

'Sofia told me,' I said.

'I was old enough to have looked out for her better,' he said. 'I should have been more caring of Sofia too. I didn't really look out for either of them.'

'You were a child yourself. Thirteen is so very young.' I dared to touch his hand where it was wrapped around the coffee mug. 'We don't have to talk about it any more, if you'd prefer.'

'We never did *have* to talk about it,' he said 'and we never would have if you weren't you.'

I took a sip of the cold, putrid coffee. 'Thank you,' I said.

I was afraid to say any more. I'd never been good at saying the right thing at the right time and couldn't decide if the time was right now, either, to say something.

'Coffee tasting better?' He raised an eyebrow.

He'd a fiendishly sexy way of raising a quizzical eyebrow. I couldn't even tell him this, much as I wanted to.

'Worse,' I said.

I left to visit the bathroom, a need for some time alone as great as the call of nature. My hair was manic and so, in the three-inch-square mirror over the basin, was the expression on my face. I applied mascara and lipstick. I would have washed my teeth if there had been water in the tap. I used a breath freshener instead.

Alex Borodin was standing, talking to the sad waitress, when I got back.

'Rain's stopped,' he said.

The waitress smiled at him as we left.

A rising wind was full of the sound of screaming gulls and the smell of salt sea water. The frazzled charms of Coney were growing on me; I'd an urge to try my luck at the Bonanza Shooting Gallery or visit the Bizarre Beauties of the Deep in the Aquarium. A stroll along the boardwalk would have been even better but I thought it might have been pushing it.

'I could get to like this place,' I admitted.

'You're a woman of taste.' He put his arm about me again. 'How about a walk along the boardwalk?'

Which was what we did, not once mentioning his mother or how she'd drowned beneath it. We stopped talking too about brutal fathers and orphaned children. All we did was hold hands while we walked, looked at the sea and laughed at a fake palm tree on the beach. We stopped and took shots at sitting ducks until I won a panda bear. We watched a sailing boat, and wished we were on it.

It was the best part of the day. Even the clouds were moved to clear a space for a flagrant yellow sun as we headed for Stillwell Avenue and the subway back into the city.

By the time we got off the train in Manhattan there was no question of my not going back to Alex Borodin's place.

24

I offered to cook us something almost as soon as we were inside the door of his apartment. Not that I wanted to eat. I was just afraid that without something to do I might hurl myself at him.

'What have you got in your cupboards?' I asked. 'Or I could go downstairs, do a bit of shopping.'

He lived over an old-style greengrocer's. I'd had time for a quick look before he hurried me up narrow stairs. The street he lived on was hilly, full of small shops and convivial eating places.

'No cooking,' he picked up the phone, 'life's too short and there's nowhere to cook anyway. I only ever order in or eat out.'

He ordered Spanish, without asking me, wondrous-sounding things like fried king-fish and paprika-dusted chicken and octopus salad. The apartment was warm, and very small; one room on two levels, the kitchen and bathroom a couple of steps lower than the main living area. It was lined everywhere with books and had a corner devoted to music, DVDs and a telly. His bed was an unmade bundle of navy-blue linen on a futon against a wall. A life in a room.

'I wasn't expecting company,' he said, following my gaze to the futon.

I walked to the window, keeping my flushed face turned away from him, and looked across the city through the insect mesh. The mesh created an alien world of pin-prick dancing lights.

'It's forever changing,' I said, 'every corner you turn it's different.'

'New York can be whatever you want it to be,' he said. He put on a low-key piece of Bach organ music.

'Too funereal,' I said firmly and turned, desperate for some control of the situation. 'Do you have Keith Jarrett?'

'I've got Jarrett,' he said, smiling. The strains of 'Shenandoah' did a lot to calm me down.

'How long have you lived here?' I said as he produced and began to open a bottle of Chianti.

'Twenty-five years. The rent's stabilised and I like the area. There's a good mix of Ethiopians, Spanish and Chinese about and I get on with the landlord.' He poured the wine. 'Crackheads come visiting from time to time but I've got plenty of those in school so I can deal with them.' He handed me one of the glasses. Raising my glass to his I prayed, fervently, that I would remember the moves of the game we were playing.

'Sláinte,' I said.

'Here's to us,' Alex Borodin said.

Wearing just his shirt, which was dark green, he looked slighter than I'd imagined he would be. I hoped, without my jacket, that I didn't look fatter.

I looked through his bookshelves. There was a great deal on American literature, and education. He also had a couple of shelves devoted to embalming. I lifted down a slim volume on *Preserving the Body from Decay*.

'Is this a hobby?' I said. He'd been touched by evil, marked by a hideous crime; God alone knew what personal habits and hobbies he had.

'It was a job,' he said, 'once. I was a mortician's assistant for a few years, a morbid youth who thought forcing blood out of veins and embalming fluid into them would make a suitable job for life.' He grinned. 'I changed my mind. Decided to work on the living instead.'

'Glad to hear it,' I said.

He was standing very close, his shoulder touching mine. His face, if I turned, would be that close too. A kiss, I thought, a kiss would be nice. I turned.

The intercom on the wall shrilled.

We ate at the counter in his small kitchen and he talked about the public school he taught in; deprived and underfunded and where just 21 per cent of students met state standards in English and maths.

'By state measures it's a failing school,' he said. 'In the lives of the majority of my students it's a link to life.'

When he asked I told him about the Now and Again Café and about Emer, my mother and, very briefly, about Hector. He really was a good listener.

'It's Ritchie Walsh time,' I said, eventually, 'I want to know how you tracked him down and what's happening tomorrow.'

'It's time,' he agreed and poured us both some more wine. 'It'll be strange for me, meeting him tomorrow. The last time I saw him was when he came to visit me in the home where I was being cared for. That was about two years after my mother's death.'

'Was that a surprise?' I said. 'Him visiting like that?'

'Not at the time. I was fifteen and took it for granted. Ritchie Walsh was the sort of guy people took for granted. Maybe he came out of guilt, because of the row his son was the cause of the night my mother died. Things fall into place as life goes on. I suppose we just learn to read the picture better.'

There had been a row in the Walsh household too, the night Shirley Walsh died.

'What was the row about?' I said.

'It was Thanksgiving. The Walshes were eating with us and Ben Walsh brought some fish he'd caught that day off the boardwalk. My mother cooked him some of it but when my father arrived she gave it to him instead. A row developed. I don't really remember much more, except the Walshes leaving pretty quickly. My father laid into my mother then, I tried to stop him, managed to separate them and she ran from the apartment. That was it until her body was found in the early hours.'

'Shirley Walsh ran from the house after a row too,' I said.

'I know that, Fran, and so does anyone who ever listened to Ritchie Walsh tell his tale,' he said. 'Doesn't really prove anything.'

'It might mean something though,' I said.

'Let's talk about that after we meet Ritchie tomorrow,' he said.

'How does Sofia's picture of the past compare with yours?'

'As black does with white,' he said. 'She's convinced my father was wrongly convicted and my mother in the wrong place at the wrong time. It's worked for her. She's a success. My own, probably more realistic view of things has not, as you can see,' he looked wryly around the room, 'had a similar result.'

'What am I supposed to see?'

'A mean room in a mean neighbourhood,' he stood, smiling, 'inhabited by the fifty-three-year-old owner of a 'ninety-four Porsche,' the smile widened, 'who can't believe his luck at meeting someone like you.'

'I like the room,' I said.

'That's a beginning,' he said.

Together we stacked the dishes and cutlery in his tiny dishwasher. We put the condiments where they belonged, everything else in the fridge and what we hadn't eaten into the garbage. Alex then opened another bottle of wine, and poured two more glasses.

He put his arm across my shoulder, his fingers touching my neck, and we climbed the two steps back to where the books and music were, and the futon.

'I'm ashamed to tell you how few of your titles I've read,' I nodded to the book-shelves.

'It's never too late,' he said by my side, 'and never be ashamed.'

I turned to him. 'I'm not usually,' I said.

'That's good,' he said.

I started to say something but instead of listening he kissed me. It was a meeting of lips, slightly parted, slightly pressing, nothing more. I was beginning to respond, not one bit sure, yet, when he did a surprising thing. He put his hands inside my waistband and very slowly brushed my stomach with the back of his nails. And that was what did it.

Suddenly I was on fire and kissing him back, desperately and hungrily, the need in me triggered, a too-long stifled appetite bursting its dam. I couldn't believe, or deal with, how fast it was happening.

When I drew back he let me go at once. But the need was in him now too, I could see it. I lifted my glass and took a long, long drink.

'I shouldn't take advantage,' he said, grinning, stroking the side of my face. 'You're alone and in a strange town.'

'What a line,' I said, 'what a line.'

I put the glass of wine on a bookshelf. Part of me was thinking this was too precarious a perch for it as I touched his cheek, then leaned my face against his and stroked the back of his neck.

I don't know how he got rid of his glass but he did, and put both of his arms around me. When he held me against him I felt his erection.

It wasn't kind, and might not even have been wise, but I had to do it. I pulled back, again.

'I need to use the bathroom,' I said.

His bathroom was a blue shower-room, small but with a wall mirror in which I could talk to myself. I needed to rehearse how I was going to ask him to use a condom. This was New York, for God's sake, city of nine million people and thousands of ships meeting in the night. Like us, like me and Alex Borodin.

I splashed my face with cold water and cursed a world which changes but stays the same. As a young woman I worried about becoming pregnant. Now, when all should be safe and wonderful, there was bloody AIDS to worry about.

I washed my teeth and the parts of me untouched by a man for too long. I took off all my clothes so as to see, objectively, what Alex Borodin would see when he looked at me.

Objectively speaking, my breasts, in his mirror, were too large. But they always had been. They had once been better able to stand up for themselves though. My belly was the same relatively small pudding it had always been but my thighs were definitely heavier. My eyes, when I looked back up, had more crows' feet than they'd had the day before.

I wasn't falling apart, objectively speaking.

On the other hand, still objectively speaking, I was about to expose myself in a city where women exercised and dieted themselves to skin and bone and where the only F-word was fat. Alex Borodin might never have seen a body like mine. Maybe, if I lay on my back all the time, he wouldn't notice.

Fuck it, I thought, and fuck him. I would

play the condom issue by ear. Everything else too.

And with that warm thought I put perfume behind my ears and between my breasts, left my clothes where they were, wrapped myself in a large blue towel and went back to him.

He was smiling, waiting for me, unsurprised. Such a good-looking man. He'd changed the music. Nina Simone was singing 'I Want a Little Sugar in my Bowl.' He took me by the hand and led me to the still-unmade futon and lay me down beside him while he unbuttoned his shirt, slowly. I liked the way he hadn't felt the need, or maybe hadn't even remembered, to straighten the bedclothes he'd slept in the night before.

This wasn't the kind of man who wanted a wraith in his bed. But I'd known that all along anyway, in a non-objective and uncertain way.

He stretched beside me on the tangle of bedclothes and traced his finger across my face, down under my chin, to the base of my neck.

'Hi, there, Frances Shaw,' he said and kissed me, gently, while his finger went on down, down between my breasts and kept on going.

I closed my eyes. 'Talk to me,' I said.

'I didn't sleep last night,' he said. His finger was joined by others. They spread across my belly.

'Nor did I,' I said, 'sleep, I mean...' The fingers were parting my legs.

'I thought about your mouth when you laugh,' he was going in with his fingers, 'and about your eyes looking at me...'

I opened my eyes and met his as his fingers moved into that soft and so willing part of me.

'I thought about doing this with you,' he said.

With me ... not to me. A lifetime's wait for the right words, the right way of doing things.

'Is this all right?' he said.

'Oh, yes.'

'And this?'

'Yes ... please...'

He knew what he was doing, Alex Borodin, his fingers finding a spot never found before, not even by Hector. Everything I wanted he did. All thoughts of Hector, almost all thought, went. There was only now, and now...

'We should...' a single thought surfaced.

'It's all right,' he said.

He slipped the condom on easily. Then he slipped inside me, easily too and slowly. He moved that way too, at first, his eyes on my face until I arched my hips and caught his behind and pulled him deeper into me.

Then it was summertime, rivers of warm gold and sweet, sweet abandon until I came, just before he did, to the fullness, to that God-given sense of being flooded with light and life that I had all but forgotten.

He rolled away to pull me into his arms.

I cried, a little. A part of it was gratitude. He'd given me back something I'd been missing for such a very long time.

How could I tell this man how happy he'd made me? How glad I was to be in his bed? How much more complete I felt than I had for a very long time?

'I feel good,' I said.

He pulled away and looked at me. 'You look great,' he said.

Such beautiful brown eyes he had, such a welcoming mouth. How many women had he loved and left? I didn't care, because it didn't matter. This was for now, which was what we both wanted.

'Thank you,' I said.

We lay facing one another and talked for a while, sporadically, of nothing and of everything. He told how Sofia had married for money and an education. Twice. How he himself had stuck with what he knew; dysfunctional kids and their needs. I ran a finger along the curve of his kind mouth and wondered if he had ever, would ever, see that his mother's murder was not his fault, and nor was his father's execution. If he would ever grow to feel deserving of love, less wary of kindness.

'It wasn't your fault,' I said. 'You were only a child.'

'You're right,' he said, 'technically speaking. But I've done all the right things, therapy, work, writing it out. It's always been like I'm feeling my way along a path in the darkness, waiting to come into the light again. Tonight there's light,' he kissed me, lightly, 'plenty of it.'

Around midnight we got up and went out and he showed me his neighbourhood. We had brandies in a late place he liked. When we got back into bed we made love again, very slowly.

I lay beside him for a long time after he'd fallen asleep, wondering how I'd feel in the morning.

When the morning came we made love again.

25

November, 1963. Coney Island.

He has parked the car and is walking to a bar when he sees her in the line for the movie theatre. He almost walks on by.

Almost, but doesn't.

He stops and studies her pale profile, the black hair loose on her shoulders and thinks no, no I will not let this go. I will not let her go.

She is as surprised to see him as he had been to see her. Surprised and uneasy.

'I didn't know you cared for the movies,' she says when he slips into line beside her.

'Love 'em,' he says. 'Sergei not with you?'

'No,' she says, her face half turned from him, 'he's at home with Sasha and Sofia.'

'He let you out...' Bernard looks at her in disbelief, '...to go to a movie alone?'

This had to be a first, or a lie. Sergei Borodin only ever allowed his wife to go to a movie theatre with Bernard's father, Ritchie, or with one or both of their children.

'Does he know where you are?' Bernard asks.

Liliya gives a low moan and does a sort of small collapse, holding onto his arm and lowering her head and taking deep breaths. When she raises her head and turns to face him fully he sees that one of her eyes is beginning to close and that there is a cut on her forehead.

If she hadn't betrayed me, he thinks, if she hadn't taken his side against mine, I'd have killed him, before letting him do this to her. But she'd taken Borodin's side so she had it coming.

'I hope he doesn't know where I am,' she says. 'I pray to God he doesn't. I left. It was the only way to stop it...'

'The kids?'

'He won't touch them... Sasha is thirteen years old...'

She doesn't sound very sure. She has left her children to save her own skin, proving again that she is not the woman he thought she was. He is saddened but not surprised. Women build you up to let you down. It happens over and over.

The line has moved and they are close to the box-office.

'I'll come in with you if you like,' he says.

'I think I'd like to be on my own,' she says, voice muffled in her hair, which has fallen forward as she lowers her head again. He thinks she might be crying.

'I'll come with you,' he says, decisively.

He makes it sound as if he's doing her a favour, wants to look after her. He actually likes the idea of being in the darkened theatre with her, thinks it might just prove the time and place he's been waiting for.

They're showing *High Noon*. He knows she's seen it before because his father talks about it a lot. But for late-night showings beggars can't be choosers. He buys their tickets.

They sit in the middle of the theatre. He'd have preferred the back but can't do anything about it when she moves quickly ahead of him and chooses the seats. She doesn't talk to him when they sit down, just sits staring at the red velvet curtains where the screen will be.

'What's the story?' he says.

'He'll be looking for me by now,' she says, 'he's sure to be looking for me.'

'What's the story of the movie?' he says, patiently. His father has told him that she likes movies with good stories.

'It's about a marshal in the wild west who gets married to the woman he loves.'

'Not much of a story to that,' he says when she stops.

'Then an outlaw called Frank Miller comes to kill him...'

'That's more like a story,' he says, interrupting her.

Trumpets blare and the curtains begin to

open. He looks up at the midnight blue of the ceiling, at the golden stars twinkling there and thinks yes, this is the time and this is the place. He takes her hand in his.

He is shocked when she pulls hers away. He sits, brooding and angry, as the movie unfolds on the screen.

She is fixated by what is happening to the actor, has come here to live the movie and forget everything outside the theatre.

Even her children. She has abandoned them to satisfy this need.

Liliya has her hands clasped in her lap and the actor on the screen is staring through the glass of a broken window, when Ben again reaches for her. This time she allows his hand to cover her two, but without responding in any way. He realises then how truly unaware she is of him, sitting beside her.

He removes his hand. She doesn't even notice. He begins planning his next move, imagining how it will be.

26

May, 2003. New York.

It was lunchtime before we got out of New York city. It was a leisurely hour-and-a-half's drive after that before we reached the outskirts of Southampton, the Long Island town closest to Parson's Retreat.

I'd phoned the hotel to let them know I would be coming back to my room, just in case Nina or anyone else phoned. I wasn't yet ready to make contact with home myself so hadn't turned on the mobile.

The multi-laned highway which took us out along Long Island was white and wide, screaming with signs and directions. We cruised at a speed and with an ease I'd never experienced before, talked as if we'd known each other a lifetime. It felt unreal, as if the me sitting in the passenger seat of a '94 Porsche was being played by an actress, as if the passing miles, and a countryside which had survived Native Americans, Puritans and pirates, was the backdrop to some film.

Hollywood's fault, the result of too many hours in too many cinemas watching too many American movies.

I asked Alex what his mother's favourite film had been.

'She talked a lot about *High Noon*,' he said, 'the strong, silent male and doomed love, I suppose.' His tone was dry. 'I remember her singing "Do Not Forsake Me Oh My Darlin" when my father wasn't about.'

'Poor Liliya,' I said.

'She'd been to *High Noon* the night she ... was murdered,' he said. 'It played a lot during those years. Makes you wonder what she was thinking about as she died.'

'Yes,' I said, 'it does.'

We were a lot closer to Southampton when he said, 'There are a couple of things you should know before we meet Ritchie. One is that he's not always compos mentis, apparently. He's got a form of dementia which gives him good days and bad days. Let's hope today's a good one.'

'And the second thing?' I said.

'I took the liberty of telling the woman I spoke to that you were a niece of Ritchie's over from Ireland. I said you had a special wish to meet your old uncle before he died.'

'Not very original of you,' I said, 'although I'd probably have said the same thing myself. And who are you supposed to be?'

'I didn't go into that,' he said. 'As far as they're concerned I'm your driver for the day.'

'Aha. And what happens if Ritchie's

having a good day and remembers you and denounces me? He doesn't have a niece in Ireland, not one that I know of anyway. What if he turns nasty?'

'Then we'll deal with that too,' Alex said.

Driving through South Main Street in Southampton he pointed out the oldest frame house in New York State and other notable landmarks. It was all very chic and tasty, a cross between a French seaside village and the Puritan place it had probably once been.

'A retirement home in an area like this costs money,' I said. 'I wonder who pays for Ritchie's keep?'

'I wondered that myself. Could be his sons and nieces pay it between them.'

'Perhaps.'

The Parson's Retreat, when we came to it, was itself something of a landmark building; a white house at the end of a tree-lined avenue with a small lake in front. The car park was a distance from the house and by the time we came to ring the doorbell we'd walked away any stiffness from the journey.

The woman who opened the door was close to six feet tall and quite lovely. She wore white and her golden hair was caught in a golden net under a neat, boat-shaped hat. She had almond-shaped eyes of an aqua-marine colour and magnificently pink pouting lips. She wasn't a lot younger than me.

She focused the aqua-marines on Alex. 'Hello there,' she said, 'what can I do for you?'

'I'm Alex Borodin,' he smiled, 'we're here to visit Richard Walsh.' He stepped past her into the hall. 'I called two days ago.

'Ah, yes. We've been expecting you,' she said, 'you've brought the Irish niece, I see.' She didn't look at me. 'Our guests don't often have mid-week visitors so you *will* be discreet? And quiet as possible?' Her accent was quintessential southern states.

'We'll do whatever you say.' Alex went on smiling, oozing a deliberate charm I hadn't seen him use before. It worked too. The woman took him by the arm as she led us to a reception desk, a kidney-shaped monstrosity with inlaid mirrored panels.

'I am Nurse Clark,' she produced a silver pen which she whirled while she spoke, 'and I must first ask you to sign our visitors' book. Then you will follow me.' Alex signed and I looked around. Chintz, in a word, described The Parson's Retreat style. The curtains on the several windows were chintz, the armchairs scattered around the high, wide hallway were chintz covered and the carpeting on the wide stairs had a cabbage-rose design. The place smelled of hyacinth and had an echoing silence.

The views of the lawned garden and lake through the long windows were spectacular and completely uninterrupted by either animal or man. I wondered where the residents of The Parson's Retreat took their airings and walks.

'Nice place,' Alex said as he signed.

'We aim to please,' Nurse Clark said. 'Our guests deserve the best.' She looked at me then, and nodded in the direction of the visitors' book. 'Perhaps you would sign too?' she said.

I signed. She glanced briefly at our names and turned briskly. 'Follow me,' she said.

We followed her up the cabbage-rose stairs and along a cabbage-rose landing to a door at the end. She knocked and turned to Alex.

'You'll have been told that Mr Walsh is not always with us, intellectually speaking?' she said. Alex nodded and she went on. 'Richard chooses to whom and when he will speak and that is his prerogative. One of the few he can exercise, at this point in his life. Some days he talks a great deal, others he chooses to be silent. He is physically frail.' She looked from one to the other of us, frowning. 'He could leave us any day. He was told about your visit but did not seem inclined to respond. I myself have found that he speaks only when he has something he wishes to say.'

She looked at me without much interest. 'Visits from his family are rare. We must hope that he finds himself able to appreciate this occasion. Someone from the old country...' she shrugged, '...is a treat indeed. He's never had a visitor from Ireland before.'

'His sons don't come to see him?' I said. 'Nor his nieces?'

'There is no need for them to do so.' Nurse Clark gave the door a gentle tap and put a hand on its rose-embossed porcelain knob. 'Our guests have everything they could wish for here in The Parson's Retreat,' she turned the knob, 'that is why their families bring them to us. We undertake to give them the peace and contentment they deserve coming to the end of their days.'

The Parson's Retreat, in other words, absolved those who could afford it of all responsibility for ageing, in-the-way, relatives.

Nurse Clark opened the door and we followed her into a bright, primrose-coloured room with gold curtains and a violently green carpet. A neatly made bed had a white bedspread.

Ritchie Walsh, sitting by the window with a rug about his knees, didn't look like a man who cared much about his room's decor, much less that its colours were those of his country's flag. He was wasted to a wraith and his head was sunk on his chest. He appeared to be asleep.

'Hi there, Richard,' Nurse Clark sat on a footstool and took one of his hands, 'how're you feeling today?' She rubbed the hand between hers and spoke to him with gentle affection. 'Your visitors are here, Richard, your niece from Ireland and her friend. I'll leave the door open when I go. That way you can call me if you want anything. I won't be far away. I won't even go downstairs. Is this all right with you, Richard?'

She was very good with him, watching his face closely as she spoke, gently massaging his hand between hers all the while. Nurse Clark was a woman whose heart was in her job. Richard Walsh didn't give any response that I could see but she appeared reassured when she patted his hand and stood. When she spoke to myself and Alex she was again brisk and businesslike.

'He's actually very well today. But be considerate with him. It will upset him if you fuss for memories, anything like that.' She put a hand on Ritchie's shoulder. 'Richard perfectly understands everything you say to him. But please remember that whether or not he decides to respond is entirely his choice.'

As promised, she left the door open when she left the room.

I sat on the footstool, facing Ritchie Walsh. Alex pulled up an armchair and sat with his back to the window, blocking the spectacular view – but also ensuring that Ritchie couldn't see his face against the light.

Ritchie Walsh, in old age, had grown to

look like his sister Concepta. The hair which had looked so black in the newspaper pictures was a wispy white around a face shrivelled to become as bird-like as hers. His skin was eaten into by huge age and sun-marks and his eyes were half closed. It was hard to tell what, if anything, he was looking at.

'My name is Frances Shaw,' I said, slowly and clearly, 'Thaddeus Shaw is my father-in-law. He sends his regards.'

Lie number one had little effect. Ritchie Walsh gave no sign he'd heard, or was even listening. I put my hand over his veiny, skin-and-bone one where it lay on the rug about his knees.

'I met Concepta last week,' I said, 'she's keeping well. She said she hadn't heard from you in a long time and would like a word from you, if I managed to see you.'

Lie number two brought as little response as the first. I lifted his other wafer-like hand and held both of them together in mine in the way the nurse had done.

'There's been another murder in Dun Laoghaire, Ritchie,' I spoke without looking at him, keeping my eyes on his hands, 'another young woman. She was nineteen and her name was Alannah Casey. She had a small daughter and was pregnant with another baby. She was stripped naked and her body left on the morgue steps.' I looked up then, into Ritchie Walsh's open, colour-less eyes. 'I found her, Ritchie,' I said. 'Please help me.'

He dropped his eyes, so quickly I won-dered if I'd imagined meeting them at all. I held onto his hands and he made no attempt to pull them away. Maybe he didn't feel them being held.

Alex put a hand on my shoulder. 'Give him time,' he said, quietly. 'He's got to go a long way back to find you. Could be he's blanked out a lot of what happened. Maybe everything.'

'I don't think he has,' I said.

I watched Ritchie Walsh's face. Devoured it might be, by time and wear, but there was something happening on those threadbare features. An ancient muscle trembled, moisture gathered at the side of an eye, the mouth opened, then closed again. Then opened again.

'Who did you say you were?' His voice was like paper crumpling.

'I'm Frances Shaw. I married Thaddeus's son, Hector.'

'Did you, indeed.' It was a statement, with wonder in it.

His accent was unbridled Irish still and his breathing difficult. He gathered himself to speak again and I waited. When I heard Alex move behind me I shook my head without turning and he went quiet.

'You're here because Thaddeus is in trouble again, is that it?' Ritchie Walsh said. 'He drowned a girl, is that it?' His eyes were spilling what might have been tears. They never left mine.

'No,' I said. 'No, that's not it. I'm here because a girl was strangled and left on the morgue steps, the way Shirley was. We don't know who did it.'

'It's none of my business,' he said. 'I didn't drown her.'

'I know that, Ritchie,' I said. 'I was hoping you could remember something about Shirley's death, and Liliya Borodin's, that might be a help in finding who killed Alannah Casey.'

'I didn't drown Shirley either.' His hands moved in mine. I loosened my grip and let them go. He dropped his eyes and plucked fretfully at the rug. 'Shirley was a nice woman to look at but mad as a hatter.' He spoke in short gasps. 'You had to watch her all the time, make sure she was behaving herself. She was the author of her own misfortune.'

'Who drowned her, Ritchie?' I said.

'She drowned herself,' Ritchie said. 'Whoever drowned her was driven to it. He'd never have done it if she wasn't the way she was...' he gave a thin sigh. '...She was a mad bitch, when all's said and done.'

'You wrote to Thaddeus after Liliya Borodin was drowned on Coney Island,' I said.

'Do you know who drowned Liliya?'

'Another mad bitch.'

I held my breath but couldn't hear a sound from behind me. 'I thought you liked Liliya,' I said.

'She was a beautiful creature. I never had much luck with women. My wife was a harridan. She was born a harridan and for all I know she died one. I often think about her. She didn't treat the boys good. She treated them bad. He couldn't have turned out any other way.'

'Who, Ritchie?' Alex was on his hunkers beside me, voice gently coaxing. 'Who couldn't have turned out any other way?'

Ritchie didn't answer and I thought we'd lost him. I put my head in my hands and gave a low moan. 'Oh, Jesus God, Alex, why did you have to...' I began.

Ritchie's voice interrupted me. 'Life's all down to the way we treat our children. I learned that much in America. It wasn't his fault. It's always the mother's fault. I learned that too. My own mother was a hard woman. But she wasn't a harridan and she wasn't cruel. No. She was never cruel. And she stayed with us.'

Alex would have said something again but I put a hand on his knee.

'You wrote about him to Thaddeus, didn't you, Ritchie? Thaddeus shared your burden, didn't he?'

'I've carried a terrible burden all these years,' Ritchie said. 'A burden no man should have to carry. Inhuman, it was, but I carried it. As he knew I would. He always knew I wouldn't betray him. And I didn't.'

'Who knew?' Alex asked.

'My brother didn't drown his wife,' Ritchie said. 'Our mother was hard but she wasn't cruel. She didn't put it into Jimmy to go drowning women.'

He fell silent again. So did we, waiting. Alex, on his hunkers still, must have been aching to move but didn't, not even when Ritchie's silence stretched on, and on. I was the one who broke it.

'He's done it again,' I said, 'he's drowned another young woman, Ritchie. Who is the person you've kept silent about? What was too horrible to even think about?'

'Did Thaddeus send you to me?' Ritchie's voice was stronger than it had been. 'Is that why you're here? What lies has he been telling now?'

'Thaddeus didn't send me, Ritchie. But he has been talking about you. So has Concepta.'

'Tell them I'm dead. I might as well be anyway. I'm not living, that's for sure.'

Alex got to his feet. I was afraid he might be reaching the end of his patience but he pulled over the armchair and sat, comfortably and thoughtfully, facing Ritchie.

'You're right, Mr Walsh,' he said, his voice sympathetic, 'in the sense that you might as well be dead.'

Ritchie had become very still. He'd long stopped plucking the rug but now his eyes were focused too, on Alex.

Alex smiled at him. 'I'm Alexander Borodin, Mr Walsh,' he said, 'do you remember me?' His tone was even and mercilessly insistent. 'You used have dinner in our apartment. My dead mother used to cook for you. She used to go to the movies with you too, sometimes. You liked to talk with my sister, Sofia.' He leaned forward. 'You remember, Mr Walsh, I know you do. You remember how my mother was drowned and how my father died in the chair for her murder. I know you remember, Mr Walsh.'

Ritchie Walsh went on looking at him, silently. Alex allowed him three or four minutes of silence, then spoke to him again. His tone was harsher. 'You might as well be dead, Mr Walsh, because if you know who really murdered my mother and your brother's wife then your life is a betrayal of both the living and the dead. My mother knew who took her life. Your brother's wife knew. But they're dead and can't tell us. You can.'

Ritchie made a low sound, a sort of moan, and was silent again.

'All we want to know,' Alex said, 'is if the

right men, my father and your brother, died for their deaths. Set things right, Mr Walsh, while you still can.'

Ritchie moved. He put his hands on the side of the chair and thrust his head forward. 'Talk to Thaddeus,' he said, 'Thaddeus will know what to tell you.'

'Thaddeus is frightened,' I said, and wondered why this hadn't been so clear to me before. 'He's drinking again, Ritchie. Drowning himself in whiskey.'

'Blood of his blood,' Ritchie said, 'and bone of his bone. The image of him in every way as she grew. Every way. That's how I came to know, for certain sure.'

The back of my neck prickled. An involuntary reaction to what I was afraid of knowing. 'You mean Thaddeus's daughter?' I said. 'You mean your niece?'

'Melanie. We called her Mel. She was plain but grew pretty. Bone of his bone with a sharp tongue on her. And he never saw her. Never came after her. He couldn't have anything but bad luck, letting a child go from him like that.'

'Where is she now?' I said.

'Gone,' Ritchie Walsh said, 'gone this long time. I never told her. That was another thing to keep silent and inside of me. Not natural.'

'But Thaddeus knew?' I asked.

Ritchie didn't answer. Alex sat in his chair

without a word. In the extreme quiet of the room a clock ticked. A door closed with a soft click somewhere nearby. Alex asked the question, at last.

'Did one of your boys drown your brother's wife, Ritchie? Is that your burden?' He made it sound like an everyday query about the weather.

'He had a mean streak in him, always. He was the kind would throw water on a drowning man. A monstrous child. His mother was the same. He was a lonely, monstrous child and she left him.'

'He had you,' I said, when he stopped and to prevent another silence developing. 'He had you,' I said again.

But Concepta Walsh's phrase had crept into the room. Shadows will fall, was what she'd said about the damage done by a vile and uncaring mother. Shadows will fall...

'Thaddeus knew my fear. He didn't disagree with me. He'd seen the lad with his eyes on Shirley. He knew in his heart that Jimmy couldn't have done it. He didn't want the guards poking around too much. He didn't want his secret to be out.'

Ritchie Walsh's body shook and his lips pulled back from his teeth. He was weeping. I touched his hands on the rug. When he didn't pull away I lifted and held them between my own, again. He wept for a good while, quietly for the most part, weak tears wandering around the broken map of his face. Between his tears he said, 'She was the better of the two of them and he never saw her.'

'Which of your sons was the lonely one, Ritchie?' I asked.

'That was Bernard,' Ritchie said, 'Bernard never was right. When he came home to me that night I knew by him that he'd changed, crossed a bridge and couldn't go back. He stood full square in the kitchen and told me to make food for him. I was afraid not to. I didn't know then his aunt was dead but I knew he had changed. I was never sure enough about what had happened. I let my brother take the blame for want of being sure, for fear of being wrong. And unnatural.'

'He was sixteen,' I said, softly.

'Only a few months past his sixteenth birthday,' Ritchie agreed.

'But you knew when he drowned Liliya Borodin, didn't you?' Alex said. I couldn't look at him.

'There was no doubt in my mind but that he'd drowned the Russian woman. I swore to the police that Bernard and myself had put in the night playing cards. He was gone till three in the morning and he was wet through with sea water when he came in. Her husband was a bad case, a worse case than my son ever was.'

'So you said nothing?'

'The world was better off without the husband. She was a grand woman in many ways but she was dead and there was no bringing her back. The husband was an evil in the land and better off dead.'

'You gave us a murderer for a father,' Alex said, 'me and Sofia.'

Ritchie nodded. 'I did that too,' he said.

'Your son would be sixty-six years old now,' I said. 'Where is he, Ritchie?'

'Living a lie,' Ritchie said, 'like he always did.'

'In Ireland? In Dun Laoghaire?'

'This long while now. He took another man's name and went back.'

'Why?' My blood was cold in my veins. The only other time I'd felt so icy inside was on the morning I'd found Alannah Casey's body. 'Why did he go back to Ireland?'

'He said the place had changed and that now it suited him.'

'Is he living in Dun Laoghaire?'

'He might well be.' Ritchie's gaze drifted to the window. 'It was hard for a man alone with first two and then the four youngsters to look after.' His voice had become low and hard to hear. 'I tried to control them. I tried to show them right from wrong. I didn't do a lot of good in the end. I worried, that was all I did, I worried.' His hands became agitated and I stroked them. 'Then I took to the drink and was as bad or worse than

Thaddeus Shaw ever was. They had no regard for me at all then and they were right. They went away, one by one, and left me to my solace.'

'Who pays to keep you here?' Alex asked the question gently.

'He does.' Ritchie took a breath that almost caved in his body. 'And now ye have it all. I've no more to say.'

Ritchie Walsh's head sank down and his eyes closed.

'What name does he use now, Ritchie? What does he call himself?' I was too urgent. He gave no indication he'd heard me. I would have shaken him if Alex hadn't taken hold of me.

'Let it go, Fran,' he said, softly, 'he won't talk any more now. He's tired and he's bought himself some peace. To give us the name would be a final betrayal. He won't go that far.'

He was right, I knew he was.

We stood side by side, thinking our thoughts about a man whose lifetime of silence had allowed two women be drowned when at least one of them might have been saved, and two men to die wrongly convicted.

Whose silence had denied Melanie Walsh any knowledge of her father and allowed Thaddeus to live a lie.

And, very likely, been the cause of Alannah Casey's death too.

27

I didn't spend another night with Alex Borodin. We drove from Southampton to the Jameson Hotel and from there to JFK Airport where I changed my ticket to a stand-by for the next flight for Dublin. There was a three-hour wait. The flight would take six hours. Give or take time gained and lost to tail winds and traffic it would be eleven to twelve hours before I got home.

Alex and I agreed, following the messages on my mobile when I finally turned it on, that this was the best, if not only, course of action open to me.

Hopefully I would get home before Bernard Walsh, or whatever name he was now using, discovered I'd met with and talked to his father.

In time to stop Thaddeus doing anything which would warn him off, have him running for cover and another identity, give him further years of freedom to pursue his murderous way.

Reality had kicked in somewhere on the highway coming back to New York from Southampton but, before that, we'd had a meal in Southampton. Alex had chosen the food, fish and expensive and mostly uneaten for my part. The restaurant was stiff with white linen and dark wood and we'd talked through all that Ritchie Walsh had said, and not said, trying to make sense of it, to put it in some sort of perspective. The truth, if Ritchie had been telling the truth, was hard for Alex to digest. It would take him a while to accept, finally, that his father had not murdered his mother. For my own part there was the reality of Melanie Walsh to get used to, the fact that somewhere in the world there was a fifty-six-year-old woman who was Thaddeus's daughter, Hector's half-sister and an aunt to Emer.

'My guess is he was never sure whether she was his or not,' I said, 'Shirley seems to have put it about quite a lot...' I nudged my grilled sturgeon to the side of the plate and attempted the vegetable mignonette. 'Also, he was drinking...' I knew I was making excuses for my beloved, idiotic Thaddeus. 'He was probably afraid of knowing the truth anyway, and of the police knowing the truth. He'd have come under suspicion and he had a six-month-old son and new marriage to think about...' I trailed off. None of it excused what he'd done.

The mignonette was more than I could handle too. The wine, a Chablis, was good. I drank quickly.

'Ritchie Walsh kept quiet about it too, as

she grew and he realised the truth, and for the same reason,' Alex said. 'He wanted the past good and dead, no more looking back, no more questions.'

'But of course it doesn't die at all,' I said.

Alex refilled my glass. He was driving and had barely touched his own. 'It sure explains his predicament when this recent young woman turned up dead on the morgue steps. Long-ago guilt, long-ago nightmares. As good a reason as any to hit the bottle again.'

'He could have said something,' I said. 'He could have told me, or Hector.'

'Told you what? That he might have a daughter alive somewhere? That he had suspicions that Bernard Walsh, at sixteen years old, might have drowned his aunt Shirley? He couldn't tell you, Fran, he was afraid of losing your regard, his grand-daughter's regard, all the respect he'd built over the non-drinking years. Your ex would have certainly condemned him, been pretty unforgiving from the sound of him.' He put a hand over mine. 'Your Thaddeus's life collapsed when that girl was murdered.'

'God only knows what he's doing now,' I said, 'God only knows.'

That was when I lost my nerve and turned on my phone and listened to my messages. They were many and they were angry.

The first, made the day before, was from Nina who said Derek Moran had phoned.

He wanted to talk to me and he wanted us on site a week earlier than planned. She reminded me that she hated to lie, said it wasn't good anyway to start in business with a lie. She'd told Derek Moran where I was.

The next two were from Emer. She'd called to the house and found Nina feeding the dog. She'd wondered about this, queried why Lucifer wasn't in the country with me so Nina had told her where I was. She wondered if I'd completely lost it. In the second message she said she'd spoken to Hector. He'd said he hoped I was enjoying New York. He did not recommend Coney Island as a place to visit.

The fourth was from Hector himself. He hoped I was enjoying New York, did not recommend a visit to Coney Island (again) and said the investigation had taken my concerns on board. This meant, I presumed, that they'd discovered something for themselves about 1953 and were pursuing it. Good news, maybe.

The last three almost incoherent messages were from Thaddeus. He warned me 'not to try finding Ritchie Walsh' but, if I did, not to talk to him. 'He'll have nothing but ill to talk about that will bode no good for anyone,' he warned. 'He'll open up a can of worms that'll do terrible harm.'

He continued this theme in the second message. In the third he said he 'had things in hand', that he 'knew what had to be done' that the problem, as he'd feared, was in Dun Laoghaire. All that was required was for him, Thaddeus, to do what had to be done.

'Sounds as if he knows, or thinks he does, what identity Bernard Walsh has taken on,' I said. I'd given Alex the gist of the messages as I listened to them. Now I put the phone on the table where I could hear it if it rang again. 'I have to presume Thaddeus has spoken to Hector by this stage,' I said.

When a waiter arrived with a dessert menu I'd a sudden and terrible craving for the sweet and wholesome reassurance of carbohydrate. I was looking at it when a fearful thought struck me like a blow to the head.

'Oh, God!' I wailed. 'If Bernard Walsh realises what Thaddeus is up to he may try to get at Emer...'

'He won't do that.' Alex was curt. 'He's not going to expose himself. If he does anything at all he'll run. Call your ex now. Better to do something than become hysterical.'

His cold, rational slap of common sense was what I needed. It also showed me another side of him; the severed survivor who knew how to keep a distance.

Hector answered on the first ring. It was after midnight in Ireland, the time of night he was at his liveliest.

'Nice to hear from you,' he said.

'Has Thaddeus been talking to you?' I said.

'If you could call it that, yes.'

'Has he told you about Bernard Walsh?'

'That name hasn't come up, no,' Hector said.

'I think you should bring it up with him, Hector. I've spoken with Ritchie Walsh. Bernard is his son. He says he's in Dun Laoghaire. He says his son murdered Shirley Walsh.'

'Ritchie Walsh is in his eighties, Fran,' Hector was using his reasonable tones.

'Just talk to Thaddeus, Hector, see if you can get any sense out of him. Please, Hector. Talk to him now, or in the morning, early. Tell him what I told you. Tell him I said to tell you everything. Tell him it's going to be all right. That's it's all over now.'

'Are you all right?' Hector sounded alarmed.

'I'm fine. Keep an eye on Emer. And on Thaddeus. The man who killed Alannah Casey is in his sixties, Hector, and Thaddeus may know who he is.'

'I'll talk to Thaddeus,' Hector said, slowly. 'Soon as I can.'

'Do that, Hector, please.'

We were in the car and on the highway before we spoke about the consequences of Ritchie Walsh's revelations for Alex and Sofia, how knowing who had murdered their mother changed history for both of them.

'Sofia is vindicated,' he said. He had a relaxed driving style and smiled at me as he spoke. But his knuckles were white on the wheel. 'Our father the saint will become even more hallowed. Sofia herself will be released from the stigma of having a convicted murderer for a father. It'll do wonders for her socially.' His tone was light, bantering.

'I can imagine,' I said. 'What about you? How're you going to deal with it?'

He shrugged. 'Way I deal with everything, I suppose. Take a look at it, dissect it a bit, talk about it a bit then put it somewhere in my head where I can live with it.'

'Will it be so very difficult to accept him as victim?' I said.

He shrugged again. His shrugs were very eloquent; they said he wasn't going there and I shouldn't either.

'It will all have to be proven,' he said, 'and I'd bet everything I own, down to this beauty,' he took a hand from the wheel and thumped the dashboard, hard. Then he thumped it again, for good measure. He seemed to have forgotten what he was going so say so I prompted him.

'What's the bet?'

'I'm betting Richard Walsh won't ever open his mouth again. He relieved himself of his burden to us and that's it, as far as he's concerned. He's not going to give evidence or convict his son in a court of law, anywhere.'

'He may not have to,' I said, hopefully. 'If Bernard Walsh is caught, and he will be, then there won't be any way he can deny responsibility for the ... earlier murders. For drowning your mother and Shirley Walsh.'

I stopped then, feeling strangely clammy, a cold sweat breaking out on my palms and forehead. I closed my eyes and a wave of nausea came, and thankfully went. Bernard Walsh *had* to be caught.

'It's all down to Thaddeus,' I said, 'he's the only one can finger him and recognise him. And he will, I know he will.'

'What will he do, Fran? Finger him or recognise him?'

'Both.' I was firm.

'Bernard Walsh has been walking around Dun Laoghaire for a while now and he hasn't recognised him,' he pointed out.

'He wasn't looking for him.'

'Right. So now he recognises him. But all he has by way of proof are feelings and circumstantial evidence. Ritchie didn't even come up with tangible evidence which could be used in a court of law.'

'The mud on his clothes, the late hour he came home the night Shirley was drowned...'

'The clothes are long gone and everything

319

else depends on Ritchie Walsh hanging his son, so to speak. It's not going to be easy.'

I had a sudden, violent hatred of his rationality. 'It's not going to be impossible either...' I heard my raised voice and stopped.

'Take it easy,' Alex said and lifted one of my hands and held it, tight, for a minute. The road sped by, the traffic seeming to come and go around us like shoals of fish, sometimes crowding in, sometimes drifting by. We drove for a long time in silence, both of us with too much to think about. My own thinking was fairly circular and kept coming back to one thing.

'I'll have to go home straight away,' I said. It was dark by then and the city coming up ahead. 'Tonight. I'll have to change my flight.'

'Yes,' Alex said, gently, 'I think you do have to do that.'

This time I was the one reached out, to touch the side of his face with my hand. In the light of an oncoming car I saw his wry grin. There was something resigned about it.

New York, all lit up and radiant, mono-polised the skyline more and more as we came closer. The wonder of it, the sheer, powerful wonder, hit me.

'It's a right old mickey dazzler,' I said and he laughed; a wonderful, transforming sound I hadn't heard from him before. We hadn't laughed half enough together, Alex Borodin and I. Maybe we would, some other time. Maybe.

He held me for a moment in the hotel bedroom, after I'd finished packing, and kissed me very gently. Then he lifted my bag and opened the door and we went downstairs together in the dare-devil of a lift.

At the airport I changed my flight for one going at midnight, then texted Emer and Hector to give them my flight number and time of arrival. When everything was done, and the three-hour wait stretched ahead, I told Alex I didn't want him to wait with me. I couldn't bear it, I said.

He couldn't either, obviously, because he didn't take much persuading. He put his hands on my shoulders and kissed me on the forehead.

'We'll meet again,' he smiled.

I resisted an easy 'don't know where don't know when' and smiled instead and said, 'Yes, yes we will. Soon.'

I watched him go. He might have looked back; a sudden swarm of people came between us and swallowed him up and it was hard to tell.

I sat to wait and pondered the possibles. Impossible to think of anything else. Was it possible I'd met Bernard Walsh without knowing it was him? He'd gone back as another man, his father had said. He would also have been upwards of forty years older. No one had seen him over the years, who would recognise him?

Almost seventeen per cent of the population had left Ireland between 1946 and 1961, huge numbers of them from Dun Laoghaire. Huge numbers returned in the early 1990s, drawn by the full-belly roars of the Celtic Tiger. John Rutledge was an example of someone had come back, for God's sake. He'd gone in the 1950s. Ted Cullen had been away too and so had Derek Moran, making his money on the lump. Gerry Fuller had also worked abroad, according to Hector. There were hundreds like them, all the right age too. Who was to say which one of them was Bernard Walsh, using a name and identity he knew and could respond to? Only Thaddeus would have recognised an imposter, surely? Thing was, would he have said anything if he had?

How many knew I'd been in New York and met with Richard Walsh?

It was three a.m. in Ireland when Alex left me. It was six a.m. in Ireland by the time I boarded the plane taking me home. I stopped myself making a last phone call by telling myself my loved ones were safe, in their beds and asleep.

A call wouldn't have changed anything, anyway. Wouldn't have prevented anything that happened happening.

It was just after midday when the flight touched down at Dublin Airport. The land was a washed, clean emerald and the sea a shining blue as we came in over Lambay and Howth and the bay, all of them lazily inviting. Summer had arrived in my absence.

It was Wednesday and I'd been away five days. It felt like a lifetime.

I knew, as I came through Customs and out into the arrival hall and saw Emer standing waiting that more than the weather had changed in my absence. Something terrible was wrong. She had her hair caught back and she was white faced and shaking with the effort to be calm.

'What is it?' I took her hands in mine and my first thought, God forgive me, was a penetrating gratitude that she was okay. Whatever had happened it hadn't happened to her, not to my beautiful daughter.

'Thaddeus is dead,' she said. 'Hector found him this morning, in the apartment.'

'What happened?'

'Oh, God, Fran, you don't want to know...' She began to shake in earnest and I caught and held her.

'I have to know,' I said, 'tell me.'

'His head. It was ... bashed in,' Emer said.

28

November, 1963. Coney Island.

He knows the film is over when there is a general shuffle around him and the audience begins to rise. The lights go up. Liliya stands and begins pulling on her gloves.

'It's perfect. It doesn't matter how often I see it, it's still perfect. Did you like it?'

'Yes,' he lies.

Outside the theatre the night is clear and starry. The crowd disperses quickly and leaves them alone on the sidewalk.

'I'd like you to see where I caught the fish you cooked tonight,' he says. He smiles at her.

'You are a strange young man,' she looks up at him, 'you should have a girlfriend to show such special places to.' She sees something in his face and places a hand on his arm. 'I'm sorry, that was insensitive. You may be suffering from a broken heart for all I know. Or maybe you're like Gary Cooper, a one-woman man waiting for your true love.' She turns her collar up around her face. 'I would very much like to see where you fish. But we will have to be quick. I must go home.'

Though it is colder on the boardwalk she will not allow him to hold her close as they go along. It doesn't matter. He is resigned now, knows what has to be done and what kind of woman she is.

He takes her to where he caught the fish, a sheltered niche to the back of a shooting gallery. She pretends to be impressed, says how clever of him to find his own place. 'The water is so dark,' she looks out, across the sea's shining swell, 'I have always been afraid of great oceans of water. I was brought up where there was no sea, only mountains and woods. I have got used to this and I like the beach but sometimes I think I would like to go with my children away from here. There is so much water.'

She turns to him. Her bruised eye is quite closed now and the side of her face swollen. When she smiles it is a lopsided thing, jeering and childish.

'Why are you looking at me like that, Bernard?' she says.

He doesn't trust himself to speak so just does what he has to do.

She is a small woman and has no strength in her at all. She tries, feebly, to stop his hands when they go about her neck, under the collar of her coat. Her good eye stares at him, black and disbelieving.

He holds her away from him, both of his

hands around her neck, tight and tighter with her hands trying to pull his away all the time. Lucky for him she's wearing gloves. She might have scratched and marked him otherwise.

He squeezes until he hears a sort of cracking sound and her neck loses its tautness. So does she, becoming limp and sagging in his hands.

So far so good. All he has to do now is to make sure, for her children's sake, that she gets a proper funeral. Then they will always know where she is. It won't be like it was for him, never knowing where his mother was, even whether she was, or is, alive or dead.

He didn't understand, the first time, that what he did to Shirley was for the girls. He knows now. He is sure of the moral need to do away with women who are unfit to be mothers.

He knows that Liliya Borodin is dead when he shoulders her body and takes her down and under the boardwalk, to the place where lovers meet on warm nights. He puts her into the water, cleansing her as Shirley was cleansed.

Because she is small and he knows Coney's alleyways so well, it is not difficult to carry her back to the car unseen. Because it is a cold, late night in November it is not difficult to find a quiet place to park the car and strip her of her wet clothes.

326

The area around is desolate of life and movement too when he lays Liliya Borodin's body on the steps of the morgue.

Sergei Borodin will be blamed. He is known for beating his wife and the cops have been after him for years about his racketeering. He, Ben Walsh, will be a distraught witness, a young man who caught fish and brought them to the Borodin Thanksgiving supper.

He goes home and to bed in the room where his father lies sleeping until the cops arrive in the early morning. They want to know about the dinner-table argument the night before. They have already arrested Sergei Borodin for his wife's murder.

29

May, 2003. Dun Laoghaire.

He sits in the barber's chair, asking the female barber to be careful, joking that a man his age doesn't need to lose any more hair than is necessary.

'You've got a great head of hair still,' the girl enters into the spirit of the thing, telling him that he's unlikely to go bald, that, 'it's all down to family genes in the end of the day. Is your father bald, or any of your uncles?'

'My father's got all of his hair,' Bernard smiles at her, 'the only uncle I had died young so we'll never know about him, will we?'

'I suppose not,' the barber agrees, un-easily.

She finds his smile and the way he stares at her in the mirror unsettling. He's not a regular and she's alone in the shop so she drops the banter and gets down to business, wanting him out of there as quickly as possible. She asks him how he'd like his hair cut and drapes a towel around his shoulders. He's the last customer of the day and she's put him into the chair closest to the window, only feet away from those passing on the footpath outside. She's not a nervous person but it's better to be safe than sorry. Far better.

'As I was trying to explain,' Bernard senses her nervousness and is curt, 'I don't want any unnecessary cutting. Just a trim. Your sign says old-style barbering and that's what I want.'

'It's your hair and you're paying.' The barber doesn't want an argument and her tone is light. She smiles at him in the mirror as she begins what she's decided will be a tidy-up job, nothing more. 'Great the way the weather's changed, isn't it?' she says, chatty in the way she is with all her customers. 'Looks like we're going to have a summer after all.'

'It's taken a change for the better all right,' Ben says, making an effort to be affable. He likes to fit in, when possible.

The barber relaxes, thinks to herself that he's probably having a hard time with his wife or girlfriend. Older guys like him all seem to be pulling younger women these days.

'Do you want me to razor the back?' She puts a hand on his shoulder and smiles at him in the mirror.

'No. Just use scissors,' he says. 'That's the way I used to get it done and it's what I prefer.' He smiles. 'Old ways are best.'

The barber picks up the scissors, puts her hand on his head and exerts the smallest of pressures. 'Bend forward,' she says, 'just a little.'

Bernard puts his head down and she begins to snip at the back hair, quick precise movements which quickly sort out the straggling bits.

She is almost finished when there is a darkening in the window. The barber is used to this and doesn't look round. People stand and look in all the time, as if cutting hair was some sort of stage-show.

Bernard turns however, without warning and almost, but not quite, causing her to snip a bit of skin.

'Please keep you head still and look down,' she says, alarmed, 'I'm almost finished.'

But Bernard keeps his head turned to the window, staring at the man who is looking in at him. He stares and sees the recognition in Thaddeus Shaw's eyes.

Bernard has known, since he killed the Casey girl, that something like this might happen. But he knows too that Thaddeus is drinking again and that he is drunk now. He begins to plan.

Thaddeus, on his way back to the apartment with the evening paper, decides to have his pony-tail trimmed in the barber's. He stops by the window. The customer having his haircut turns to look at him. He recognises Bernard Walsh.

Thaddeus is a bit under the weather but has no doubt that he has found the man he's been looking for. He might never have found him but for the situation; sitting there, with the blond girl barber working on his hair with her scissors, Bernard Walsh is once again the boy whose hair Shirley used to cut in the kitchen. There is no mistaking him.

Too late now to get the pony-tail cut.

It's a warm day, and sunny. Thaddeus watches as Bernard Walsh turns and talks to the barber. He sees the girl hesitate, then shrug, then hurriedly take the towel from around Bernard's shoulders, brush him free of hairs and begin making up his bill.

Thaddeus moves away, down the street a little to the hoarding around Fran's burned-out shop front. He leans against it and opens the newspaper. He makes a show of reading the headlines.

He knows he might never have recognised Bernard Walsh if his mind hadn't been so fixated on finding him. But he has him now, by a fluke and the greatest of luck, and he is not going to let him out of his sight. No point going into the barber's shop, putting the little blond barber girl in danger. He'll have to do what he can here, when Bernard comes out into the street. Either that or follow him.

Thaddeus wishes to Christ he had his mobile phone with him. If he had it he could call Hector. But he's left it in the apartment. He curses the drink which has fogged his mind and he curses Bernard Walsh, mightily, wishes a pox of suppurating pustules on him and the horse he rode in on. He hears the barber's door close and the heavy shutter come down.

'Hello, Thaddeus,' Bernard Walsh is standing beside him, 'you're looking fit and well.'

'I could say the same for you,' Thaddeus says.

It's true. Bernard Walsh is all of sixty-six and looks ten years younger. Proof of the Dorian Gray theory, or something like it. He's filled out, of course, and the years have changed his face a great deal. If he hadn't turned in the chair like that...

Bernard is smiling.

'Have you been in Dun Laoghaire long?' Thaddeus says.

'A while,' Bernard Walsh says. 'The new Ireland, you know. Draws her prodigal sons back.'

'You'd call yourself a prodigal then, would you?' Thaddeus says.

His mind is a fever of wondering how he can hold onto Bernard, how he can keep him by him until he gets word to Hector, or any Guard for that matter. Bernard has to be stopped before he makes a run for it, which is what he will do as soon as he walks away from Thaddeus.

Thaddeus knows that Bernard knows that Thaddeus realises what he is and what he's done. It's in the cruelly smiling eyes, in the way he's playing with him.

'Would you not call me a prodigal, Thaddeus?' Bernard asks the question in a friendly way, his head to one side, smiling his smile. He hadn't smiled much as a youngster. Thaddeus had thought him a muted, lifeless sort of boy.

'It's not the word comes to mind, no,' Thaddeus says. He folds the paper, wishes he could think more clearly.

'Do you live on your own these days?' Bernard asks. 'Or did you find yourself another lady companion?'

Thaddeus feels sure that Bernard well knows the answer to this question but plays along anyway. 'I'm on my own. It's more peaceful that way.' Thaddeus smiles. He is making a gigantic effort to suppress the effects of the whiskey he's been drinking. 'And you, Bernard, do you have a wife and family?'

'Unlucky in love,' Bernard shrugs, smiling too. He looks about, as if seeing the street, the shops, the apartments opposite, for the first time. 'Nice part of town. Things have changed, hardly recognisable most of it. Are you living around here then?'

'Across the road,' Thaddeus says, and has a flash of genius. 'Why don't you come up for a drink? It's been a long time.'

It doesn't once occur to him that he has been walked into something. He's totally convinced that the idea is his.

'Just the one then,' Bernard Walsh says, feigning reluctance, 'all right if I put my car in your garage?'

'Fine. Just bring it round and I'll let you in the back way.'

Thaddeus, crossing the road to the apartment ahead of Bernard Walsh, suppresses the warning bells ringing in his head. He has no choice, he tells himself, he cannot let the man go. Once he has Bernard safely in the apartment he'll ring Hector from the bathroom, on the mobile.

He tells himself too that this is where his life has been heading for a long, long time. He did a wrong and he must make right. This is a man who has, very likely, killed three young women. Murderers have a form and they stay true to it. He's unlikely to kill a man, to kill him.

Thaddeus is wrong.

30

It was the evening of the day that I arrived home from New York before I was finally able to sit and talk with Emer and Hector.

I told them, again, all that I'd already told the police about Ritchie Walsh and what he'd called his 'monstrous child'. I told them about Alexander and Sofia Borodin's memories of the Walsh family, of their mother's drowning and father's execution. The rest: Alex and I, our walks, talks and love making, seemed just so much history, something I had imagined and which had happened to someone else.

I left a gap in the statement I gave to the guards too. I didn't say anything about Thaddeus's daughter by Shirley Walsh. I couldn't bear to have Hector learn he had a half-sister in so nakedly public a fashion, in front of his colleagues.

So while the three of us talked and tried for some sort of coming to terms with what had happened to Thaddeus, I waited for the best, and gentlest, way to tell Hector he wasn't quite the only child he'd always thought he was.

'How *could* he be out there, still? Why

hasn't he been caught? What's *happening?*' Emer kept asking the same thing, coming back to the nightmare fact that the man who'd murdered her grandfather was still free, and a threat.

Now that he'd gone beyond the murdering of young women, Bernard Walsh was an even more lethal threat than before. He was exposed now too; the police might not yet know what he looked like but they knew enough to get their computer and tracking systems doing what they had to identify him.

'Everything possible's being done,' Hector said.

We were in my house. Hector, in a break from pacing, was sitting by the window, an arm's length from the phone, his own mobile ringing repeatedly in his pocket. His face was a shade of ash and his control icy.

He'd held me, for long, long minutes, when I arrived with Emer at the garda station. We went there directly from the airport.

'I'm sorry I couldn't pick you up,' he spoke into my hair, 'sorry I wasn't the one to tell you.' He felt thin and tired and let me go reluctantly.

'I know,' I said, 'I know you are.'

Hector's only way of dealing with his father's murder was to concentrate every-thing on finding and punishing the person who had done it. How he would deal with life after that had happened was tomorrow's worry.

'Have you arrested anyone yet?' I said.

'Not yet.'

'Have you any idea who did it?' I said.

'Not yet. Thaddeus was last seen crossing the road to the apartment after buying an evening newspaper. Whoever killed him must have been in the apartment when he got back upstairs. Either that or Thaddeus let him in soon after.'

That was when I began to tell him, when the statement-taking began. Before I left the station the American police were on their way to visit Ritchie Walsh in Southampton. I didn't much reckon their chances of getting anything more out of him than Alex and I had.

They had also stepped up the urgency about finding and talking to Bernard Walsh's younger brother and cousins. I was wildly hoping that the news that Melanie Walsh was his half-sister might, in the long term, be a positive thing for Hector. I couldn't see it being anything other than immediately shocking though.

Hector had been the one to find his father. He'd been phoning Thaddeus's apartment throughout the evening before, wondering if an arrangement had been made to pick me up at the airport. By midnight, when he hadn't been able to get a reply, he drove round to see what was wrong. He'd expected to find Thaddeus in a drunken stupor, nothing more. He let himself in with his own key.

Thaddeus, his head caved in, lay dead on the kitchen floor. The large, bronze heron he'd kept on top of the fridge stood bloody and upright beside him. It had taken more than one blow to kill him. A great many more. His shipshape kitchen dripped with his splattered blood, his head was a bloody pulp on his spotless floor.

I hadn't been to see Thaddeus's body yet myself. I couldn't bear to until after they'd reconstructed his head.

'How could whoever did it have got away so completely?' Emer wouldn't let it go.

'He hasn't got away,' Hector was coolly patient. 'We'll get him. He's good at this. He's been hiding and dodging, living another life for a lifetime. He becomes whoever he wants to believe he is and we don't, just yet, know who that is.' He looked at me. 'We've got a guy profiling him. A psychologist. It's his belief that Bernard Walsh becomes whoever he needs to believe he is.'

'His need will be great at the moment,' I said, 'he'll be angry and frustrated. Bad things if you're trying to be careful to avoid drawing attention to yourself.'

'How could he walk out of Thaddeus's apartment, covered in blood, and not be seen?' Emer demanded. 'How did he get in? Thaddeus was fussy about the people he invited up.' She walked to the window where she stood with her back to the room and hands on the sill. Her profile glared at the garden. 'Fuck him. Fuck him. Why did he have to be such a crank? Why couldn't he have told us about fucking Bernard Walsh? Why?'

'One of the reasons was *because* he was a crank and people wouldn't have believed him,' I said.

'I'm going to miss him so much...' Emer said and gave way to great, gulping sobs. Her father went to her.

'We'll all miss him,' he said. He watched me over her head, his policeman's brain taking note that I'd said there were reasons for Thaddeus's secrecy but only given one.

'What was Ritchie Walsh like?' Emer said after a while. 'Did you like him?'

'I think I might have,' I said, surprising myself. 'He seemed to me a gentle soul, too gentle to deal with the battering life dealt him. It was a tough one, taking on the responsibility for teenage sons and younger nieces, going off to America to give them new lives. All the time knowing in your heart that your older son had more than likely killed his aunt.'

That your younger niece wasn't your niece at all, I thought but didn't say.

'Did he talk much about Thaddeus?' Emer asked.

'Yes, he did,' I said. 'They were friends because of Thaddeus's friendship with Ritchie's brother, Jimmy. Thaddeus was friendly with Shirley too.'

'How friendly?' Hector asked.

'Very,' I said.

'Do you mean they were lovers?' Hector was impatient, but resigned too.

'Yes. Probably for years. There's something I didn't put in my statement, Hector.'

'I'm waiting,' he said. He looked me straight in the eye.

'Thaddeus was the father of Shirley's second daughter, Melanie,' I said. 'She was called Mel growing up and looks like Thaddeus, Ritchie Walsh says. He doesn't know where she is, she hasn't been in touch for years. She doesn't know. She has no idea Thaddeus was her father.' I hesitated. 'Nor that she has a half-brother.'

'Did Thaddeus know?' Hector said.

'It seems he did...'

'He knew,' Hector was harsh, 'and he as good as knew that the wrong person was convicted for the murder of her mother.' He stood. 'He's better off dead,' he said.

Emer stayed with me that night.

'He'll find his sister, you know,' Emer said. 'If it takes him ten years, he'll find her. And

340

he'll make up to her for Thaddeus's rejection.'

'I know he will,' I said.

A guard spent the night in the house too. Security, Hector said, just a precaution, he said, nothing to worry about. He didn't need to say it was because Bernard Walsh could by now have found out I'd visited his father in the Parson's Retreat. I didn't think myself that he would be so stupid as to ring Ritchie. Nor that he would care enough about his father.

A garda group was painstakingly going through records of everyone in a certain age group who'd taken up residence in Dun Laoghaire in the 1990s. Everyone would be questioned.

I thought about ringing Alex. Then I thought how difficult the call would be, how much I would have to explain, and put it off until the next day. I did dream about him, though, him and Thaddeus both.

They were walking across Manhattan Bridge in the rain and I was calling after them.

31

Emer went for a walk next morning, a habit she picked up from me. She took Lucifer with her. Nina arrived five minutes after she left. She was very agitated.

'It's the end of my life here.' She paced the same patch of floorboards Hector had trod the evening before. 'My peace is gone. I thought I had escaped from trouble of this kind. My life is going backwards. Damn him for doing this to me...'

I cut her short, snappily. 'I'm tired, Nina, and I'm upset about Thaddeus,' I said. 'Just tell me who is doing what to you?'

She slowed and looked at me cautiously. 'Emer will be gone for a while?' she said.

'You waited outside until she left,' I said, 'didn't you? What's happened, Nina, that can't be said in front of my daughter?'

'You are in bad mood,' Nina gnawed her finger-nails, 'too much has happened to you.'

I was in my dressing gown and she was right. Too much had happened. Because of Thaddeus's death I hadn't even had time to assimilate the emotional roller-coaster that had been New York. I was punch drunk.

These were the excuses I made for myself, afterwards, for the decision I made to go along with Nina that morning.

'Who has annoyed you, Nina?' I said tiredly.

'Dimitri,' she said, 'Dimitri Sobchak has annoyed me.'

'He has always annoyed you,' I said.

'Yes, that's true,' Nina said, 'and I have annoyed him. But now he needs me.'

She went to the front window and I realised she was checking to see if Emer was coming back. She gave a small grunt and began pacing again. 'He is afraid. He is afraid for himself. He came to talk to me last night.'

'What about?'

She took a deep breath. 'He was calm and very sure of the path he has chosen. He says he knows who the man is who drowned Alannah Casey. He wants to talk to you and to me, together, to tell us. He has decided to go away because the guards will make things hard for him and because he says there is nothing left for him here. First he wants to tell us who the man is and also other things about him.'

'Is he mad? Are you mad? Why didn't you go to the police?'

'I told you why,' Nina was patient. 'He knows people he shouldn't know, and he has been involved in things he shouldn't have been involved in. He doesn't want any more trouble for himself but he wants the man who killed Alannah Casey punished. He will tell you, and me, who this man is. Then he is going away.'

'Where is he now?' I picked up the phone. I was having none of this. 'We'll have to tell the guards...'

'I will deny everything I've just told you,' Nina said, calmly. 'And I don't know where Dimitri is, anyway. But I do know that he will go, and his secret with him, and it will be your fault. I believe him. I know his type.' She shrugged. 'I told him you might not come with me.'

I put the phone back down. 'Who are these other people he doesn't want the guards to know about?'

'I don't know,' Nina was testy, 'I don't involve myself with Russians like him and their business.'

She gnawed again at a finger-nail. She was puffy-eyed and looked as if she hadn't slept much. I could only begin to imagine the sort of *déjà-vu* experience this must be for her.

'Why doesn't he tell his solicitor, or his solicitor's pay-cheque, Gerry Fuller? They'll believe in him.'

'Because he is going away,' Nina said, 'because he doesn't want them to know he is going away. They will try to stop him. I have already asked him all of these questions.'

'Why doesn't he leave them a letter and just go?'

'Because he cannot write English and there is too much to explain. I told you, I have asked him everything. He says we must come this morning, he will be gone away by midday.'

'But why doesn't he just go? Why is he bothering to tell us, to tell anyone?' I looked at her closely. Nina had always been honest with me; she didn't look like a woman who was lying now, either. Why would she lie, in any case?

'Dimitri Sobchak says that what he and Alannah Casey were is dead to him,' Nina spoke slowly, as if to a dim child. 'He says that he has let her go. And this is true, in his head. His heart says something else, and his pride. So to free himself of guilt and make things right in his heart he must speak before he goes.'

'Let me think about this for a minute,' I said.

Nina looked at her watch. 'It is after ten o'clock. Emer will be back soon with the dog. We should go before she gets here. She will ask too many questions.'

I went to the phone. 'I'll come with you. But I want to phone Hector, at least, before we go. If Dimitri really does know who murdered Alannah then I should...'

Nina, moving quickly across the room,

reached from behind me and depressed the phone button.

'You cannot do that. I promised Dimitri it would be just us two, no police. Not even your husband.' She paused. 'Especially not ... Hector. I have been talking with him while you were away. Your husband is a passionate policeman.'

'Hector's my ex-husband,' I said, automatically. 'And why would you make a promise like that to someone you don't even like?'

'Because he is my countryman and, in this one thing, I believe him. You went to America to find out about the past,' Nina said, 'and now you will not even come down the road with me to find out what has happened today.'

'Where is Dimitri?' I said.

'He said he would go to Morrissey's pub at ten thirty. He said he would wait for us there.'

'I'll come with you. I'll give him twenty minutes. Then if I think he's lying or playing games I'm leaving.'

Morrissey's was one of those small, friendly pubs where boys go for their first drink at seventeen and keep going for a lifetime. Dimitri was ensconced in the back snug, more miserable and furtive looking than ever. He scowled at me.

'Good morning,' he said.

'Good morning, Dimitri.' I sat opposite him. 'I'll have a cup of coffee, please.'

'I would prefer to talk somewhere else,' he said, 'it is too quiet here. What we say will be heard.'

There was something of the sepulchre about the place all right, but nobody much to hear us. Still, I'd come this far so I humoured him.

'Where do you suggest?' I said, wearily. Nina, who was still standing, looked at him in fury.

'You are always making things difficult,' she said. 'We are here and that should be enough. Frances is mourning her husband's father. She is not in a mood for you, Dimitri, I warn you.'

Dimitri stood. 'The apartment I am staying in is close by,' he said. 'It would be better to talk there.'

He shoved his hands into the pockets of his leather coat and walked from the pub, sure we would follow him. We did too.

In the lobby of the Ocean Vista apartment block, waiting for the lift to arrive, I thought idly that Dimitri must be making money somewhere. The Ocean Vista was one of the more expensive developments in town, built in the early 1990s and owned by thriving young professionals and property-invest-ment types.

I knew all this, and should have been suspicious, but still I got into the lift, and went with Dimitri Sobchak and Nina to the eighth floor and apartment number 801. Dimitri opened the door and stood back to allow Nina and myself to go in ahead of him. Then he stepped inside himself and locked the door after us.

'Don't you think you're carrying the paranoia a little too far, Dimitri?' I said, sharply.

He ignored me and walked ahead of us, down a blue-carpeted, bare-looking hallway. He opened a door at the end and went through.

Nina raised her eyebrows, shrugged and went after him. I followed. The curtains in the room were closed but there was light enough to see what was to be seen. The carpet was a paler blue than in the hallway and covered in blood. A table in the centre of the room was covered with an old-fashioned lace cloth. The armchairs were black leather.

Gerry Fuller, the businessman paying Dimitri Sobchak's legal bills, sat in one of them staring at the door. His eyes were sightless, his face a waxy grey and as still as wax too. His body was propped up and completely rigid in the armchair, the blood covering the part of his chest where his heart would have been beating were he alive congealed and drying.

32

Nina screamed and screamed, the sound echoing and loud enough to waken the dead. Gerry Fuller didn't move.

I leaned against the wall as waves of dizziness came and went, then gave in and slumped to my knees. Nina began a demented wailing in Russian as I leaned my back against the wall and stared numbly at Gerry Fuller.

I've no idea how long she went on, and I've no idea how long I was unconscious before I felt her kneeling beside me with a cup of cold water. After I had had some to drink she dipped a tissue in the cup and dampened my forehead.

'Please get up,' she said, and helped me.

I sat at the table with the water. Nina sat beside me.

'You killed him?' I said to Dimitri. He was leaning, with his arms folded, against the wall behind the dead man.

'He killed Alannah,' Dimitri said, 'and he killed my unborn child. He also killed your husband's father.'

'Ex-husband,' I said.

If Dimitri Sobchak was right then the

dead man in the chair was Bernard Walsh and he'd also killed Shirley Walsh and Liliya Borodin. There was no reason to doubt Dimitri Sobchak's claim. There was no reason to believe it either.

'I had no choice,' Dimitri said, 'I did not know she was carrying my child when he killed her. When I heard this I knew I must kill him.' He shrugged. 'If I had not waited so long your husband's father would not have died too.'

Nina, hugging herself and rocking in her chair, was weeping and directing a stream of Russian invective at him. He took it from her, seemingly impassive.

I felt very cold, but not afraid any more. It seemed to me that everything which could happen had happened, that nothing was going to happen to me, now. I was more dumb than numb, operating on auto-pilot and very clear in my head about some things, at least.

I tapped the table to get Dimitri Sobchak's attention.

'Why did he kill Alannah?' I said.

Dimitri was quite expressionless when he looked at me.

'He said it was because she laughed at him. But it was also because he feared she was taking me away from my work with him.'

'Alannah knew him?'

This surprised me, until I thought about it. The guards hadn't come up with any connection between Alannah Casey and Bernard Walsh, alias Gerry Fuller. But they'd known very little about Gerry Fuller in any event; he wasn't even Gerry Fuller.

'Of course she knew him,' Dimitri said. 'I worked for him so he knew everything in my life. Packing boxes onto shelves was not my real job.'

Nina stopped rocking and hurled what was clearly a series of questions at Dimitri. Her voice was harsh and hoarse. When she stopped he looked briefly at Bernard Walsh's body in the chair and began to speak in Russian. Nina's hand came down in a table-shaking thump.

'In English,' she screamed, the words full of a ragged hysteria, 'you will tell us all you have to say in English, Dimitri Sobchak. Frances Shaw must be told *everything*.' She turned to me, her face so bleached of colour even her lips were white. She spoke so quickly it took all of my concentration to understand what she was saying.

'I have told him what I didn't yet tell you. Early this morning I talked with a man in our community here, a good man, who knows Dimitri Sobchak and his kind and what they do. I told him we were meeting with this son of a bitch. I told him that if he did not hear from me on the telephone by one o'clock then he must go to the police. I said where we would meet Sobchak and when we were leaving the pub I told the barman where we were going. You must have no worry that Dimitri Sobchak will harm us.'

'Right,' I said and looked into Dimitri's hardened, indifferent eyes. 'Right,' I said again. Until then I hadn't really been afraid. Now I was, very. Now I realised he might harm us, too.

Everything Nina said made me feel worse instead of better, and for two reasons. The first was the knowledge that Nina had believed there was so much danger in what we were doing, the second was that she was lying. She hadn't told the barman anything. She'd walked ahead of me out of the pub, keeping her eyes on Dimitri and without detouring or looking to left or right.

I couldn't see what Dimitri had to gain by hurting us. He'd killed the man who'd killed his lover and now wanted to explain himself, and betray Bernard Walsh/Gerry Fuller for what he was, before absconding.

Or so it seemed to me. I couldn't for the life of me, unless he was a sadistic bloody pervert, see why he would hurt Nina and myself.

He could, of course, be a sadistic bloody pervert.

I wondered if he had a gun. He'd used a

knife to kill Bernard Walsh so maybe a knife was all he carried.

'Did you know this man...' it was difficult not to look at the body, 'for a long time? Did he ever tell you that ... Gerry Fuller wasn't his real name?'

'I knew his passport was false,' Dimitri Sobchak said. 'I thought of course that there was a reason for this. But it was none of my business.'

Nina started to pace. I wanted to scream at her to stop. I asked Dimitri Sobchak my next question.

'How did you know his passport was false?' I said.

'Because I am an expert in such things.' Dimitri said this with a certain amount of pride. 'I make passports. This is why Gerry Fuller first came to me.'

Dimitri's own passport was probably false; God knows what he'd left behind him in Russia.

'Gerry Fuller came to you to make him a fake passport?'

'Not for himself. He already had his own fake passport, a very good one made many years ago. But I am not a fool and I could see what it was. He came to me because he needed someone to make passports and other documents for his business.'

'His business...' Nina stopped, put her face very close to Dimitri's and hissed,

'...tell Frances what his business was, Dimitri Sobchak. Tell her...' She stepped back. She looked capable of murder.

'He is very important and very rich.' Dimitri looked around the room. 'He owns many apartments and land. He buys and he sells, a businessman of property. That is one of the things he does.'

He ran a quick hand over his eyes. It was the first indication he'd given of distress. He went on, still in the present tense, as if Bernard Walsh were alive.

'Gerry Fuller also brings people to this country, and to Britain, from my country and from Ukraine, other places. They come to work for his friends who own factories and hotels and farms. He promises them much. He tells people he can get their immigrant papers for them, get them work when they get here. I make the papers and they pay him, a lot of money. When they come to Ireland they must live in caravans or all together in rooms and bad houses. I make the documents too for the friends of Gerry Fuller when they go to work for them. Sometimes passports for people who are not allowed to travel. Many hundreds of people come, more and more every year. The employers pay Gerry Fuller and the workers pay Gerry Fuller so he makes a lot of money.'

'This is called human trafficking,' I said slowly, 'Gerry Fuller can't have been organising all of this alone, with just you to help.'

'There are others but I don't know their names,' Dimitri shrugged, 'it is better for me, Gerry Fuller says, not to know.'

Better for him to get away too, now Gerry Fuller/Bernard Walsh was dead. The nameless others would get him long before the guards did.

'What sort of work do they do, the people you make papers for?' I said.

'Work that Irish people will not do. They go in the cold picking potatoes in fields and to work in kitchens and factories where the bosses want people for cheap pay.' He shrugged. 'There are plenty of bosses who want cheap workers.'

This was the Ireland Bernard Walsh had told his father suited him. The land of new opportunities.

'I want you to tell the police Gerry Fuller killed Alannah, and your husband's father,' Dimitri said.

'They'll want to know why,' I said.

'It is simple.' He was impatient. 'Alannah could not understand why I had to have secrets all the time and I did not want, after a while, to keep secrets from her.'

Nina muttered something and he turned to her, face tightening, and replied. She gave him a steady, compassionless stare and he turned away.

'I decided I would marry Alannah,' he

said. 'She wanted this. After a while I wanted this too.'

His shrug was cynical; it said that Alannah might have been hopeful their love would survive but he, Dimitri Sobchak, had seen it all and knew better. It said he couldn't believe, screamed a fatalism that was learned and would not go away.

'When I asked Gerry Fuller to find another person to make his documents he said he would like to meet Alannah. I told Alannah I had a businessman friend who would like to meet her and she came with me to this apartment to meet him. He liked her, of course. He said he was sorry he had never married, that marriage might have given him a daughter like her.'

He stopped to think for a minute. I did a bit of reflecting myself. Bernard Walsh the kindly uncle figure was a frightening proposition. I wondered what Alannah Casey had made of him.

'She didn't like him,' Dimitri went on, as if reading my mind, 'she said he was a man of secrets and she was suspicious because he was so alone in life. He said he had a family but she said why did no one ever see his family? I had no answer. I did not want to see his family anyway. She said he made her skin creep. She said all of this but still she said we must use him because he had money and knew people. Gerry Fuller said to me that I should be careful of Alannah, that a woman who had a child by another man was not to be trusted.'

When he stopped this time it was for longer than before. In the sky outside a seagull cried, just once, and Dimitri Sobchak started to talk again.

But the telling had become harder for him. It showed in his face, which had become haggard, and in his voice, which had become spiritless.

Nina saw these things too and stopped her pacing. She sat at the table again, her arms folded, taking care to be where she didn't have to look at the dead man's body in its chair.

'I saw that he liked her,' Dimitri said. 'That he would like her for himself. He said he did not want her for me because she would know too soon what I was doing and betray us, and this was true too. But as he knew her more and more he wanted her himself too.'

'What happened?' I prompted when he stopped again.

'He never met me in a public place. Always in this apartment, or some other apartment. The night ... he killed her he asked us both to come here. We would have some drinks, he said, and talk about the future. I said I was working in the warehouse but he said to Alannah she must go anyway, that he wanted to talk to her. She did not want to go but I said she must. I said he wanted to help us.'

He looked at the man he'd murdered then, for the first time. It was an indifferent look, but long. After a minute he put his head in his hands. They were long-fingered hands, and slim. Very lovely hands. When he took them away he had grown bleak.

'He told me she laughed at him. That he offered her money to go away and she laughed. I do not believe him. What I believe is that he offered her himself and she laughed and said no and he killed her. He told me she knew things, that she had found them out, and that if he didn't kill her someone else would have anyway. Very late in the night he took her down in the lift to his car and took her to where you found her and left her there, naked.'

'Did he tell you why?'

'He said it was so that the police would not think of me and begin questioning my life here. He said it would lead them to think it was a local person, someone who knew about the other woman who was murdered and left on the morgue steps.'

'But you didn't believe him?'

'I think that was part of the reason. But he smiled when he told me this and I could see he wanted to do it too.'

'Did you know he had murdered the other women?'

'How could I?'

How could he, indeed? It wasn't as if Bernard Walsh was going to tell him.

'Was he not worried you would tell the police he killed Alannah? You loved her...'

'He knew I valued my life. She was dead. I could no longer have her. What was there to die for? He was a man used to living many lives. If I told the police he would disappear with his money and I would be alone to blame for the passports, the documents, for everything. Then I would die, either in jail or out of it, he would see that I did. The only future for me was to kill him. It is the only way I can forget Alannah.'

I had started to understand Bernard Walsh, a little. I thought I could see why he'd killed as he did, behaved afterwards as he did.

'Gerry Fuller put Alannah on the steps of the morgue so as to divert the police enquiry,' I said, 'to make it seem this was some mad, copy-cat killer obsessing with the past. Didn't he?'

'That is not what he said,' Dimitri said, 'he said it was because he had respect for her, that he wanted her body to be found and given a good funeral before it decayed. He said if she had betrayed what we were doing both of us would have died, that it was our lives or hers, that there were others involved who would have first killed Alannah, then me and then him if she had betrayed us. He said he had to kill her. He said that he had no choice.'

Nina erupted into life. 'You are a pitiful creature,' she said. 'He killed your woman and you play his game for him still. You allow him to protect you with a civil rights solicitor who will make difficulties for the guards looking at your life.'

'If they examined me and my life they would have found him,' Dimitri said.

'Why did he burn down my café?' I said.

'Because of the same reason,' Dimitri said. 'He said it would make the police look more to racist people for the murder. They would think Alannah had been murdered because of me by an insane person who looked to the past and did not want new people, like Russians, in Ireland. He also said...' Dimitri straightened up and Nina, watching him, straightened in her chair.

'He said too that he did not like the people who went there,' Dimitri said. 'The old man Rutledge and your husband's father.'

'You sold your own people when you made false documents for him,' Nina said.

'Do you think the lives they ran from were better?' Dimitri turned on her. 'I do not owe Russia anything.'

'You must pay for what you have done.' Nina stood and faced him. She was very calm. 'You have killed a man and you have helped make slaves of many people. You must pay.'

'I have paid,' Dimitri said, so softly it was hard to hear him. 'I have done what had to be done about Alannah.'

Nina said something fierce and pitiless sounding in Russian and he smiled and shook his head. She said just one more word to him before turning to me.

'We will go now,' she said. I stood up beside her.

Dimitri Sobchak moved quickly. Before we had taken even a step, before we had even realised what he was doing, he had passed us and was standing in the open door.

'*I* will go now,' he said. 'You will leave later.'

It was Nina who realised what he intended and made a wild leap for the door. It was Nina who stood banging on the inside of the door with her fists after he pulled it closed and turned the key on the other side.

'When I have saved myself I will tell the guards where to get you,' Dimitri called through the door. 'They will come.'

Then he was gone, the hall door to the apartment opening, closing with a click and the turn of a key in the frightening silence.

'I hope he tells the guards we're not alone,' I muttered and sat, swallowing something that tasted like that morning's scone coming up my throat.

'I am not looking at that thing for the rest of the time.' Nina took off her denim jacket and dropped it over Bernard Walsh in the chair. It covered the bloodier part of him.

'You're tampering with evidence,' I said, the remnants of a policeman's wife still in me somewhere. Nina looked at me as if I were mad. Which I may well have been.

It was more than eight hours later when, ears tuned to even a change in air current, we again heard a key turn in the outer door.

'Better leave the jacket where it is,' I said when Nina eyed her denim. 'Forensics will need to include it as evidence.'

'I don't think I will wear it again anyway,' Nina said.

Hector was the first of the guards through the door.

'You all right?' He held my shoulders and looked at me. He was shaking.

'I'll live,' I said, then wished I hadn't. 'I want to get out of here,' I said.

Hector pulled me close and held me tightly against him; I wrapped my arms about him and clung on. It was just what and all that I needed, the warmth of fearlessly living flesh and blood. So much the better that it was Hector's.

The guards had brought blankets to wrap us in and water. Nectar and a golden fleece. When a young guard began to gag at the smell in the room I realised how inured

Nina and I had become to the side effects of sharing a 12ft x 6ft space with a corpse, how dead in ourselves. The need to survive will do that to you.

Hector dropped the denim back over Bernard Walsh's face with a loud and ugly obscenity. He roared at the men with him, looked at the walls and ceilings as if he would tear them apart. I'd felt that way myself during some of the eight hours. It was a long, long time since I'd seen Hector in a state of such out-of-control fury.

I put my arm about Nina as we went down the stairs. No one had hugged her and I could hardly ask it of Hector, not in front of her anyway.

For brief moments, as we came out into the early evening and fresh air, she leaned against me and closed her eyes.

Then she straightened and walked to the police car, the loneliness in her heart still intact.

Epilogue

I pretend to listen and pay attention as Hector tells me how the police are doing all they can to put the life story of Bernard Walsh, alias Gerald Fuller, together. Tells me how they are trying to account for every year of his life since he left Dun Laoghaire as a teenage murderer, how nearly impossible it's proving.

There are gaps, Hector says. They will never be certain that the four accounted-for murders were the only ones he committed.

Hector uses this kind of police language all the time. It distances him from what happened to Thaddeus.

The truth is, I don't care to know too much. Shirley Walsh, Liliya Borodin, Alannah Casey – it is enough to know who killed them, and why.

And Thaddeus. My flawed but lovely friend, my daughter's grandfather, dead because of the same man's sick understanding of what it is to be human.

Hector takes my hand. 'There's no going back, I suppose, for us?' he says.

I shake my head and touch the side of his pale, unshaven and much-loved face.

'There's no going back,' I say.

I am very certain of this. Have been since the eight hours spent waiting, and thinking, in the room in the Ocean Vista apartment block. The proximity of death had remarkably sharpened my thoughts.

Drink and distrust and unhappiness had destroyed what Hector and I had had in the beginning. The long years apart had restored trust and friendship, but not passion. There was nothing left that made me want to be with him, wait for his phone calls, lie in his arms the night long.

And I want all of those things.

Alex Borodin plans to visit Dublin next week. My anticipation makes me very much fear that what Concepta Walsh said was right, that there is no escaping my 'lack of wisdom in regard to matters of the heart'.

Nina drops by after Hector leaves. She takes charge of a great deal of the business these days. I can afford to take time out: Thaddeus's will has seen to that.

'How are you today?' I ask. I ask this question every day but today she gives me a longer answer than I expect.

'I'm happy as anyone could be,' she says.

I pondered the 'could' but let it go. Nina is young. Maybe she will some day substitute should.

I have. I am definitely as happy as anyone should be in the circumstances.

The publishers hope that this book has given you enjoyable reading. Large Print Books are especially designed to be as easy to see and hold as possible. If you wish a complete list of our books please ask at your local library or write directly to:

Magna Large Print Books
Magna House, Long Preston,
Skipton, North Yorkshire.
BD23 4ND